D1566531

Also by John Banville

Nightspawn
Birchwood
Doctor Copernicus
Kepler
The Newton Letter
Mefisto
The Book of Evidence
Ghosts
Athena
The Untouchable
Eclipse
Shroud
The Sea
The Infinities
Ancient Light
The Blue Guitar
Mrs. Osmond
Snow
April in Spain
The Singularities
The Lock-Up

JOHN
BANVILLE

The
Drowned

A NOVEL

HANOVER
SQUARE
PRESS

HANOVER
SQUARE
PRESS™

Recycling programs
for this product may
not exist in your area.

ISBN-13: 978-1-335-00059-0

The Drowned

First published in Great Britain in 2024 by Faber & Faber Ltd. This edition published in 2024.

Hanover Square Press
22 Adelaide St. West, 41st Floor
Toronto, Ontario M5H 4E3, Canada
HanoverSqPress.com

Printed in U.S.A.

1

He had lived alone for so long, so far away from the world and its endless swarms of people, that when he saw the strange thing standing at a slight list in the middle of the field below the house, for a second he didn't know what it was. In the gloaming, two red lights glared at him out of the long grass like the eyes of a wild animal crouched and ready to spring. His heart gave three dull slow thumps; he felt them in his ears, like the beating of a distant drum.

But it wasn't an animal. It was a motorcar, low-slung, sleek and expensive looking, painted a burnished shade of dark gold. In the gathering shadows it gave off a muted, sinister glow. The engine was running, and thick gray-white smoke was trickling slowly out of the exhaust pipe at the back and dispersing in ghostly wisps.

The door on the right-hand side, the driver's door, stood

wide-open on its hinges. Again he thought of an animal, jaws agape, bellowing in pain and fury. But there was no sound to be heard, except that of the faint breeze rustling through the bowed grasses and the leaning brambles still loaded with overripe blackberries.

A car sitting in a field below someone's house. So what? No concern of his. The wise thing to do would be to walk on, past the gateway, as if he had seen nothing, and go home and mind his own business. Yet something held him there. Later, of course, he would regret that he should have paused even for a second. But by then it was too late, and he was caught up among people, again.

People, the bane of his life.

It was bound to have happened, sooner or later. The one thing the world would not do was leave you alone, in peace, by yourself. Always it had to draw you in, insisting you take part in the fun and games like everyone else. Children: the world was full to bursting with children. Not real children, those magical, achingly precious creatures, but stunted, ill-developed homunculi all marching up and down stamping their feet and gesticulating. He had been frightened of them when he was little and they were all still children or pretending to be, and they frightened him now more than ever, when they were pretending to be grown-ups.

Yes, life, so-called, was a birthday party gone wild, with shouting and squabbling, and games he didn't know the rules of, and one lot ganging up on the other, and knocking each other down and dancing in a ring like savages, the whole mad rampage going on in a haze of dust and noise and horrible, hot stinks.

That was the world for you, all right. Their world.

He put his things down behind the gatepost, his fishing rod

and his old floppy shoulder bag—not much of an afternoon's catch, three medium-sized bass, and a pollock he would fry for the dog—and the old tin cashbox that he kept his sandwiches in. He hesitated a moment, but then, even though his heart was still going like a tom-tom, he went in at the gate. *You fool,* he told himself, even as he advanced, *why can't you mind your own business?*

He walked along the grassy hump that ran between the twin ruts of the driveway, his legs moving as if by themselves, leading him toward—what?

The house was some way off, at the top of the rise, and he could see only the roof and part of a gable end.

He came to the spot where the car had abruptly veered left and plunged deep into the field, and he turned and followed in its twin zigzag tracks through the tall grass.

It was a sports car, a Mercedes SL, so it said in raised letters on the lid of the trunk, with a retractable roof of stiff black canvas. He knew little about cars, but enough to know this was no run-of-the-mill model. Who would have left such a costly machine sitting in the middle of an overgrown field, with the lights on and the engine running? There was a mingled smell of exhaust fumes, hot metal and leather upholstery. Also a trace of a woman's perfume, musky, slightly rank— or was he imagining it? He leaned down and looked inside.

A silver key ring dangled from the ignition, and on the ring was a leather tab bearing a small round metal shield stamped with the three-pointed Mercedes logo. The little thing struck the one intimate note among so much steel and chrome and glass. Someone owned that ring and its key, someone kept it in a pocket, or in a purse, someone twirled it on a finger, and sat in behind the steering wheel and leaned forward with it pressed between a finger and a thumb and inserted it in its groove and turned it and made the engine roar into life. Someone.

He found the switch for the lights and turned them off, then turned off the engine too, leaving the key in its slot. When he swung the door to, he used too much force and it slammed shut with a thud that seemed to him as loud as a thunderclap. Then the silence crowded in around him once more. There was the sense of everything pressing forward eagerly, like bystanders at the scene of an accident, or a crime.

Yes, there must have been an argument, that must be what happened. A person would have to have lost the run of himself, or herself, to leave a Mercedes SL sports car standing here like this, with the key in the ignition, even on this lonely stretch of coast. There were some wild fellows going about here, real yahoos, half-wild farmers' sons, day laborers, now and then an IRA man down from the North to lie low after yet another botched bomb attempt or an inept raid on a customs post. Those boyos wouldn't hesitate to hop in and take this gilded beauty for a spin, and more than likely leave it wrapped around a tree trunk along the road somewhere, steaming and smoking, or nosedown in six feet of water in some hidden rocky inlet.

The field, or meadow as he supposed it should be called, rose at a shallow angle in the direction of the house. He made his way to the top of the slope, and stopped and looked about him. The late-October evening was fading fast, yet in the sky in the west a long bar of cloud was whitely aglow, so bright that he had to put up a hand to shade his eyes. It had been an uncommonly fine month so far, and the weather seemed set to last for a good while yet. He dearly hoped it would. Not that he had much time for summer and sunshine and games and all that nonsense, but the thought of the winter coming

on made his heart shrink. Would he be able to hold out, living like an outcast—but wasn't he an outcast?—seeing not a
soul and hearing from no one?

He would have to manage somehow. There was no going
back. He couldn't be trusted, in the world, among people,
among—

Stop! He shut his eyes and struck a fist against his forehead.
Take a deep breath. Another. And another. Now.

He opened his eyes.

To his left, the surface of the evening sea was chopped,
metallic, faintly aglitter. Not a thing to be seen out there, no
ship or sail, nothing between here and the Welsh coast, invisible beyond the horizon. He turned his gaze inland. The
house stood at the end of the grassy track leading up from the
gate. It was a fair-sized, two-story farmhouse, built of granite, with a steep slate roof ashine now in the light from the
west, two tall chimneys, and a wrought iron weather vane
in the shape of a cock crowing.

Why was he hanging about here? What business was it of
his, he asked himself again, what had he to do with this abandoned car and whoever had abandoned it? He told himself
again that if he had any sense at all he should go, should turn
on his heel this very second, walk back down to the gate and
gather up his rod and his bag and his sandwich box, and take
himself off smartly, before the owners of the car returned
from wherever they had gone to and drew him inexorably
into some ghastly, complicated mess of their own making.

At that moment, as if the thought had conjured the thing,
he heard a voice call out behind him. He spun round to see a
figure wading toward him up through the meadow, from the
direction of the sea. It was a man, lanky-looking, with un-
steady legs and rubbery knees. He was waving an arm above

his head, urgently, like someone drowning and coming up for the second time. Again came that call, but the words were lost in the immensities of land and sky and sea.

What to do? Oh, God, what to do? Turn and run, as he should have done already? The bag and the fishing tackle he could come back for another time, no one would think the stuff worth the taking. He could pretend he hadn't seen the man, with the light fading, and hadn't heard him either.

But it was already too late.

Trapped!

"Listen, listen—you've got to help me," the man gasped, stumbling up the last few yards of the slope with a long pale hand pressed to his heaving chest. "I think my wife has drowned herself."

His name, he said, was Armitage. He was tall and very thin, with bony shoulders and a concave chest and a high narrow head and small dark eyes set too close together. His oiled hair was combed straight back from his forehead: it looked, to Wymes's eye, like a Channel swimmer's tight black rubber cap. Under a gabardine raincoat he wore a navy-blue blazer with brass buttons, and wide, cream-colored trousers that flapped loosely around his skinny shins. The sharp-pointed collar of his shirt was open. His narrow patent-leather shoes, dainty as dancing pumps, damp from the dew and stuck with sand, were as black and shiny as his hair. His white socks were streaked with grass stains.

He stopped, out of breath, leaned forward from the waist and braced his hands on his knees with his head hanging and made a kind of mewling sound. Was he weeping? After a moment, he straightened up. No sign of tears. Oddly, he seemed more excited than distressed.

"And you are——?" he asked.

His fruity accent sounded put-on.

"Wymes. Denton Wymes. I——"

"Weems?"

"Yes. Spelled W-y-m-e-s, pronounced Weems."

It annoyed him that he always felt obliged to offer this trivial clarification, even to strangers. Armitage stared at him in silence for a moment, then stepped forward and grasped him by the upper arms.

"You're not a Paddy, then," he said, with a sort of laugh. "Thank Christ for that."

"Actually, I am Irish, if that's what you mean," Wymes said stiffly. "But not——"

"Not bog Irish. That's the point. Good man!"

Wymes blinked. This all felt unreal. Had the fellow really said that about his wife having drowned herself? Maybe it was intended as some kind of grotesque joke.

Suddenly, the fellow twisted his face to one side and gave a sort of strangled howl, as if for a moment he had forgotten about his wife and had just now remembered her again. He was still holding Wymes by his upper arms, but now he let go of him and wiped the back of a hand across his mouth.

"She's gone!" he keened. "She's gone in the sea, I'm sure she is."

It seemed a piece of bad acting, but then, Wymes told himself, that's mostly how people behave when there's a crisis and they're distraught.

"Look, calm down," he said, with a mounting sense of desperation. "I'm sure there's been some——"

"*She's gone!*" It was almost a scream. "I'm telling you, she threw herself off the rocks down there."

"Did you see her? I mean, did you actually see her throw herself into the water?"

At this Armitage paused, and took a half step back, narrowing his little, crafty eyes.

"You're right," he said, grown thoughtful suddenly. "I didn't see her jump, there is that."

"You mean she fell? It was an accident?"

"No no no no!" Armitage said, shaking his head violently. "She got out of the car and ran—" he gestured behind him with a vaguely flapping hand "—and ran down to the sea, and—" He stopped, and tilted his head to one side, as if attending to a voice speaking softly just beside his ear. "I suppose," he said slowly, "I suppose she could have hid behind the rocks, to make me think she had jumped." He smiled, almost wistfully. "It's the kind of thing she'd do, you know."

He seemed to consider this possibility for a moment, then to Wymes's horror he reached out and took him by the hand, actually grasped him tightly palm to palm, and turned and set off in the direction of the sea, drawing him along behind him.

Once, as a boy, Wymes's parents had taken him to the circus. He had found the whole thing terrifying—the squeals and farts of the three-piece band, the whooping shouts of the acrobats, the lights glaring through the talcum-laden darkness—but then came the worst of all, when a clown singled him out. He was tall and gangly, a bit like Armitage, in fact, with a face painted stark white and a carroty wig on which was stuck at a crooked angle a bright red porkpie hat. He came barging up long-legged through the first four rows of benches, pushing people aside and even stepping on one or two of them, and seized young Wymes by the hand and dragged him down into the ring.

He had never forgotten the experience, the hot fingers

clutching his, the smell of greasepaint and sweat, the crazed laughter.

Armitage, he thought, would make a good clown, skeletal, mocking and maniacal.

"Come on," he said now, pulling harder at Wymes's hand. "If she's hiding, we'll soon find her, the little minx. She'll show herself eventually—she was always afraid of being on her own in the dark."

Yes, the man was mad, Wymes decided, mad, or drunk, or both. He snatched his hand away and stepped back and stopped, planting his feet wide, determined to stand his ground.

"I'm sorry," he said, "I'm afraid I can't help you. I have to—" He searched for a plausible excuse. "I have to let my dog out."

Armitage stopped too, and turned and looked at him, frowning.

"Your dog?"

"Yes. He's locked in the caravan, he'll think I've abandoned him. He's a Border collie. They're very highly strung, you know, Border collies. The trouble is, he barks and barks and frightens the fish."

"He what?"

"He frightens off the fish, with his barking. That's why I don't bring him with me."

"Because he frightens the fish." Armitage nodded slowly. "I see. So you're a fisherman."

"Not really. It's to eat. The fish. I mean I fish for food, not sport." Stop babbling, for God's sake. "I live on my own, away from—away from shops, and so on."

Armitage pursed his lips and squinted at the sky.

"My wife," he said with studied calm, nodding again, more

slowly still, "my wife has either drowned herself, or has run off and come to some mishap, probably fatal, but your dog has to be let out for a piss. I see."

"I'm sorry, I—"

"No no, don't apologize. I quite understand. You're in a predicament. Lassie of the Bulging Bladder will be fretting while you stand here wasting your precious time listening to me speculating on the sad fate of my lady wife. Perfectly reasonable, perfectly. Off you go. Don't mind about me— don't mind about *us*."

Cracked in the head, definitely, Wymes thought. I'm trapped with a lunatic out here on this bleak shore.

"Look, Mr.—Mr. Armitage," he said gently, "why don't you go up to the house—you see the house, up there?—and ask them to phone for help."

"I could do that, yes," Armitage said, stroking his chin and looking at the ground and frowning. "That is a thing I could do."

Wymes began to say something more, but all at once Armitage wheeled about and marched off up the slope, his knees pumping and his arms swinging. He looked like nothing so much as a life-size mechanical doll.

"Wait!" Wymes called, but not as loudly, or with as much force, as he might have. Here, after all, was his chance to escape.

And yet.

What if the fellow's wife really had fallen into the sea, or had thrown herself in, or had run off into the night, furious, or drunk, or whatever? She might have slipped on the slimed rocks and broken something, an arm, a leg. And Armitage, however unappealing he might be—there was something of the slacker about him, despite the clipped vowels and the fancy shoes—was a human being, after all, a man, like Wymes himself, a man in desperate need of assistance. One couldn't just walk off and leave him on his own, out here, in the gathering dark. Could one?

Armitage had stopped, and stood looking about him wildly. The grass came almost up to his knees.

There was a wind now, and they could hear the sound of the waves breaking on the rocks at the shoreline. If she really had gone into the water, Wymes told himself grimly, she would be well drowned by now, her body broken, her face smashed, her clothes ripped and half torn-off. He had seen drowned people. A sight not to be forgotten.

Behind them a light went on, making the air around them seem abruptly darker. A window in the gable end of the house glowed yellow. That meant there was someone at home, a farmer, probably, and his family. Surely they wouldn't refuse aid to a man searching for his lost wife. He would ask them to phone the Guards, or the lifeboat, and while they were doing that, he could slip away unnoticed. Scamp would be glad to see him. They would go for a walk together, man and dog, down the lane through the dunes and off along the beach.

Or no, not the beach. The woman's body might be washed up there already. Imagine stumbling on it, the pulpy, phosphorescent flesh, the face swollen and cut, the hair twisted like seaweed, the eyes blindly staring.

He set off determinedly up the slope, toward that lighted window. He must get help. He heard the man call out again behind him.

"You! Weemess! Wait!"

It was always the same. No matter how clearly he spelled it out and explained it, everyone always got his name wrong.

"Come on!" he called back, beckoning with his arm. "There's no time to lose!"

How banal a thing life is, he thought, even at its most dramatic, its most melodramatic. Now he seemed to be the actor, making exaggerated gestures and spouting bad lines.

2

He had thought matters couldn't get any more strange, and then they did. As he climbed the slope, making his way cautiously in the gloom over the uneven ground, he heard Armitage behind him sobbing quietly, or so he thought. Then he realized the man wasn't sobbing, but laughing, softly, to himself. That would be hysteria, surely? The sounds stopped after a moment, and Wymes glanced back and saw Armitage making an effort to pull himself together, squaring his shoulders and clearing his throat and passing a hand over his face.

"Sorry," he said. "Something just occurred to me."

And despite himself, he gave another piping little laugh.

When they got to the house, they saw through a downstairs window at the front a man seated at a table in the kitchen. There was a glass of something in his hand, whiskey, by the look of it. He was smoking a cigarette, too, leaning back on a wooden chair with one knee crossed on the other. He had broad shoulders and a high, somewhat brutish-looking handsome head, and a shock of curly dark hair tumbling over his forehead. He wore a vaguely military-looking dark green sweater, a checked shirt, and light brown corduroy trousers. Even at this distance, he gave an impression of confidence and ease: the man of the house.

At the other side of the room, a woman stood at a big black range, stirring something in a deep copper saucepan. She had long straight dark hair tied back with a red bandanna. She was dressed in an oversize white shirt, loose like a painter's smock, and a pair of baggy slacks.

Now she turned, with a wooden spoon held aloft in her hand, and was about to say something to the man, but stopped, and looked to the window, frowning.

She must have seen them at the gate, despite the darkness, Wymes thought, or must have sensed their approach somehow. Despite his limited experience of them, women, he believed, were in general more alert than men, more keenly receptive of the tiny signals the world sends streaming out endlessly. It made sense, since they were more vulnerable and therefore had to be always on their guard. The same as children, only children were more trusting. Oh, yes.

He lifted the latch of the gate. A little woolly terrier bitch bounded forward out of the shadows, snuffling welcomingly. Some guard dog, Wymes thought—about as useful in that regard as his own Scamp. Armitage made a kick at the creature, but it would not be discouraged. Wymes leaned down and tickled the matted fur behind its ears.

The front door opened and the man they had seen in the kitchen appeared, standing slightly sideways and outlined against the light behind him in the hall. He was large and muscular, more so than he had seemed when seen through the window. There were beige-colored leather patches sewn onto the elbows and onto the shoulders of his pullover.

A city slicker, Wymes thought, a weekender playing at being the country gent, or—those shoulder patches—a soldier home on furlough. He doesn't know what's about to descend on him and his little idyll, Wymes thought, not without a touch of malice, and he immediately felt ashamed.

The man dropped the butt of his cigarette on the stone step and crushed it under the toe of his shoe. The little dog ran around his ankles in a circle three times, then abruptly sat down, quivering with excitement.

"Hello?" the man said into the darkness.

The voice was deep, the tone neutral, unchallenging. He was not worried. He was in his own place, standing proprietorially in his own doorway. Again Wymes felt a pang of foreboding. Something, he knew, something really was coming to upend this man's world, something, to be exact, in a blue blazer, shiny shoes and white socks with grass-green stains on them.

The man spoke again.

"Can I help you?"

Armitage stepped forward, into the crooked parallelogram of yellow light falling from the doorway onto the cobbles with the man's shadow framed in it.

"Sorry to intrude like this," he said. "Bit of bother—I seem to have lost the missus."

The man peered more closely at him, and Wymes thought he saw a look of startled recognition cross his face.

"Your wife?"

"I think she might have drowned herself," Armitage said. "Pretty sure she did, actually. Or fell in, if not."

He sounded oddly unfocused, as if the real matter were not the missing woman, but something else, some other matter off to the side.

"Good God," the man in the doorway said, but he too seemed distracted, and puzzled in some way.

Armitage introduced himself—"Armitage, Ronnie Armitage"—and held out a hand. The man looked at it as if he didn't know what it was.

"Drowned, you say?" he said. "You think she drowned, your wife?"

"So it seems. I mean, that's how it looks. I searched and searched, but not a sign. So it's a fair bet she went into the water. Poor thing. Very dark, down on that shore."

Wymes came forward now, edging Armitage aside.

"Have you a phone?" he asked of the man.

"A phone?"

"Yes, a telephone. To call for help. For assistance."

The woman had appeared at the far end of the hall, and stood there, still holding up the wooden spoon, scepterlike.

"What is it, Charles?" she asked.

Charles. Just a name, a perfectly ordinary name, yet it sounded unnatural, somehow, uttered like this, sharply, in a South Dublin accent, here, with the night all round and the man standing with his back to the light and the cobbles gleaming. Charles, in his ribbed green sweater with its neatly applied patches, and Mrs. Charles, almost as tall as her husband, slim, attractively flat-chested, with an oval face, a fine thin nose and vivid jade-green eyes. The perfect couple, Wymes thought, seeing the words in print, as in the headline above a photograph accompanying a crime report.

"It seems there's been an accident," Charles said to his wife, not turning to her, but still facing Armitage, and staring at him as if mesmerized. "Someone has drowned."

"Good God," the woman said, echoing her husband, and sounding, as he had, not so much shocked as puzzled. To Wymes, it seemed more than ever as if the whole thing had been rehearsed beforehand, and that everyone was acting, himself included.

"Come in," said the man, and he turned aside, lifting a hand with the palm turned upward. "Get out, you!" he snapped suddenly, in a hardened voice. The little dog whined and slunk out at the door.

"It's all right, Raggles," the woman said, and the dog cast back at her an accusing glance and went off into the darkness.

"Please, come in," the man said again, almost vexedly. "The name's Ruddock, by the way." He was addressing Wymes. "And this—" indicating the woman "—this is Charlotte, my wife. I'm Charles and she's Charlotte. Everyone laughs." He had a big man's slightly shambling walk. Halfway along the hall, he stopped and turned to Armitage. "By the way—how did you get here?"

"Eh?" Armitage said, blinking.

He was taking everything in with the keenest interest, the bog-oak hall table, the wood-framed mirror, the backing of which was crumbled to a yellowed laciness around the edges, the red and gray floor tiles. He was humming to himself, making a low, buzzing sound. He ran his fingers along the stippled Anaglypta wallpaper below the chair rail.

"How do you come to be here?" Ruddock asked again.

"Car," Armitage answered. He jerked a thumb over his shoulder. "It's sitting in the middle of your field, back there, where Dee abandoned it, and me along with it—charmed, dear lady," he broke off to say to Ruddock's wife, proffering a hand and assuming an oleaginous expression, more a leer than a smile, the corners of his thin, whitish lips stretched out and up at each side and almost reaching his earlobes. Yes, very like a clown, Wymes thought.

Mrs. Ruddock juggled the wooden spoon and took his hand, and quickly let go of it again, as if it were hot, or slimy, or both. Wymes noticed that she was barefoot. Her feet looked strange to his already confused eye. They weren't like feet at all. They could be a pair of undersea creatures, tentacled, unnaturally white, yet pretty in their eerie, unearthly way.

He paused at the hall table, on which a telephone stood. But already the others had gone on, into the kitchen, and he had no choice but to follow them—he wasn't going to take it on himself to summon help. *Remember,* he told himself, *you have no business being here, no business at all.* It wasn't his wife who was missing.

And it couldn't be, since there was no Mrs. Wymes. There never had been, and never would be. Mrs. Denton Wymes— what a thought! It almost made him laugh. For a second, there rose up before him the image of a giantess, mottled of arm and muscled of leg, with bulging breasts and a pair of hips the size of a dresser, a creature painted, curled and corseted, exuding moist warmth and an overpowering odor, bearing down on him glassily, irresistible as a ship's figurehead. *Faugh.*

The kitchen was tiny, square, low-ceilinged. It reminded him of the illustrations in a book his mother used to read to him from when he was a little boy. *Winnie-the-Pooh,* was it, or the one about rabbits, by that woman? The neat and cozy look of everything—the broad squat black range, the checked curtains, that vase of chrysanthemums on the scrubbed wooden table—seemed false, somehow, seemed fake. It was as if someone had arranged it all and then discreetly withdrawn, leaving the place to this tall, rangy couple with their drawling accents, their casual but expensive clothes, their undisguised, lazy air of privilege and languid disdain. Or not a picture book, no. Yet again, he had a sense of theater. The room was a stage set, and these people the players acting on it.

But then the thought came to him, bringing with it a mild shock, that he and the Ruddocks, this Charles and his Charlotte, were of the same class—was not his accent as fruity as theirs, did he not have about him the same aura of privilege, despite everything?—while Armitage was unmistakably the intruder. Just look at the white socks.

And yet it was Armitage who seemed most at ease, looking about the kitchen as he had looked about the hall, as if he were putting a valuation on the place, with an eye to a possible purchase when the moment was opportune.

"A drink?" Ruddock asked.

He had addressed the question to Armitage, bypassing Wymes, as if he were beyond consideration in the matter of alcohol, or anything else. Wymes was accustomed to being thus disregarded. Like an elderly clergyman, say, or a maiden aunt come for a visit at Christmastime.

"Don't mind if I do," Armitage said, eyeing the three-quarters-full bottle of Bushmills on the table.

Ruddock took down a tumbler from a shelf of the dresser that stood by the sink, turned, then hesitated. He looked at Armitage with his head to one side and one eye half-closed.

"Sure you haven't been hitting the bottle already?" he asked, intending it to sound light and humorous, and failing.

"Oh, indeed, I have," Armitage said, with the mildness of a man entitled to take offense but declining to do so out of a native magnanimity. He tittered. "I had a dry sherry on New Year's Day, like I do every year."

Charlotte Ruddock gave a short bark of laughter and then clamped her lips shut and glanced quickly at her husband. She had at last relinquished the wooden spoon, but stayed close by the draining board where she had put it down, as if she felt that at any moment she might have to snatch it up again and wield it in defense of herself or of her husband, or both. She had the look of a woman on whom something was slowly dawning. She glanced from her husband to Armitage and back again, her eyes narrowed.

There was the smell of stew. The copper pot on the range was making a low rumbling sound.

It struck Wymes who it was that Ruddock reminded him of. It was a fellow he had known at Oxford—what was his name?—a hearty, of course, and a persecutor of the weaklings below him in the junior classes. Ruddock had the same look of arrogance and calm stupidity, along with an occasional, fleeting frown, as if the thought had crossed his mind that, unlikely as it was, tonight might be the night when one of the many things he knew nothing about and cared nothing for might rear up out of nowhere and put a stop to him, as he made his broad-shouldered, heedless way through the world.

Armitage accepted the glass of whiskey and took an appreciative sip.

"Of course, as I said to my friend Whymass here, she may just have run off—the missus, I mean." He sipped again. "Mmm," smacking his lips, "I do like a drop of—" here he put on what he imagined was an Irish accent "—the *craythur.*" He paused, and cocked one eyebrow at Ruddock where he stood by the table with the whiskey bottle still in his hand. "She didn't come up here, by any chance?"

Ruddock stared at him.

"Your wife? Why would she?"

"Oh, you know."

"What?"

"How women get. Time of the month. March hares. *You* know."

Charlotte Ruddock's mouth tightened. She turned to Wymes.

"Were you in the car?" she asked.

"No, no," Armitage answered for him. "He was just passing by. He's a fisherman. His dog is locked in." He swiveled on the chair and looked up at Wymes. "Speaking of which, the bugger will have pissed all over your place by now. Maybe you should—"

"There's a phone in the hall," Charlotte Ruddock said, clipped and cold. "You can call the Guards and tell them your wife is missing. The wireless is forecasting high winds tonight."

Armitage smiled at her, the sharp pink tip of his tongue pressed to his lower lip. Of the four people in the room, he was the only one sitting down. He seemed thoroughly at his ease, with the tumbler of whiskey in his hand and one bony knee crossed on the other and one foot in its narrow shoe jiggling lightly.

"We'd had a bit of a row, you see," he said, to no one in particular. "She can be a tartar, when she gets going, our Deirdre. I remember one time—"

Charlotte Ruddock walked out of the room, her bare soles slapping on the floor tiles. Armitage looked to her husband, then glanced at Wymes again and lifted his eyebrows.

"Was it something I said?" he asked with mock innocence.

They heard from the hall the sound of the woman cranking the handle of the telephone. After a moment she spoke, but they could not make out the words. Ruddock had still not put down the bottle. It seemed as if he might at any moment hurl it at the wall, if not at someone's head.

Wymes looked again from one man to the other. What was going on here? He had the distinct impression that these two knew each other, and, further, that there was something between them, some hidden grudge or grievance. The wife, too, was part of it, he felt. It was as if he had stumbled into the midst of a muted but dangerous quarrel, between distant relations, say, over the contents of a will that had just been read out to them, to their general surprise and dismay. But also there lingered that sense of the theatrical.

Charlotte Ruddock came back. She stopped in the doorway.

"The Guards are on their way," she said, in a voice that was at once tense and toneless. "They're going to call out the lifeboat."

She looked at her husband where he stood, bottle in hand, still frowning in that baffled, sulky way. She knew that frown, Wymes could see, knew it all too well.

There was a soft click, and a door in a far corner of the room that Wymes hadn't noticed until now began to open slowly, in small, hesitant stages, creaking. He assumed there must be a draft there, since no one seemed to be pushing the handle, but then he looked lower down and saw a child of four or five edging its way into the room.

Was it a boy or a girl? Wymes couldn't tell at first. The mite was dressed in a loose white shirt—it was a miniature version of the woman's smock—black velvet knickerbockers, white ankle socks and neat little shoes of dark pink suede, complete with brass buckles.

"Heard people talking."

It was a boy's voice.

He was a creature of ethereal, of unnatural, beauty. Yellow tresses, like polished gold, framed a small, heart-shaped face. The lips had the curve of Cupid's bow, the huge eyes were deep blue and glossy. A tiny, perfect Grecian nose descended in a straight line from a flawless brow. He stood there, this tiny immaculate creature, taking in the adults one by one, as if they were strangers to him every one, but not at all threatening, and of no particular interest.

None of the four people before him stirred or spoke—even Armitage, sitting at the table with his knobbly knees crossed and the whiskey glass forgotten in his hand, was silenced for the moment. Then, suddenly, he roused himself.

"Why, if it isn't the Little Lord Fauntleroy!" he crowed.

And laughed his squeaky laugh.

Wymes, with a pained look, was blinking rapidly. He felt himself to be—dear Christ, no—on the verge of tears.

Outside, a gust of wind struck the house a large soft blow. The gale that was forecast was coming on.

3

The Garda sergeant's name was Crowley. Thomas Crowley, known as Toss. Toss Crowley was well-known in the neighborhood. He was not a tall man, but he was wide, and looked as if he had been carved from Galway granite.

He had been a Civic Guard since the force was set up, and should be retired by now, but no one, it seemed, could work up the courage to tell him it was time to go. Over the years he had been stationed at a number of Garda barracks up and down the country, never staying long in any of them, since his rough and often violent way with suspects resulted in frequent, hurried transfers.

In the Civil War he had fought with de Valera's crowd, and had a reputation as a crack shot. There were rumors he had been involved in the assassination of Michael Collins, de Valera's one-time ally and later opponent. Maybe he was, and maybe he wasn't. Toss Crowley was not a man to share a secret.

When Wymes heard the dog barking outside and saw the familiar figure shouldering his way in at the back door, he turned pale. The two men had a long acquaintance. Crowley came round regularly to the battered old caravan where Wymes was living, with his smile that wasn't a smile but a sort of knowing smirk. The pretexts for these visits were always flimsy. He checked repeatedly that Wymes had a license for Scamp, mentioning darkly that a dog with the same markings had been spotted worrying sheep. He would bring him forms to sign, about things that had nothing to do with him, the control of noxious weeds, or the leakage of contaminants into the water supply, or new restrictions on the lighting of fires in cornfields to burn off weeds.

He would stand outside the door of the caravan, with one foot on the step and his Garda cap pushed to the back of his head, making desultory comments between long silences, squinting up at Wymes in the doorway and sucking his teeth at one side. Sometimes he would drop a cigarette butt on the scrap of balding carpet at Wymes's feet and crush it out with the toe of his boot, and smile that smile, waiting to see what Wymes would do. Wymes never did anything, of course, and Crowley's smile would turn nastier still.

Tonight, he had a rumpled aspect. Two of the buttons of his tunic were unfastened, and the knot in one of his shoelaces had come undone. Wymes caught a sour whiff of porter—Crowley was a drinker, though usually he managed to cover up the telltale signs. He would not have expected to be called out this late at night—it was heading for eleven o'clock, and the atmosphere in the kitchen had become increasingly strained. Earlier, Mrs. Ruddock had taken the child off to bed and stayed upstairs for a long time, returning only when she heard the wheels of the squad car crunching on the gravel outside, and the little dog barking.

"Evening," Toss Crowley said, taking off his cap.

His close-cropped, grizzled hair glittered with beads of sweat, and the pink of his scalp showed through it. There was stubble on his cheeks and in the cleft of his chin. His glance was smeared, and he blinked frequently. He exuded a dampish, cottony odor. Probably he had taken to his bed early, Wymes thought, to sleep off an afternoon session in the pub, and when the station called him he had to struggle up and throw on his uniform.

Charles Ruddock was still seated at the table, where the by now almost empty bottle of Bushmills stood—it was Armitage who had drunk most of it, after which he had moved to a big old armchair in front of the fireplace, and was sprawled there now, asleep. Someone had thrown a checked woolen blanket over him.

The sound of Crowley's voice woke him, and he sat up blearily, wiping his mouth on the back of his hand.

Now another, younger Guard appeared in the doorway. He had a long neck and a small head and remarkably large, translucent pink ears that stuck out at right angles, like the trafficators on a motorcar. He was holding his cap nervously in his hand. He glanced shyly about the room.

"Shut the door," Crowley growled at him.

Armitage yawned, the joints in his jaws making a crackling sound. He gave himself a shake and rose unsteadily from the armchair, regarding the sergeant with lively interest. Ruddock too stood up. Crowley was eyeing the whiskey bottle.

"Will you take a cup of tea, Guard?" Charlotte Ruddock inquired of him, reaching for the kettle. He ignored her.

"Whose wife is it that's gone missing?" he asked of the room.

He looked questioningly at each of the three men in turn. He came to Wymes last, and frowned. He had not registered him until now.

Armitage stepped forward, a hand extended.

"Thank you for coming, Constable," he said. He glanced pointedly at his watch. "Long way, was it? Long drive? Sorry to bring you so far. The name's Armitage. I'm the one whose missus has gone AWOL."

This last he said with a shrug and a lopsided smile, as if losing a wife were a matter of small account, and quite droll, in its way.

Crowley, allowing his hand to be shaken, looked at him warily. It was plain he did not care for what he saw. An Englishman, too tall and too thin, speaking as if he had a mouthful of marbles. The accent was so refined it had to be phony. He appeared to be more or less drunk.

Wymes moved back a careful pace, out of the light of the shaded bulb above the table. He was wondering if he might manage to sidle around the room all the way to the door, keeping to the shadows, his back to the walls, and that way make his escape. *Fool!* he told himself. *Hapless fool! You're here now, and stuck here, and it's your own fault for stopping at that bloody car.*

"The thing is, it seems there's been some sort of accident," Charles Ruddock said. He was standing with the steepled fingers of one hand braced on the tabletop and the other hand on his hip. "My wife explained it to whoever it was she spoke to on the phone. This man—" indicating Armitage with a lift of his chin "—as he says, thinks his wife may have drowned. Or run off, or something."

The furrows in Toss Crowley's brow deepened.

"Are you related?" he asked suspiciously.

"Sorry?" Ruddock was frowning too. "You mean—?"

"I mean," Crowley said, "is this man—" he turned to Armitage and redirected his words at him "—are you a family member?"

"Oh, no," Armitage said, and this time laughed, as if the possibility of his being related to anyone here were the unlikeliest thing in the world. "Not at all, not at all."

His eyes shone glassily, and there was a small pink circular spot over each of his cheekbones. He should be footless, Wymes thought, after all the whiskey he had downed, but instead he seemed only excited, to the point of feverishness. It was how he had seemed earlier, when he came wading up through the meadow in the twilight, calling out, and waving his arm like a drowning man. What was the matter with the fellow? *Was* he unhinged in some way?

Crowley undid the button of the breast pocket of his tunic and brought out a dog-eared notebook with a black oilcloth cover.

"Can we start at the start," he said. He looked Charles Ruddock up and down, as if he intended to make a sketch of him in his notebook. "You're the householder, are you?"

"Yes. Ruddock. Charles Ruddock. This is my wife."

Charlotte Ruddock did not look at her husband. She was still by the range. It was, Wymes thought, as if an invisible aura kept drawing her back to that spot, and held her there, like an enchanted maiden in a fairy tale. Crowley had turned to speak to her, but now looked past her, frowning, to where the pinheaded young Guard hovered, a silhouette against the light from the hall.

"Didn't I tell you to shut that door?" he snapped. "Are you deaf, or what?"

"Sorry, Sarge," the Guard stammered, then corrected himself, "sorry, sir. It's stuck, or something."

"It's warped shut," Charlotte Ruddock remarked indifferently. "Like most things in this place," she said, glancing at her husband.

Armitage had fetched his glass from where he had left it standing on the mantelpiece, and now he approached the table and put out a hand eagerly toward the whiskey bottle. Ruddock grabbed it by the neck and drew it out of his reach.

"Don't you think you've had enough?" he said. Armitage lifted again that overly mobile eyebrow. "You seem to be forgetting about your missing wife."

"Oh, no," Armitage said, on a note almost of gaiety, "the darling one is ever in my thoughts."

Toss Crowley was looking from one of them to the other. He was plainly baffled. He turned to Wymes.

"And you," he said, "what are you doing here?"

Before Wymes could answer, Armitage lifted a hand in a sweeping flourish and said, "This, Constable, is my Good Samaritan. I met him back there—" he gestured toward the window with his other hand, twiddling his fingers "—there on the side of the hill, when I—"

"Whose is that car down there," Crowley demanded, cutting him off, "the one parked in the middle of the field?"

Armitage heaved an exaggerated sigh.

"That's what I'm trying to tell you, Constable."

"Stop calling me Constable. I'm a Garda sergeant. You're not in England now."

"Sorry, sorry." He swallowed, giving a sort of gulp. "The car is mine. Well, it's my wife's."

"What's it doing there?" Crowley turned to Ruddock. "What's his car doing in your field?" Ruddock looked at him with lofty disdain and said nothing. Crowley turned to the young Guard. "Dessie, go down and have a look at that vehicle. And stay by it, in case Mrs.—in case the woman comes back."

There was a search then for a flashlight. In the end, Ruddock went out and fetched one from the garage. It was a big bulky thing shaped like a flat iron, with a plastic handle. Dessie the Guard set off into the night, a white beam dancing before him like a will-o'-the-wisp.

Suddenly, Charlotte Ruddock spoke.

"Look, shouldn't there be a search party, or something? We can't just stand here doing nothing."

Her voice was constricted, as if an invisible cord had been pulled tight around her throat. Wymes watched her. She seemed in a fury, one she must have been working herself into, unnoticed by anyone, as she stood trapped there in her magicked circle by the range.

Sweat had oozed up now on Toss Crowley's forehead, and on his upper lip. He produced the stub of an indelible pencil, licked the tip of it and turned over a blank page in his notebook. He made to write something, but stopped. He turned to Ruddock with an almost pleading air.

"This man—" he turned his grizzled head in Armitage's direction "—he's a friend of yours, then, is he?"

"No, no. He just appeared at the door. He and—he and this person."

Wymes took a further soft step backward. Oh, if only he could melt through the wall and be gone. The sense of foreboding he had first felt on the hillside when he heard Armitage call out to him was creeping steadily, coldly, along his veins. He couldn't go back to prison—no, no, he couldn't go back there. Last time, he had been beaten up three times—

the last time, he had got two broken ribs and a dislocated jaw and black and yellow bruises the size of saucers all over his chest and his back. Another stint inside would be the end of him. He would do himself in, if one of his tormentors didn't do it for him first.

"All right," Crowley said, and he wiped the side of an index finger across his upper lip. "Sit down here at the table, all of you, and we'll try to get this thing straight."

He was breathing heavily, and his movements were clumsy. He's out of his depth here, Wymes thought, and furthermore is badly in need of a drink.

Charlotte Ruddock stamped her foot.

"Isn't someone going to *do* something?" she as good as shrieked. "For God's sake!"

There was a moment of silence, then from upstairs came a faint, querulous cry, light as a thread of cobweb floating down upon the air.

"Christ," the woman muttered, "now we've woken the child."

It was close to midnight when Toss Crowley licked the tip of his pencil for the last time and went through the motions of making a final entry in his notebook, then put it away in his breast pocket and did up the button. The wind now was pummeling the house and making the window frames rattle. Armitage, in the midst of telling his story, had broken down and wept for "my darling Dee." His tears, Wymes could see, sprang less from sorrow than from the effect of the alcohol he had consumed.

Charlotte Ruddock had gone upstairs to tend to her son, and had not returned.

Her husband was seated at the table again, upright and

watchful. He had the air of a sentry on the battlements waiting for the first flare to shoot up, signaling the start of the
siege. He was holding on to the neck of the Bushmills bottle
as if it were the barrel of a musket. He kept his eye on Armitage, with what seemed a continuing, puzzled surmise.

There was, there *was* something between these two men,
Wymes was certain of it, some angry, bitter, rivalrous thing.

He had a sense of the night crouched outside the windows
like a sleek dark animal, attending with an animal's indifference upon the lamplit human scene within.

Toss Crowley had gone out to the hall to phone the barracks in Wicklow. The people in the kitchen listened to him
asking if the lifeboat had returned yet, and if there had been
any trace of the woman. After some moments he came back
into the room and glared in turn at Wymes, at Ruddock
and at Armitage, as if they were all three equally to blame
for everything.

"Go on," he said to Armitage, "take yourself off home.
Leave me your number. When there's news, I'll call you."

Armitage blinked, then shook his head.

"No," he said, "no, I'm not going anywhere until Deirdre is found. I won't leave her." He gave a loud, accusatory
sniffle. "She's somewhere out there in the dark, all on her
own—how could I go?"

Ruddock had not spoken for some time. Now, he said,
"The pub down the road has a room to let. He can lodge
there for the night."

Armitage gave him a wounded look.

"You want me to check myself into some hostel, at this
hour?"

Crowley turned on Wymes an almost complicit glance.
Could it be the man's eyelid fluttered, in something like a

wink? There would be, Wymes realized, with bitter amusement, no talk of dog licenses this night. In certain circumstances, even the most unlikely ally will do.

4

Every morning the postman arrived at the door of the house on Mespil Road at eight o'clock sharp. Always at eight, or at most a minute or two before or after the hour. Strafford couldn't understand how the fellow managed to maintain this almost military regularity. After all, not every house received post every day, which would mean, surely, that the time taken to complete the day's round must vary. But it didn't.

Whether he was still in his room, dressing, or in the bathroom, shaving, or soaking in the tub, Strafford would hear faintly from below the surreptitious creak as the lid of the letterbox was pushed open, and then the tinny clack when it sprang shut, and he would check his watch. Eight on the dot, or seven fifty-nine, or a minute, two minutes, past. It was one of the smaller markers of his day: creak, clack, followed by the glance at the watch, and the head shaken in mild wonderment.

But they were both creatures of habit, the detective and the postman—whom, strangely enough, Strafford, in all the months he had been lodging here, had never seen, not even glimpsed, not once. Strafford too had his matutinal rituals, and never set out for work before half past eight.

Perhaps, he sometimes thought, perhaps it wasn't a human being at all who delivered the mail. Perhaps it was a machine of some sort, a fantastically intricate robot invented by a crazed genius in the employ of the Post Office. A ridiculous notion, of course, the stuff of cheap science fiction. All the same, it was a strange phenomenon, this impossibly punctual, phantom postman.

Strafford rarely bothered to check the mail when it arrived. There was hardly ever anything for him, except the usual circulars and a few bills at the end of each month. Anyway, he would never be able to get to the half-dozen or so envelopes strewn on the hall mat before one or other of his landlord's furtive yet omnipresent daughters had darted out and jealously gathered them up.

When he came in this evening, though, he was surprised to see the single letter, addressed to him, propped against a vase on the hall table. He recognized his wife's handwriting. It was the first time she had written to him—before this, in the long interval of their separation, all their communications, such as they were, had been by phone. He was surprised at how far and with what a jolt his heart sank when he saw those familiar fat loops, the erratically crossed *t*s and the *i*s topped not with dots but tiny circles.

He picked up the envelope and studied it for some moments. No thoughts, just that sinking sensation, and the sudden onset of an obscure, hardly palpable ache.

All was quiet. The Claridges, whose house it was, conducted their lives in an uncanny hush, in their quarters on the ground floor. Always, when he came in, he imagined them, stout Mr. and Mrs. Claridge and their thin, taciturn daughters, falling silent the instant they heard his key in the lock, and listening intently to his footsteps as he walked self-consciously along the hall and mounted the stairs to his room.

Sometimes he would pause on the landing and stand outside his door for a few moments, listening too, hoping in his turn to hear them, down in their burrow, as they began to twitter tinily, excitedly, discussing him. But either they were habitually silent, or they had the patience to outwait him, and at last he would fish out his key and go into the room and shut the door behind him and put a record on the gramophone and vindictively turn the volume as high as it would go.

It was odd that no one complained about the music, not even Mr. Singh, the young man who lodged in the room next to Strafford's. Mr. Singh was almost as quiet as the Claridges. It was, all in all, a troublingly tranquil household. Troubling, he realized, because it wasn't really tranquility, but a stealthy, tireless vigilance.

Anyway, probably it was all in his imagination. Probably the Claridges didn't even notice when he came or went, and God only knew what matters preoccupied the mind of the scrupulously incommunicative Mr. Singh.

Yes, Strafford thought gloomily, he was just being a fussy old bachelor. Although in fact, as he had to remind himself, he wasn't a bachelor, but a fussy, no longer young, solitary but unquestionably married man.

He put the letter on the mantelpiece and poured out a small

measure of whiskey. He had never been much of a drinker, but he always kept a bottle on hand, and in recent months had been surprised to find himself most evenings indulging in a modest glass of the fiery stuff, or even two.

It wasn't clear to him why, but he took this mild resort to the bottle as the mark of his having arrived definitively at middle age. That very morning he had spotted a gray hair, just the one, in his left eyebrow. He had tweezered it out, re-membering, too late, his mother observing that if you pulled out one gray hair, two would grow in its place. Was it true? Time would tell. It would give him something to do, he told himself with a bleak grin, the monitoring of his slow but in-evitable engrizzlement.

He turned down the volume on the gramophone—it was childish to have it on so high, especially as no one seemed to mind.

This evening, he had chosen Wagner. The *Siegfried Idyll*, performed by the Berlin Philharmonic, under Furtwängler. Though the melody was nice enough, he couldn't like the piece. He supposed this to be a failure of taste and musical discrimination.

Among the Germans, Mahler was his favorite. Though in fact, he reminded himself, Mahler wasn't German. His birth-place was in Austria, or Bohemia, or somewhere like that, somewhere in Mitteleuropa. What was it the anti-Semites called the Jews? Rootless cosmopolitans?

Late one night, as he was listening to the final movement of Mahler's first symphony, he had a sudden insight. It came to him, with the force of a profound and irrefutable truth, that Mahler's music wasn't really music at all. Certainly, it was not what Mozart or Bach or even Beethoven would have recognized as such. It was something else, something unique, individual, a grand, magnificent and chaotic medley of disparate and frequently dissonant noises.

He would never claim to be a thinker, but this formulation pleased him. He was proud of the insight, which he believed to be original. Of course, he would not dream of sharing it with anyone, ever, not because he feared being laughed at, but because he did not want to have to feel sorry for the idiots who could not understand what he was talking about.

But perhaps he might try it out on Phoebe? He could at least count on her not to laugh, and she would certainly grasp what he meant. Like him, Phoebe gave to such matters the grave, careful and only slightly lugubrious consideration she had no doubt they deserved.

He was, so it seemed, in love with Phoebe. Or at least, he seemed to love her, which might seem to be the same thing but wasn't. For instance, one could love one's sister, if one had a sister, but not be *in* love with her, not unless you were Lord Byron, or one of the pharaohs.

Thinking these thoughts, he glanced again in the direction of the mantelpiece and the letter. He had set it leaning against a porcelain figure of a twenties flapper in a green gown, slim, pale, reclining on a delicate little porcelain chair. Mrs. Claridge again, and her execrable taste.

It felt somehow as if the letter were looking back at him, with a narrow stare, beady, tight-lipped, impatient.

He rose and went to the gramophone and lifted the stylus and turned over the record and read the label. The *Meistersinger* overture. He rather thought not. He closed the lid and put the record into its brown-paper sheath and stowed it among its steadily swelling rank of fellows. He was becoming quite the collector. Next thing he would be joining a club of like-minded music lovers. Wouldn't that be jolly.

The letter was not dated, but it would have been sent yesterday, or at most the day before—the smudged postmark was indecipherable. *Dear Johnners*, it began, and was signed *Mag*. Her name was Marguerite. A pretty name. Daisy, in French. Daisy my sometime darling. Though his wife was as unlike that particular flower as any woman he had ever known.

He looked away from the sheet of notepaper and turned his gaze to the window and the deepening twilight outside. The western sky was still aglow, and on the other side of the road the surface of the canal had a silvery glare, as if the water had turned to polished metal.

Johnners. She only addressed him by that parody of his name when she was annoyed at him. And she was often annoyed at him, at his detachment, at what she considered his infuriating diffidence. Though she claimed it wasn't diffidence, not really, but a veiled and twisted form of arrogance.

He thought that, on the whole, she was probably right. Though if he was arrogant, he never seemed to get any of the benefits that were supposed to flow from it, such as the satisfaction of effortlessly crushing his enemies. But then, he had no enemies, that he knew of. Dr. Quirke, in whose company he found himself with unaccountable and annoying frequency, was these days displaying toward him an unrelenting—though for the most part unexpressed—animosity. The cause of this, Strafford knew, was jealousy. Phoebe was Quirke's daughter, and it enraged the father that she should have started up an affair with Strafford, of all people.

An affair. What a strange term, he thought, at once vague and businesslike. A man of affairs. A fine state of affairs. The Phoebe Affair.

Dear Johnners—

She hoped he was well, she wrote. She was well herself, now, for she seemed at last to have shaken off a cold that had been plaguing her for a fortnight. Her mother had recently turned seventy—"seventy, imagine!"—but showed no signs of slowing down. Yesterday, however, she had tripped over one of her dogs and sustained a badly sprained ankle.

Strafford couldn't but smile at that, if shamefacedly. He wondered which one of the yappy little brutes it was that had brought the old girl down.

He read on.

The farm was ticking over. The harvest was late, but the yield would be up on last year. One of the horses had a frightful cough, and sounded just like a child with croup, only louder. The vet said it would pass, and administered an injection, for which he charged three pounds, no less!

We have to meet, she wrote. *We have to talk.* He was to call the moment he received this letter, and they would set a day for her to come up to town. It must be soon.

The matter is urgent. I want you to understand that. Extreemly urgent.

Her spelling had always been erratic.

Mag. No *love*, no Xs. Only in letters did she use the diminutive of her name. It was what the family had called her when she was little.

The light had faded in the west. The house seemed even more somnolent than usual. When he listened like this, really listened, the silence became a kind of hollow roaring in his ears, as if there were a raging torrent somewhere nearby.

He telephoned her, as bidden, standing in the hallway with a hand cupped over the mouthpiece.

"Why are you whispering?" she demanded crossly.

"The walls have ears," he said, and laughed a hollow laugh.

He pictured the Claridges in their living room, vigilant as ever, the four of them standing in a row, crouched, with their ears pressed like stethoscopes to the flowered wallpaper, straining to catch what he was saying.

He really must put a stop to these absurd fantasies.

"What's so urgent?" he asked.

"What? I can't hear you." He spoke more loudly. "Oh, surely you know," she said.

He did, surely.

She would come up on the ten o'clock train in the morning, she said. He could take the time off work and meet her at Kingsbridge station. Her tone said, *It's the least you can do.* It was a given, by her lights, that he was always, in general, to blame.

5

He watched her approaching along the platform with small, rapid steps, her head bent and her eyes scanning the ground, quick and darting like a bird's, as if she were looking for something to snap up. The sight of her, of that familiar, hurried gait, set up a small ache inside him, the same as the one he had felt when he spotted her letter on the hall table last evening. She carried a handbag but no suitcase—she would not be staying, then. A raincoat was slung over her left arm. She always reminded him a little of her almost namesake, Princess Margaret. Poor Margaret, the party girl, with her cigs and her gin and her failed loves.

How many months was it since he and Marguerite had last met? He had lost count. Had they been together at Christmas? No use, he couldn't remember. He tried to, but his mind was blank. It was really too bad, forgetting, like this.

He had expected her to be changed since he saw her last, but she wasn't. Perhaps she was a shade slimmer. At any rate she looked quite svelte, in a dark blue two-piece outfit, the jacket nipped sharply at the waist, the skirt narrow and reaching to midcalf. Her legs were shapely—they were one of her best features, as she was well aware. The seams of her stockings were always straight, but all the same she checked them frequently, glancing quickly back and down, in what he had come to think of as a sort of tic.

The least of remembered things are the most affecting. That walk, the birdlike turn of her head, those trim ankles.

"God," she said, "this city is even filthier than I remembered."

"Yes, you'll miss the fresh country air."

She glanced at him sharply, suspecting mockery. He kept a straight face—it was naturally straight anyway. He felt dispirited already. *Vehement* was one of the words he associated with her. That, and *relentless*. How in heaven's name had they ever thought to marry? It was a question he had put to himself over and over, during the months of their separation.

She wore a black felt hat that for some reason made him think of archery. It was molded to a point at the front, and there was a curl in the brim at the back and a feather in the band. The heroine in some film had worn one like it. Fetchingly boyish in a wasp-waisted jerkin, extratight tights, pointy-toed boots, the jaunty little hat. Gene Tierney? Maureen O'Hara? It was a long time since he had been to the pictures. He and Phoebe should go, some night. Or he could go on his own. It was always restful, sitting alone in flickering darkness, his mind emptied of all thought by the nonsense being enacted up there on the screen.

Outside the station, they had to wait a good ten minutes at

the taxi stand. They did not speak. Marguerite, tapping her foot, gazed off in the direction of the Phoenix Park, where the Wellington monument rose massively above the trees. The sun was shining, the day was calm. They could smell the river, its greasy, sour stench.

Strafford sneezed.

He was wondering when to raise the question again as to what the matter could be that was so urgent she had to come up in person to discuss it with him. He knew, of course, or at least guessed. She wouldn't bring it up before he did. She had certain codes of behavior, which, though she never stated them, she expected those around her to comply with, and emulate. It was the man's place to do the heavy lifting. That was in the order of things.

He looked up at the sky, with its delicate powdery pale blue tint. Autumn. He experienced yet again that pang of— of what? It felt like a sort of diluted woe. He missed so many things he had never possessed.

The woman beside him sighed irritably, craning her neck and peering down now along both sides of the river. Not a taxi in sight.

"You'd think they'd be here, waiting," she said vexedly. "It is a railway station, after all."

He caught a fleeting waft of her perfume—or was it her face powder? Whatever it was, he remembered it.

She was going to leave him, for good this time. He did know it, had known it for some time, without being told. Indeed, she had already left; all that was required was an official announcement. That was why she had come up today, that was why she was so tense, tapping her foot on the pavement and scanning the taxiless quaysides and sighing. She wanted it over and done with. That was the urgent matter.

★ ★ ★

They went to Bewley's on Grafton Street. He couldn't think where else to take her. When he suggested it, she shrugged—as well there as anywhere. Yet they were hardly seated before she began to complain. The place was horribly crowded, and the smell of roasting coffee beans made her feel nauseous, she said. She took particular exception to the number of students lounging at the tables roundabout—"so scruffy, my God."

She had taken off her Robin Hood hat. Her gleaming black hair—another of her good points—was drawn back tightly into a neat bun, leaving a perfectly straight, chalk-white parting down the middle. She removed her gloves of soft black kid, finger by finger, and arranged them carefully beside her plate. She liked things to be in their proper place, just so. *Meticulous*: there was another word for her.

A waitress came and took their order. Coffee for Strafford, Darjeeling tea for Marguerite, with a jug of hot water on the side—"*hot* water, mind."

At every movement they made, the dingy crimson plush of the banquette where they sat gave off invisible puffs of weary-smelling dust. The room was loud with talk and the clatter of cups and saucers and cutlery. A loud crash made them both jump—someone had dropped a tray—and the students with one voice sent up a ragged cheer.

Strafford fingered the tarnished little spoon in the sugar bowl, piling the sugar to this side, then to that.

"I wish you wouldn't fidget," Marguerite snapped. He put down the spoon. "How are you?" she asked testily. "You look pale. Are you eating, and so on?"

"I tend to forget to cook when I come in, and then it gets to be too late and I can't be bothered."

"You are hopeless, you know that?"

"Yes, I suppose I am." He risked a smile, and, at last, the question. "Care to tell me why you've come up today, in such a hurry?"

She said nothing, only picked up her gloves, glared at them, and dropped them back on the table.

The waitress came, carrying a tray, and set out the tea things and the coffeepot.

"Thank you," Strafford said.

"You're welcome, sir, I'm sure," the girl replied, and gave him a perky little smile and blushed.

He filled his cup, to the brim, mistakenly, and the coffee slopped over and splashed into the saucer.

"What's the matter?" Marguerite demanded. "Are you nervous, or just being your usual clumsy self?"

"Both."

She delved in her handbag and brought out a cigarette case and a small gold lighter, and set them on the table beside the teapot. He thought of a nurse setting out the instruments before an operation. The cigarette case he recognized. He had given it to her some years ago, for her birthday. Or was it a Christmas gift? Again, he couldn't remember. She was fading, for him, fading already into the past.

"I don't see what's so amusing," she said.

"Nor do I," he answered, startled.

"Then stop grinning in that ridiculous way."

"I didn't realize I was."

"Well, you are."

"I think it's more a grimace, my dear."

"Whatever it is, please stop doing it."

She poured out the tea and added water from the little dented pewter jug. Strafford watched her hands. How graceful she was, even when she was irritated, as she was now. Or perhaps it wasn't irritation, perhaps she too felt discomfited, and oddly hindered, somehow, as he did.

"How is your mother?" he said.

"I was wondering how long it would take you to get around to asking. She's all right. I told you she sprained her ankle."

"Yes, you did."

"Her hands are giving her trouble, too, the joints. The doctor, old Squires—you remember him?—thinks it might be gout. I thought gout was something old men got, in their toes, from drinking too much port after dinner at their clubs."

"I'm sorry to hear she's unwell."

She paused with the jug of water still in her hand and frowned at him.

"I didn't say she's unwell."

"Gout is quite painful, I'm told. And there's her sprained ankle."

"She doesn't mind pain. Pain she can put up with." She set down the jug and touched the backs of her fingers to the side of it. "Lukewarm, of course. I did tell that girl—you heard me tell her, twice, that I wanted *hot* water."

Strafford, looking aside, pressed the heels of both his hands hard against the edge of the table.

"Can we stop?" he said quietly.

She gave him a stare of large but plainly fake surprise.

"Stop what?"

"Come on, old girl—"

"Don't call me that."

"Just tell me why you're here, and we can get it over and done with, whatever it is."

She drew in a long breath, flaring her nostrils.

"I've met someone."

This was an unexpected turn.

"Oh, yes?"

Now she too put her hands against the table and pressed hard. It was, he thought, as if they were playing a children's game, struggling against each other, from their opposing sides, one pushing and the other pushing back. Her gray eyes had a flinty glitter.

"Is that all you can say? 'Oh, yes?'"

"I'm waiting for you to tell me more, and then I'm sure I'll have more to say."

She selected a cigarette from the silver case and lighted it. Her fingers shook a little, and the flame wavered. What was making her shake, anger or distress? She was human, after all, he reminded himself, human like him.

"You're the most callous person I've ever met," she said, and turned her face away and blew a stream of smoke in the direction of the students at the next table. "Look at you, just sitting there. My mother warned me about you, all those years ago. Why didn't I listen to her?"

He reached out and touched the fingers of her right hand where they were braced on the table's edge. She would not relax them, and he drew his hand away and let it drop limply into his lap.

"I say again," he said, "let's not do this."

"Do what?"

"This. In a minute, I'll be remarking on how flat Norfolk is." She blinked. She didn't understand the reference—she had no time for the theater. "I mean, it's so banal, like in a mediocre play. You'll say cutting things, and I'll pretend not to mind and be debonair, and it will all be just—I don't know. Just—banal."

She gazed at him for some moments in silence, the cigarette forgotten in her fingers and busily smoking itself.

"Aren't you even going to inquire?" she said, and for a second she sounded almost plaintive.

"All right," Strafford said, suppressing a sigh. "Who is he?"

She was silent again. Then she reached across the table, ignoring the ashtray the waitress had brought, and doused her cigarette in the puddle of coffee in his saucer with a violent turn of her wrist, making the cup joggle. He said nothing. She spat at him a word he did not catch, pushed the table forward, rose quickly and strode away, pressing her handbag against her midriff with both palms.

He leaned back on his chair and looked about. She was right, there were a lot of young people in today. Trinity students, he could tell. Perhaps it was the day when examination results came out. That would account for the stridency and the false cheer.

At a table a little way off, a girl with vivid red hair tossed half of a bread roll at the young man opposite her. The fellow threw up his arms in exaggerated fright, whinnying laughter through flared nostrils. How shallow the young are, Strafford thought. Had he been the same? His mother used to say he had never been young—"born old, like that fellow in the story." *What story?* he wanted to ask, but didn't. Probably she meant Rip Van Winkle. She never could get things straight.

Lunchtime was in full swing by now, and the noise in the room was growing ever louder. They used to come here, he and Marguerite, when they were students. They didn't go in for throwing bread rolls, however. Marguerite in those days had been if anything more intense and severe than she was now. She had very little sense of humor, even then. He recalled, with a flush of not untender nostalgia, how when someone made a joke and everyone was laughing, she would glance about worriedly, afraid that the joke, the point of which she couldn't understand, might be at her expense.

Had he loved her? Had she loved him? The question seemed redundant now. He thought of Phoebe. It was all so difficult.

Marguerite came back briskly and sat down at the table.

She had applied fresh powder to her cheeks, but under it her skin was faintly blotchy. He examined her eyes to see if she had been crying—if she had, it would have been more in anger than in sorrow, he could be sure of that—but it seemed she hadn't. She had put on lipstick, too, somewhat crookedly. She was unnaturally calm. *Glacial*, he thought—there was a whole lexicon by which to describe her.

Had he been unfair, in their years together, to be forever watching her, judging her, thinking her callous and cold? If she was cold and callous, might it not be that he had made her so?

She opened the cigarette case flat on the table, then abruptly shut it again. She stared hard at the lighter she was holding in her hand.

"His name is Tom," she said, then quickly corrected herself. "Thomas. You probably know the family."

This last was spoken with a small toss of the head. She had always resented the fact—she took it to be a fact, and a fact of consequence—that his people were grander than hers. Her family had come over with Cromwell, whereas the Straffords could trace their roots back to one of the robber barons attendant upon Henry II when he came over at the start of the 1170s to put manners on the invading Anglo-Normans and the native Irish alike. That original Strafford had stayed on after the king's departure and acquired a sizable estate, where

Strafford's father, after all those centuries, still had his house and where he lived, though nowadays precious little of the land remained in the family's possession. Strafford *père* managed to be at once miserly and profligate—a miser to his family and profligate for himself—and over the years had sold off the property piecemeal to fund his various and always eccentric self-indulgences.

"What is his family?" Strafford asked, in as neutral a voice as he could manage.

"Spencer. They have a place in Waterford, outside Lismore. I believe they're related to the poet—what was his name?"

"Edmund Spenser. With an *s*, not a *c*. That how your chap spells it?"

Marguerite drew in a hissing breath.

"You're an utter pig, do you know that?" she said.

Strafford was looking at the brownish mess her cigarette had made in his saucer. He tried to mop it up with a paper napkin.

"I don't know them, the Spencers of Lismore, with or without an *s*."

This was true only in the strictest sense. His father had hunted with Rupert Spencer—*sic*—when the old boy was master of the Waterford Hunt, and returned the hospitality by inviting him to Roslea House each October, for the shooting. No doubt this Thomas Spencer of hers was old Rupert's son, or even—good Lord!—his grandson.

"What age is he, this fellow?" Strafford asked.

"He's not 'this fellow,' or 'my chap,' for that matter." She opened the cigarette case again and this time took out a cigarette. "I know what you're up to—don't think I don't."

"You do?"

"Yes, I do."

"Then maybe you'd tell me."

She gave her head another, dismissive toss.

"You know very well, with your insinuations, your sly disparagings." She did one of her little feline smiles. "Thomas is younger than you. Younger, more alive, more—" she hesitated for effect "—more vigorous."

She rolled the tip of her cigarette on the edge of the ashtray. Suddenly then she seemed to relax, as if the calming thought had come to her that, in this confrontation, she was the one who had, and would continue to have, the upper hand.

"We met at a gymkhana, of all places," she said, with a bright little laugh. "Can you imagine?" He could. Dumpy little girls on dumpy little ponies, mingled smells of dung and crushed grass, the trailers being unhitched, strident voices, far calls. "He has an adorable little girl, Fenella, and another one, who's older."

Strafford had finished his coffee, and now he considered the dregs in the bottom of the cup.

"What's her name?"

"What's whose name?"

"The sister, the older one."

"What does it matter, for Christ's sake!" Marguerite said in a fierce whisper, leaning forward and extending her head toward him on the long pale column of her neck.

How lovely she is, after all, in her brittle, princessy way, he thought. He used to call her his ice maiden, in the time when they could say such things to each other and still laugh.

Again, he put the question to himself: If he had been less cold, would she have been more warm? Futile speculation.

"Anyway," she said, drawing back with her chin and eyebrows lifted, "I hear you have *someone* too."

He felt himself blush. Phoebe—how did she know about Phoebe? Who could have told her?

"What do you mean, 'someone'?"

"Oh, don't play the innocent. I'm told she's half your age. Don't you feel just a little bit ridiculous?"

"Don't you?"

"Tom is a grown-up person, not like your bit of fluff."

He wondered how much she knew. Did she know, for instance, that Phoebe was Quirke's daughter? Marguerite had always loathed Quirke, or so she said, though Strafford had his doubts. On the few occasions when she had met the man, Strafford had not failed to notice the flush that spread slowly up from her throat and turned her cheeks a glowing pink. Loathing, or something else? He couldn't see anything attractive about Quirke, but many women did, and always had done, it seemed, even before he was a widower and winningly in need of soothing words and a shoulder on which to lean that big square head of his.

The waitress returned and began to clear the table. Strafford saw her registering with distaste the sodden napkin and the remains of the cigarette butt in his saucer. She would think it was he who had dropped it there. She asked if they would be wanting anything else. He smiled and shook his head, but Marguerite ignored her, and she went away, swinging her hips derisively. Perhaps he would have been happy with someone like her, Strafford was thinking, someone bright and bouncy who wouldn't care a fig for all the Spencers or Spensers in the land. Oh, yes, seduce the kitchen maid and have her turned out of the house to sell herself on the streets. His people had always been good at that kind of thing.

Marguerite was again fiddling vexedly with the cigarette case.

"Why are you being like this?" Strafford asked, without rancor.

"Being like what?"

He spread his hands.

"Being cross, and snarling at me."

"I'm not snarling! I don't snarl." She was sitting up very straight, and again she extended her head, upward now, Alice-like, on its long neck—it was a thing she did—until it was high enough for her to be able to look down on him. "I'm 'being like this,'" she said, "because you don't love me any more. If you ever did."

"Do you love me?" he not unreasonably inquired.

She made an impatient gesture, and stubbed out her cigarette, in the ashtray this time.

"I want a divorce."

"You forget, my dear, in Ireland divorce is forbidden by law."

She did her cat's smile.

"Yes, but we were married in England—had *you* forgotten?"

He had not, of course. At the time, her insistence on a London wedding had puzzled him, though he had made no protest. Had it been foresight on her part? Had she known even then that one day they would come to this? Or maybe it had been her mother's idea, the evil-minded old bat, that her daughter should have an escape route. He said nothing, only sat musing.

"Christ," Marguerite exclaimed, "you could at least pretend to be shocked—to be upset."

Delicate skeins of smoke from the squashed cigarette undulated above the ashtray and slowly dispersed.

"I am shocked," Strafford said flatly. "I am upset."

Now she would not look at him at all. Some moments passed. They were like wrestlers disengaging and taking a step back to catch their breath and plan new holds, new stratagems. Not that Strafford had a strategy, or anything like it. He felt hollow, hollow and starkly askew, like the stump of a burned-out tree.

"Everything is arranged," she said, still avoiding his eye. "You'll have to come to London. Just for a night. Tom will book a hotel, and arrange about—about finding someone to—"

She frowned at the tablecloth, biting her lip.

"Someone to what?"

"To be with you, at the hotel."

"Ah," he said. "I see. And your Tom will arrange for me and this someone to be caught in flagrante by someone else."

"You won't actually have to *do* anything," Marguerite said in a sulky whine, "just—be there." She paused delicately. "We thought *you* might be able to find a person to—to see you together, with—with her—and give evidence in court."

He reared back, and puffed out his cheeks and released a breathy laugh.

"You want *me* to find some grubby little man in a trench coat and a slouch hat, who'll hang around a hotel lobby and spy on me in guilty company with a tart and testify to having nabbed me in the act of adultery?"

She pouted.

"Well, you are a detective," she said simply. "Surely you have contacts at—I don't know—at Scotland Yard, or wherever. Oh, don't look at me like that! It can all be very simple and straightforward. It happens all the time, and Tom says this is how it's done. Everyone understands."

"Everyone except me, perhaps?"

"Please. It will be as easy as anything, and over before you know it."

"You make it sound like a visit to the dentist."

The students at the next table were departing noisily. One of them, a hulking fellow with a mop of matted hair and very little forehead, paused in pulling on his coat and gave Marguerite a bold, appraising stare, then glanced at Strafford and smirked. Marguerite had noticed neither the stare nor the smirk. Just as well—she would have expected Strafford to leap up and hit the fellow.

"Darling," she said, softly now, reaching across and patting the back of Strafford's hand, "you're not going to make a fuss, are you? It's over between us. It's been over for ages, we both know it—we've known it since I went away to stay with Mother. Even before that, we knew." She stopped, and then said, stumbling over the words, "I'm sorry—I am, you know, really."

"Yes," Strafford responded mechanically, "so am I."

But was he, really?

Thinking this, he was overtaken by another, tremendous sneeze. The hulking student paused among the tables and glanced back at him and laughed.

6

When he got back to the station, curiously unruffled—was Marguerite right, was he a coldhearted pig?—he found a message from Chief Inspector Hackett, summoning him to his office, which was beside his own on the top floor. He found the chief sitting in his swivel chair with his back turned, gazing out of the small square window behind his desk. Strafford gave a little cough, but the old man let some seconds elapse before he roused himself. Gathering his wits with a visible effort, he related the facts, such as they were, of the disappearance of Deirdre Armitage, and the events that had followed it at the Ruddocks' rented house.

"Queer business altogether," he said. "Gone without a trace, it seems."

By now, Strafford knew he had caught a cold. Colds were rare with him, which was probably the reason he suffered so when the sniffles did set in. And this was going to be a bad dose, he could tell. Extraordinary how quickly it had come on. So far he had used up two handkerchiefs, the one he always had with him and the spare one he kept in a drawer in his office. What had been crisp white squares of linen had become wet cold clumps the size of golf balls and the same dampish shade of gray. His eyelids stung, and the wings of his nostrils had already turned a rabbity pink, so that blowing his nose was an exquisitely sore and shiver-inducing ordeal.

Aching with self-pity, he treated himself with an almost maternal tenderness. At the same time, he was filled with self-disgust. He felt a pariah. He was supposed to have had dinner with Phoebe at the Russell Hotel tonight, but before coming to the chief's office he had telephoned her to cancel the date, for fear, he said, of infecting her with his germs. This was considerate of him, not to say chivalrous, he thought, and he was a little put out that Phoebe, on the phone, did not express the level of appreciation he judged his selfless gesture called for.

It was all right, she said, she would go to the Shakespeare for a drink with Isabel Galloway instead.

She and the actress had recently renewed a lapsed friendship, and had begun to see a great deal of each other. Strafford was not at all sure that he approved. Isabel must be a good twenty years older than Phoebe, and had a reputation— indeed, in certain circles she was notorious. He had once heard her described as a shameless rip. Besides, as if all that were not enough, she had been Quirke's mistress for a time.

However, he kept his misgivings to himself. He knew he would get a dusty riposte if he didn't.

Phoebe guarded her independence jealously. It was one of the things he found attractive in her, although it did tend to make for occasional and, as he considered, tiresome confrontations. These flare-ups he dealt with as best he could— another man would have lost his temper and stormed off. There were times, in Phoebe's company, when he felt he was not so much with her as circling round her, watchful and wary.

"I'm not your wife, you know," she had said to him one evening, when he had been insisting with uncharacteristic force on some point or other. "You don't own me."

Though she smiled when she said it, the rebuke, or warning, had hit home.

He needed Phoebe, needed her to a degree that at times alarmed him. If he caused her to leave him, he would not forgive himself. And yet, paradoxically, he wasn't sure she was so firmly fixed in his life that her departure would constitute leaving him, exactly.

She had her ways, and unsubtle ways they were, of asserting her independence. *I'm not your wife, you know.*

In fact, the thing had become horribly complicated by Marguerite's request for a divorce. He hadn't told Phoebe about it yet. He doubted she would expect him to marry her, yet she might.

His experience of women was limited. So many of the things they said and did left him at a loss. Phoebe knew this, and used the knowledge to tease him. She would demand that he accept some wholly absurd proposition and then laugh at him, if fondly, for his credulousness. It was trying at times. Good thing he was of an equable disposition.

"Anyway," Hackett said, interrupting Strafford's reverie, "go down there and talk to the husband. He's staying somewhere nearby and refusing to budge until she's found."

He lit a cigarette, coughed, and began to shuffle the papers

on his desk. Strafford, who had risen and was already at the
door, paused and looked back at him. There was something
odd about him today. He seemed distracted—no, *detached*,
that was the word. He was here, but his mind was elsewhere.
There were brownish pouches under his eyes, and his forehead had a damp gleam. Now he looked up.

"What?" he said.

"Nothing," Strafford answered. Still he tarried. "Are you—
are you all right?"

The chief regarded him with his froggy, bulging stare.

"What do you mean?"

But Strafford wasn't sure what he meant, and he excused
himself and went out and shut the door behind him. The
cooler air on the landing invaded his nostrils and he stopped
and gave such a violent sneeze it seemed a molar or two might
come loose in their sockets.

These days, he was without his car. Marguerite had gone
off to her mother's in it, and he hadn't bothered to ask for it
back. Now he had to wait for half an hour in the day room,
glancing through the *Irish Times*, until one of the drivers
came on duty.

At last young Davy Dolan appeared, pomaded and cocky
as always, with one hand in a trouser pocket, whistling. His
thick dark hair was combed into an elaborate coif, in the fashion of James Dean. He glanced with amused disdain at the
newspaper, which Strafford had not been prompt enough to
put out of sight. Dolan would regard the *Times* as altogether
too snooty and staid, being fit only for Protestants. His read
would be the *Irish Independent,* or something from across the
Channel, the *Daily Mail,* or even *Tit-Bits.*

I really am a dreadful snob, Strafford thought complacently.

"Where are we off to, then?" Dolan inquired, cheeky and offhand, and he lighted up a Woodbine.

"Wicklow," Strafford said.

"Nice day for a tootle down the country."

The young man sauntered away, trailing a plume of cigarette smoke, which Strafford, following him, tried not to breathe in, though nevertheless some of it got through and made him cough.

He had never been a smoker. Didn't smoke, hardly drank. "You know, you're the only married virgin I've ever encountered," Marguerite had said to him once, with one of her shaky little laughs. Now he blew his nose, making a honking noise that caused Dolan, like the lout in Bewley's, to look back at him over his shoulder with a grin. Why did everyone think a cold was funny? Did they never get colds themselves?

Two squad cars were parked close beside each other in the tiny yard at the back of the barracks. Dolan opened the green-painted gate onto Townsend Street and then came back and sat behind the wheel of the nearest car. He had to maneuver it out of its space before Strafford had room enough to open the passenger door and get in. He would have preferred to sit in the back, but that would have been too pointed an assertion of rank. Dolan was touchy, and a talker behind backs, besides.

"Remember the last time we were in this jalopy?" he said, as they drew to a halt at the lights at Tara Street. Strafford shook his head. "Quirke was with us."

Strafford frowned.

"Quirke?"

"Sorry—Dr. Quirke. We were going down to the Jerries' place, to talk to what's-his-name about the girl that got murdered, the Jewish one from Cork."

"Rosa Jacobs," Strafford said. "I do remember."

Did Dolan imagine the murder rate in Ireland was so high that this one would be forgotten?

"That was—what?" he mused now, "a year ago? Holy cow, where does it go to. You blink your eye and it's next year."

Strafford did not respond, and turned away and looked out of the window beside him. He had no wish to discuss Rosa Jacobs, or anyone else for that matter, with the irritatingly jaunty Davy Dolan.

The young man's smoky breath was filling the car with the stink of cheap tobacco. Strafford's sinuses ached. His cold was steadily worsening, and he felt as if he had been struck with something rigid across the bridge of the nose.

They swept through Ringsend and came out onto the coast road. The tide was low, and Sandymount's shallow strand was dry for a mile out, to where a fringe of white water bustled and distantly roared.

We would do well to keep ever in mind that for the horizon we are the horizon. Where had he read that? These bits and pieces, he thought, how they cling on, like wisps of lint.

The sun was shining, but a big-bellied purple-gray cloud was suspended, seemingly motionless, above the far-off breakers. To the left, gulls wheeled in wide, slow circles high up over the city sewage works. The birds were an unnatural pristine white against the murk of the distant cloud.

On Sandymount strand, Strafford thought, *I can connect nothing with nothing.* Another scrap of fluff. He smiled wanly to himself.

He sneezed, and Dolan looked at him askance and pointedly rolled his window halfway down.

At Newtownmountkennedy they were delayed by traffic. There had been a collision between a bread van and an ancient Ford driven by an even more ancient priest. Dolan swore under his breath, and sighed, and drummed his fingers on the rim of the steering wheel. He was a very impatient young man.

Strafford had once been told a joke about someone having the name Newtownmountkennedy tattooed on his penis, but he couldn't recall the punch line, unless that was the punch line. He was no good at jokes. Even if he could remember this one and told it to him, Dolan would know he was being patronized. Strafford's distaste for smut was well-known.

"Will I pull over and help your man to push the van out of the way?" Dolan asked.

"Oh, leave them to it," Strafford said, sounding sharper than he had meant to.

He felt another tickle in his sinuses, and pressed the already sodden handkerchief to his nose. The tickle subsided, but as soon as he lowered the hankie the sneeze came on anyway, with a suddenness and force that lifted him a couple of inches off the seat. He slumped back, gasping.

Dolan sighed again, more heavily this time.

After Arklow, they turned left off the Wexford road and headed toward the coast.

Strafford consulted the torn-off piece of ruled paper on which the desk sergeant had written out the directions.

The house was called Tullyrane. It was in an isolated spot, almost on the sea. They were to look out for a crossroads, where there was a pub and a garage with an Esso sign. Drive on then for a couple of miles, and they would find the place, behind a five-barred gate with granite pillars that was always open, and on up at the top of a rise. They couldn't miss it. Nothing else for miles around, only the countryside, fields of wheat and barley, and the sea, out beyond a rocky coastline.

They didn't miss it. There was the open gateway, the stone pillars, the car standing incongruously in the long grass on the side of the hill, its metal skin goldenly aglow in the sharp sea air.

"Will you look at that," Dolan said, with a professional's appreciative whistle. "That's a Pagoda, that is."

"A Pagoda?"

"That's what the car nuts call it. A Merc." He whistled softly. "Slinky-dinky."

The house, as they approached it up the track, gave the vertiginous sense of being about to topple over backward. Then they were on the level and everything straightened up suddenly and settled into place.

Tall narrow windows, steep roof, a door with a latch. There was a graveled space in front. On the right a garage wide enough to house two cars, on the left and toward the back a flourishing garden with flowers, fruit bushes and potato drills.

"Nice gaff," Dolan said, and for some reason snickered.

The cloud that had hung menacingly over Sandymount had followed them for a while, but then had gone off to rain on somewhere else. Here, hazy autumn sunlight bathed the stone frontage of the house and lit up the garden's dulled greens and ambers.

A woman in a floppy sun hat was on her knees before a bed of chrysanthemums, delving with a trowel. She wore a pale blue shirt and loose blue dungarees. When she heard the car she turned and watched it approach, with a hand lifted to shade her eyes.

"La-di-da," Dolan murmured, and again did his soft, sly little laugh.

What Dolan found funny was one of the smaller mysteries Strafford was presented with in his professional life.

A little dog that had been soundly asleep beside the woman woke now with a start and jumped up onto all fours, barking loudly.

The two men got out of the car. The woman did not rise, but knelt there, the back of a wrist pressed to her forehead.

"Stop it, Raggles," she said to the dog. The animal fell silent, and with a sheepish expression crept in behind the woman's back to hide.

"Good morning," Strafford said, approaching. "I'm looking for Mr. Ruddock."

"I'm Mrs. Ruddock," the woman said.

She thrust the point of the trowel into the ground and gave herself a push and with a small grunt rose to her feet. She was tall, as tall as Strafford. Her face was long and shapely, her nose sharp and tilted upward slightly at the tip. The sunlight shone full upon her face, and in the shade of her wrist he couldn't make out the color of her eyes. What was she—fortyish? Younger? She reminded him, a little, and disconcertingly, of Marguerite, though this woman was much taller, and more casually disheveled than Marguerite would ever allow herself to be. She wore fisherman's clogs with thick wooden soles, and no socks.

"The name is Strafford."

The woman glanced from him to Dolan and back again.

"You're the Guards, yes?"

"Yes. I'm a detective inspector. This is Garda Dolan."

Dolan had left his uniform cap in the car. The sunlight glinted on the buttons of his tunic, and on the oiled wave of hair lolling halfway down his forehead.

"You're the second lot we've had in the last twelve hours. Where's the one who was here last night?"

Strafford realized that he found her distinctly attractive, to his surprise and mild dismay. Was it the echo in her of his more dainty Marguerite? The same sharp gaze, the same air of lazy insolence.

His Marguerite?—she was not that, anymore.

"I'm not sure who was here," he said.

"One of them was called Cowley, or Crowley, something like that."

He tried to place her accent. English, or extraposh South Dublin?

"Ah, yes, Sgt. Crowley. He called us." He looked about. "He's not here still?"

"Went home in the early hours," Mrs. Ruddock said, "to sleep it off, I imagine." Strafford put his head to one side inquiringly. "He smelled strongly of drink," she said. "There were two of them, him and—" she glanced at Dolan "—a younger one, with the most enormous ears." She turned toward the house. "Come along. My husband is unpacking."

"Unpacking?"

"We just arrived yesterday morning. This place is rented."

"And you live in—?"

"Dún Laoghaire." She pronounced it Dunleary. "Vesey Place." She paused and turned back to him. "Do you know it?"

"Yes, I do."

Behind them, Dolan gave a soft, disdainful snort. He had a wide repertoire of sound effects.

The dog followed meekly after them, her tail trailing low to the ground.

At the front door, Charlotte Ruddock stepped out of her

clogs and propped them against the iron bootscraper. She flexed her prehensile toes on the slate threshold. She was looking back down the hill.

"That car is still there," she said darkly.

She led the way into the hall. Strafford with a look told Dolan to remain behind, at the door.

There was a vase of chrysanthemums on the hall table. Charlotte Ruddock touched them with her fingertips, then looked at herself in a big wood-framed mirror above the table and made a clown's face, letting her mouth droop at the corners. She caught Strafford's eye in the glass and held it for a moment.

"The man who owns the car," Strafford said, "he's lodging somewhere nearby, is he?"

"Armitage, he's called."

"Yes."

"The sergeant, Crowley, took him off to McEntee's—they have a room over the bar that they let to traveling salesmen and the like."

"You seem to know the area."

"We come every year—God knows why." She chuckled. "He was quite pissed—Armitage. He drank half a bottle of whiskey, more, and talked about his wife. Have you found her, by the way?"

"No."

Strafford was dealing with a tiny sense of shock. Women didn't say words like *piss*, not women of her class, and certainly not in the presence of a person they had just met.

They were walking down the short red-and-gray-tiled hall. He was sharply aware of her presence beside him. She moved at a long-legged slouch. He knew she was putting on a performance—the Barefoot Lady of Vesey Place—and he, despite himself, was responding to it.

There were noises behind them outside the door, a thump and a scrape, then Dolan stepped aside and a large, somewhat shaggy man appeared in the doorway, grasping in both arms an enormous leather trunk. Seeing the strangers, he stopped.

"This is Inspector Stafford," the woman said.

"Strafford," Strafford corrected her. "With an *r*."

"Oh, sorry," she said. She didn't sound sorry. "My husband—"

"Charles Ruddock," the man in the doorway said, brusquely forestalling her. He advanced into the hall and set the trunk down on one end and stood and leaned on it, panting.

"For Christ's sake, Charlie," he said to his wife, "what have you got in here—rocks?"

"That's it," the woman said. She turned to Strafford. "Never go anywhere without my rock collection."

Ruddock gave her a sour look. Strafford was staring at him. There was something familiar about him—what was it? Something best left unremembered, so it seemed. Rugby type, Clongowes or Blackrock College, University College or even Trinity. Then—what? Banker? Solicitor? Senior manager, Ruddock & Son? There was bound to be a Ruddock & Son.

"Have you found the woman?" Ruddock asked. "The one that went missing."

"There's a team out searching for her still."

"Oh. Good." He stepped forward. "Come into the kitchen. My darling wife here will make tea for us, if we ask her nicely." He looked along the hall to where Garda Dolan had taken his place again in the open doorway. "What about your batman?" Strafford gave his head a small shake. Ruddock smiled, without warmth. Strafford knew he was being mocked. "Other ranks, what?"

Ruddock walked ahead into the kitchen. His wife looked after him and then at the trunk and shook her head.

"Are you going to just leave the bloody thing sitting here?" she said to his back, and tried to give the trunk a shove with her bare foot.

"They're your rocks," Ruddock called back to her, with a laugh that sounded like Dolan's snicker.

In the kitchen, he went to the sink and began filling a kettle.

"Sit down," he said to Strafford, putting the kettle on the range. "This thing will take a bloody hour to boil."

He moved moodily about the room, taking down cups and saucers, setting out plates. His wife came and leaned a shoulder against the frame of the door, her arms folded and ankles crossed, watching him, one eyebrow arched. The air in the room seemed to buzz faintly. It was, Strafford knew, the sound of simmering marital strife. It was a sound he was familiar with. The Ruddocks were in trouble. This was how his own marriage had stumbled along, for years, until it stumbled to a halt.

"So," Ruddock said, addressing Strafford but with his back still turned, "do you think this woman did drown herself?"

The tone was casual, but there seemed to be tension behind the words.

"I don't know," Strafford said. "I need to talk to the husband."

"Not sure how much sense you'll get out of him. Seemed to me he had a screw loose. Then he drank himself into a stupor, on my whiskey." From a shelf over the range he took down a tea caddy and peered into it, then turned accusingly to his wife. "There's no frigging tea."

"I asked you to get a packet of frigging tea when you went into the village, and you forgot."

"What's the point?" Ruddock asked rhetorically of Strafford. "You keep a dog and bark yourself."

"Woof-woof," his wife said, with a sour laugh.

Strafford cleared his throat.

"This Armitage," he said to Ruddock, "can you give me directions to the place where he's staying?"

Ruddock paid him no attention. Husband and wife were staring at each other, expressionless. At the name, Armitage, something had passed between them silently, like an electric current. Then Charlotte Ruddock unfolded her arms, turned, and sauntered off. They heard her kicking something, and then giving a gasp of pain.

"Will you *please* move this *bloody* trunk!" she shouted back into the room.

From above came the mewling sounds of a fretful child waking up. Ruddock turned his eyes to the ceiling.

"Here we go," he said, putting a hand facetiously behind his right ear. "Wait for it."

At once, the child's hiccups turned to wails.

Ruddock nodded grimly, and glanced at Strafford.

"Got any sprogs yourself?"

"Sprogs?" said Strafford.

He didn't know the word.

"Children."

"Ah. No, I haven't."

"Married?"

"Yes. Well, sort of."

The child upstairs was shrieking now.

"And you're a detective," Ruddock said.

He had almost to shout to make himself heard over the noises from above.

"Uh..."

Ruddock chuckled.

"Sort of?"

The child's cries stopped abruptly.

"I am a detective, yes," Strafford said. "Detective inspector, actually."

"Actually," Ruddock echoed softly, with another little laugh.

Suddenly then he put down the tea caddy with a bang and turned, staring, his brows furrowing and his mouth falling open.

"Christ almighty," he said in dawning wonderment. "Strafford! I *thought* I knew you. You're St. John the Injun. Well, I'll be buggered."

7

And at once, of course, Strafford too remembered. The New School, Kilkenny. When he was young—how many eons ago?

It was a good school, by the standards of the day, liberal to a point, though academically undistinguished. There were one or two notables among its old boys, including a physicist of some distinction and a once-famous Arctic explorer. It was run by a well-meaning Quaker headmaster and his Quaker wife. The Nevills. Decent, tentative people.

Mr. Nevill, though, for all his seeming diffidence, must have been an authoritarian behind the scenes, for the teaching staff were a cowed and timid bunch in tired tweeds and narrow ties. There were a couple of exceptions. The science teacher was eccentric to the point of lunacy, and the chaplain was said to have been decorated for bravery in the war. These two the Nevills treated with much caution.

However, no master was a match for Charles—never Charlie—Ruddock, awash with testosterone and already, at fifteen, a burly, big-chested bruiser with a rugby player's thighs bursting out of his gray school trousers. He had arrived halfway through the school year, and it was rumored he had been summarily expelled from one of the Catholic colleges, Blackrock, or Rockwell, for injuring a younger boy. The matter was never mentioned openly.

Charles Ruddock's family was well-to-do and highly influential in the political life of the country. His father had been one of the new men brought in by W. T. Cosgrave when he was put in charge of the provisional government after independence in 1922. Ruddock Sr. later became something high up in the law, a barrister, or a High Court judge, Strafford couldn't remember which. His wife was an O'Kelly, one of the Fine Gael O'Kellys, a political dynasty since the days of Parnell and the Irish Parliamentary Party.

Young Ruddock knew his place, and expected others to know theirs, well below his. He had a large head and a large square chin. His manner was one of lowering, offhand menace. He stalked through the school as if he, and not Mr. Nevill, were in charge of the place. Always there was a knot of puzzlement at the center of his forehead, as if he were constantly trying to puzzle out why it was he had to sit in classrooms listening to half-baked fools droning on at him hour after hour, day after day, when by rights it was he who should have been telling them what was what—why couldn't that simple and perfectly obvious fact be acknowledged?

A bully, of course. There was no one to resist him, and certainly no one to challenge him. He punched jaws and boxed

ears when he felt like it, and yet he was never ratted out to
the staff. Younger boys he would grab by the hair at their
temples and lift them up, squealing, until they were teeter-
ing on their toes like ballet dancers.

He had his gang, four or five toughs like himself, though
none of them was quite as tough as he, and all of them were
in thrall to him. There was something about him, a sense
of something as yet unleashed, that held them subject to his
dull, slow-moving will.

Strafford, tall, thin, pale and gangly, seemed an obvious
target for Ruddock's brutish attentions. Oddly, however, the
bully left him alone. Indeed, it seemed the sports star was
ever so slightly in awe of the aesthetic nerd. Strafford vaguely
sensed his superior position, but did not understand it, and
kept himself at a prudent remove from Ruddock and his
band of brawlers.

And now here he was with his former schoolmate, standing together in a kitchen in a cottage in the country, the two
of them grown to manhood. Life, as Strafford had often had
cause to observe to himself, was strange and at the same time
thumpingly banal.

"How did you remember?" he asked.

Ruddock gave him a look well-known to Strafford, at
once blank and truculent.

"How did I remember what?"

"My nickname. St. John the Injun."

The entire school thought it a scream that his name should
be spelled as it was, yet pronounced Sinjun. It would be just
like his parents to play such a joke on him, but he was called
after his maternal grandfather, St. John the First, as his father
liked to call the old boy.

"You were such a little tick."

"Taller than you, though, as I recall."

Ruddock considered this.

"You always reminded me of Lord Snooty in the *Beano*. Remember Lord Snooty? All you needed was a top hat."

Above them, the child began to cry again. They heard the woman climbing the stairs. After a moment, the crying stopped.

Ruddock opened a cupboard and brought out a whiskey bottle, and swore when he saw that it was empty. "That bastard," he muttered. He knelt and reached into the back of the shelf, came out with another bottle and peered at the label.

"Jesus," he said. "Pernod. Who drinks Pernod in this godforsaken hole?" He stood up. "Oh, well, better that than nothing. You'll join me?"

Strafford was about to say no, but nodded instead. The old ways will assert themselves, no matter the years. With Ruddock and his like, a yes was always more advisable than a no.

From the wooden dresser, a massive affair as black as the stove, Ruddock got down two tall, slim crystal glasses—"Look, they even have the right glassware!"—and poured a measure into both. The sharp scent of aniseed stung Strafford's congested nostrils. He thought he might sneeze, but didn't. Ruddock topped up the glasses with tap water, and the drink turned cloudy and phlegm-colored. They sat down at the table.

"So how did you come to be a detective?" Ruddock asked, frowning, and he took a sip from his glass. "Pity there's no ice." He looked at Strafford. He had forgotten the question he had asked. "We only rent this place for the Halloween break. Just arrived yesterday, still settling in, as you see."

"Yes, your wife said."

"Cheers."

Strafford put the glass to his lips. The drink tasted as it smelled. He was reminded of childhood. What were those sweets? Aniseed balls? Bull's-eyes?

"This man whose wife went missing," Strafford said, "Armitage. He stayed the night at—where was it? McGinty's?"

"McEntee's. Pub down the road. They have a room for rent by the night." He did his dismissive little laugh. "The poor bastard—imagine the kip. Damp sheets, a chamber pot left half-full under the bed and a Sacred Heart lamp on the wall."

"What did he say about his wife?"

Three deep, lateral furrows appeared in Ruddock's brow. "That he thought she had thrown herself into the sea."

"You didn't believe him?"

"I didn't know what to believe. His behavior was peculiar, to say the least. He kept laughing. It wasn't just the drink." He paused. "I went down there this morning, to have a look along the beach and among the rocks. Nothing."

As he was saying this, he turned his face away so as not to meet Strafford's eye. Why this evasiveness, Strafford wondered. Armitage wasn't the only one behaving oddly.

"The Coast Guard searched along the coast all night," Strafford said. "They found no trace of her either."

Ruddock, still looking aside and frowning, tipped up his glass and drained it, then poured another inch from the bottle and rose and went to the sink for water. Strafford's glass was still three-quarters full.

"He said maybe she didn't drown, just ran off," Ruddock said, squinting up through the window above the sink. "I wouldn't blame her."

"Oh? Why not?"

Ruddock turned, his eyebrows lifted.

"I forgot, you still haven't met him—Armitage. When you do, you'll see what I mean."

He came back to the table and sat down.

"What is he?" Strafford asked. "What does he do? Did he say?"

Ruddock made a show of pondering this, still determined not to meet the detective's eye.

"No, he didn't. Might be a hotel manager, something like that. Awful outfit—patent-leather shoes, white socks. Imagine."

He knows more than he's saying, Strafford thought. And still he will not look at me straight.

The woman came into the kitchen with the child in her arms, its face buried in the hollow of her right shoulder. A tumble of curls, strange little hands with fingers like peeled twigs, two skinny white legs and long, narrow bare feet. It was dressed in a sort of tunic of cream-colored satin, with matching satin bloomers. A girl's outfit, but Strafford decided it was a boy. He recalled vaguely some painting he had seen somewhere, of a feyly androgynous royal child, a prince or dauphin, got up in similar fashion, not bare-legged, though, but with white silk stockings and dainty buckled shoes. Watteau? Gainsborough? He couldn't remember. Why was this child got-up in such a fashion?

"Will you heat up a bottle?" Charlotte Ruddock asked of her husband.

"He's too old for bottles," Ruddock muttered.

"Right, then," the woman exclaimed, with an angry sigh. "I'll do it."

She detached the clinging child and dumped it—him—into her husband's lap. Ruddock looked down at his son with undisguised distaste. He held him awkwardly, as if he were an unhandy parcel that had been thrust upon him.

His wife took up a saucepan and thumped it down on the range. She had tied back her hair in a red ribbon, and now a strand of it came loose and hung down over her left eye. She stuck out her lower lip and blew a breath upward, but the lock of hair only quivered and settled back to where it had been. Strafford watched her with simmering avidity. He knew he shouldn't, but couldn't help himself. If he had a type, she would be it.

"Turns out we're old chums, the inspector and myself," Ruddock said. The woman did not turn from the stove. "Old boys together—the misnamed New School."

"That's nice," Charlotte Ruddock said distantly.

Beads of moisture trapped under the base of the saucepan were sizzling and popping on the metal ring. She moved to the side, opened the meshed door of a cooling safe set into the wall, took out a china jug and poured milk from it into the saucepan.

Strafford turned his attention back to the boy. He was curled up around himself in Ruddock's lap, with his thumb in his mouth, looking up at his father out of enormous, expressionless eyes. The irises were a shade of violet so deep as to be almost black. He reminded Strafford of a wizened Christ Child, one of those tiny premature men that Renaissance artists used to set on the shoulders of their unrelievedly lugubrious Madonnas.

"What's his name?" he asked.

"Beverly," the woman at the stove said, and made a face. "After Charles's father. We call him Bunny." She gave a snuffly laugh. "The child, not the father."

He looked at the child again. Something about him was

not right. All that loveliness was sickly, somehow. No boy should be so pretty, so fragile, so otherworldly. The gods if they looked down would rush to have him for themselves. Beverly! Even the creature's name was androgynous.

"Coochy-coochy coo," Ruddock said sourly.

The child took his thumb out of his mouth and gave a shrill laugh. It came like three little bird cries—*cheep! cheep! cheep!*—then the pools of his eyes turned solemn in their depths, and he thrust the glistening wet thumb back into the hollow of his rose-pink mouth. Strafford had the feeling of something brushing against him, something brittle and chill, like the wing of a swiftly flying thing.

"Sexton Blake here says that fellow was having us on," Ruddock said over his shoulder to his wife, indicating Strafford with a jerk of his thumb. "The bloody woman isn't drowned at all, she just ran off."

Strafford thought of protesting that he had said no such thing, but didn't.

"What do you think, Mrs. Ruddock?" he asked.

The woman at the stove shrugged.

"He said himself she might have run off. They'd probably had a row." She laughed grimly. "I'd run away, if I were married to him."

She had finished filling the child's bottle from the saucepan, and now she fitted on the rubber nipple and turned up her hand and shook a few drops of the warmed milk onto her wrist to test the temperature. She came to the table, took the child from her husband and cradled him in her arms. He slid his thumb out of his mouth again and fixed his lips greedily on the dull-orange rubber nipple.

Strafford looked away. All of this, the tall slim woman with the overgrown baby in her arms, that moist pink mouth rhythmically sucking at the nipple, its—*his!*—his dimpled fists clenched and his bare toes making slow, crawling motions in the air, and Ruddock, Ruddock too, his malign schoolmate, grotesquely grown into this big baleful disgruntled muscle-bound brute—it was all somehow wrong, unclean, somehow, unclean and damaged, in a faintly repellent way.

The child let go of the rubber nipple with a wet, plopping sound.

"'Nuff," he said, and wriggled out of his mother's arms and ran out of the room.

When he had gone, the three adults remained in stillness, each looking away from the others. No one spoke. The silence creaked.

8

At last Ruddock stirred himself and stood up, rubbing his hands. "Come on," he said to Strafford, "I'll drive you over to McEntee's." It would take only a quarter of an hour to get there, but the way was complicated for anyone unfamiliar with the roads. "You'd be sure to get lost." Strafford told Garda Dolan to follow behind in the squad car.

The day was still fine, but the sky was hazed over and the sunshine had grown dense and grainy. The Indian summer was even still clinging on—along the roadside most of the trees had not turned yet, though their green was more a dusty gray. And there was that familiar tang of woodsmoke on the air. Bonfire season. Strafford had a sense of listless melancholy. Why did this time of year always conjure up childhood and the past? Well, he told himself grimly, before long it would be making him think in the other direction, toward old age and its inevitable end. He heard his mother's voice again, speaking out of the years: *You were never young.*

What did Phoebe see in him? he wondered, not for the first time. She too, though, was older than her years. Perhaps that was what they had in common, that impatience with the years, that wistful hankering after—after what? For life-in-death, for death-in-life. He shivered. He must not let himself drift into that state of incurable melancholy that had undone his mother.

The vehicle they traveled in was a station wagon, or what Strafford's father would call a *shooting brake.* It was old, and painted matte gray, and rattled tinnily over the winding, potholed roads. Ruddock drove fast and heedlessly, his left hand on the steering wheel and his right elbow resting on the frame of the wound-down window beside him.

"You're a country boy yourself, aren't you?" he said to Strafford.

His tone was not offensive, only indifferent.

"I grew up in the country, yes."

"Can't imagine what that was like. All those trees and fields and things." He waved a hand at the windscreen and the passing scenery outside. "Look at it. I can stand it for a week or so, then the boredom really sets in. I only come here because my missus insists, though God knows she doesn't seem to enjoy it much." He paused. "Your people in farming?"

"My father keeps some livestock. He's not very good at it—farming. And yours?"

"Solicitor. I work for him—with him." He made a face. "I'm a partner. Supposedly."

"Ah."

"Dull as dull, of course, but it brings in the shekels."

Rounding a bend, they encountered a flock of sheep trotting toward them along the road, tended by a boy with a stick. Ruddock drew the station wagon to a stop. Strafford watched the animals surging past on both sides, jostling each other and bleating. He admired their primly pursed mouths, their bright yet curiously expressionless eyes, their dainty black hooves. The smell of them, warm and rank, came in at the open window where Ruddock's elbow rested.

"Howyiz," the boy said in greeting as he passed by. He had a shock of greasy curls and a slight squint.

"I don't know why we keep coming," Ruddock mused. "I wanted to skip it this year, and go abroad somewhere, but Charlie said the country air would buck up the son and heir. Fat chance. Charlie is the missus, by the way. It's what I call her." He laughed shortly. "My trouble and strife."

The last of the sheep went past and he engaged the gears and they drove on.

"How long will you stay?" Strafford asked.

"Two weeks. One, with good behavior—I wish."

"Where is home?"

"Dunleary."

"Yes, of course, your wife told me already."

Ruddock glanced into the driving mirror and chuckled.

"Your fellow is still stuck in the sheep. Should we wait for him?"

Strafford turned and looked out of the rear window. All he could see was the top half of the squad car, the rest of which was submerged in sheep, and behind the windscreen Dolan's head and shoulders, stiffly upright and lifeless-seeming. Dolan, like Ruddock, would be no lover of the pastoral.

Here was a hamlet: three or four cottages, a chapel, a pub. He imagined a damp-eyed girl leaning chin on hand at a bedroom window, looking down on the deserted main street and dreaming of elsewhere.

"Tell me, what did you make of this fellow Armitage?"

Ruddock laughed shortly.

"What I made of him?"

"Yes. What did you think, when he said about his wife having drowned or at least having gone missing?"

Now Ruddock shrugged. He seemed uneasy again.

"I thought at first he was a madman. Then he got drunk on my whiskey, and cried for a bit, and then fell asleep. It was all pretty—" he shrugged again "—pretty weird. A bloody long way from Trinity."

"Trinity College?" Strafford asked.

A faint flush spread across Ruddock's forehead.

"He mentioned something about Trinity. I assume—I assume he teaches there."

"I see," Strafford said.

But he didn't.

Evidently, Ruddock knew more about Armitage than he had so far admitted. The mention of Trinity was clearly a slip, and clearly one that he regretted. Why the subterfuge, why these small, unforced efforts at deception?

They descended a hill, rounded a sharp bend and came to a crossroads.

"Here we are," Ruddock said. "The Wicklow Ritz."

McEntee's pub stood a little way back from the road. It was a tall, narrow and, so it seemed, slightly crooked building, with poky little windows on the upper floors and a steep slate roof. White smoke plumed from a tall black chimney that reminded Strafford of Abraham Lincoln's stovepipe hat. The publican's name was painted in gilt letters on a sign above the window. *Wm. McEntee. Whiskey Bonder. Fine Ales.*

What, Strafford idly wondered, is a whiskey bonder?

Ruddock drove the station wagon up onto the graveled space under the window and stopped. As Strafford was getting out, the squad car came around the bend at speed. He motioned to Dolan to slow down. The young man's cap was perched on the side of his head and his tunic was unbuttoned. It occurred to Strafford not for the first time that the young man had not been meant for the Garda force. He had the smirk and swagger of a wide boy, what the Americans would call a juvenile delinquent. Dolan, the rebel without a cause.

The pub inside consisted of a single room, cramped and dim. It smelled as all pubs smell in the morning, of stale porter, stale cigarette smoke and stale sweat. There was a particular, dank chill in the air. The place was empty.

"Shop!" Ruddock called out, and he rapped his knuckles on the counter.

A door latch rattled, and a large man in shirtsleeves and a waistcoat emerged from the shadows behind the bar, wiping his hands on a tea towel. He had a broad bland face and a smoothly receding hairline. He nodded affably.

"Morning, gents," he said. "What can I do you for?" He spotted Dolan's uniform, the buttons of which Dolan was doing up. "Aha, the long arm of the law!"

"They're here to see the fellow you have staying," Ruddock said.

"The professor? He's at his breakfast." He glanced up at the clock behind him on the wall above a row of bottles, and winked. It was almost noon. "Come through," he said, and lifted the hinged flap of the counter.

In an even tinier room, behind the gents' lavatory, they found Armitage sitting at a table by a window that looked onto the road. On a plate before him were bacon, sausages, black pudding, two eggs and a nibbled-at slice of fried bread. At his elbow was a steaming cup in a cracked saucer. A teapot stood nearby. He was pale, and there was stubble on his cheeks and chin. He was contemplating the food queasily. As they came in, he looked up with a pained expression.

"These arresting gentlemen," McEntee said, "have come to call on you, sir."

Armitage peered at Ruddock, then at Strafford and the young Guard behind him. He said nothing.

"How are you doing?" Ruddock asked of him.

"Bit of a headache," Armitage responded distractedly. "Otherwise, tip-top."

It was plain to see he was anything but tip-top.

Strafford stepped forward and identified himself and gave his rank. When he was close to Armitage, he recognized him with a jolt. He had interviewed him last year, after Rosa Jacobs's corpse was discovered in her car in a lock-up garage near the Pepper Canister Church. The young woman had been Armitage's assistant in the history department at Trinity College. Today there was something different about him, however—what was it? Yes: he had shaved off the ill-advised toothbrush mustache he had sported back then. His upper lip was pale and naked in the silvery light from the window, and the mouth underneath it was valvelike and faintly indecent.

Now he in his turn recognized Strafford.

"Well, well," he said. "Has Ireland got only one detective?"

Ruddock looked at Strafford and frowned in puzzlement. "You know each other?"

Both Strafford and Armitage ignored him.

"I'll get Mrs. M to make a fresh pot of tea," McEntee said, taking up the teapot.

Armitage put out one of his long white sinewy hands and Strafford had no choice but to shake it.

"I'm told your wife has gone missing," he said.

"That's right." Armitage blinked. It was clear that for a second he had forgotten why he was here, and what had happened last night, or what supposedly had happened. "Jumped out of the car, ran off, haven't seen her since. We were having a bit of a tiff."

"Do you mind?" Strafford said, bringing forward a chair.

Armitage made an ironically sweeping gesture with his left arm.

"Be my guest."

Strafford sat down, placing his hat on his lap. Ruddock cleared his throat.

"Right, then," he said. "I'll be off."

He had not once looked directly at Armitage, Strafford noted. Something was going on here, and it was up to him to find out what it was. He wished it were otherwise. He did not want to become involved with these people. He thought of the uncanny child clutching on to his mother. He thought of the mother, too, of her slender hips, of her bare pale feet.

"Thank you for the lift," he said to Ruddock, who by now was at the door. "Oh, and by the way, can you give me a phone number?"

Ruddock paused, turned.

"A phone number? For the house? Why?"

"I might need to speak to you again."

That knotted frown of ill-tempered incomprehension had appeared again in the space between Ruddock's eyebrows.

"Speak to me?" he said suspiciously. "What about?"

He was anxious to be gone, Strafford saw. He had the hurried, furtive look of a guilty man.

Dolan, at the door, had his notebook out and stood waiting, the stub of a pencil poised. Ruddock glared at him, and for a moment it seemed he would push him aside in his eagerness to get out and make good his escape. Then he relaxed, or almost.

"I can't remember the number," he said brusquely. "Sorry."

"Give me your Dublin one, then."

Ruddock growled out the number, and Dolan wrote it down.

"Thank you again," Strafford said. "I'll be in touch."

Ruddock was about to speak, but instead he reached past Dolan and yanked the door open. Going out, he almost collided with the publican, returning with the teapot and two more mugs.

"Here we are, gents," McEntee said, "the cup that cheers."

He had a fat man's wheezy laugh. A little of this fellow, Strafford decided, would go an exceedingly long way.

9

"A bit on the touchy side, that fellow," Armitage said mildly, peering out of the window to where Ruddock, looking angry, could be seen getting into the station wagon.

Strafford linked together the fingers of both hands and rested them against the edge of the table.

"Perhaps, Professor," he said, "you'd tell us exactly what happened last night."

McEntee was filling the mugs from the teapot. For such a large man, his movements were oddly delicate, even dainty. As he poured the tea, he straightened the little finger of the hand that held the mug and cocked it out. Strafford remembered an aunt of his who used to do that.

Armitage had put a hand over his own mug to indicate he wanted no more tea. He was regarding Strafford with a curiously glassy, fixed stare. It's the hangover, Strafford thought.

Evidently Ruddock was right, and the man had drunk much more whiskey than he should have. Now he gave himself a shivery sort of shake, and blinked again rapidly. When he spoke, there was the sense of a faulty engine arduously starting up.

"Dee and I—that's the wife, Deirdre—we were out for a spin in her brand-new motor. She got it off her father for her birthday." He looked out of the window again and laughed sourly. "Daddy can afford to do that kind of thing. Filthy rich, though not by the sweat of his brow—he's only a retired civil servant, if of the mandarin class. His wife's family were rolling in it since before the Domesday Book."

Too much information, Strafford thought—why is he chattering like this? The hangover again? Or something else? Despite the airy manner, he seemed nervous. Well, he would be, his wife having disappeared, but Strafford thought that wasn't the real reason—then, what was?

"How did you end up parked in the middle of the field?" Strafford asked.

Armitage shrugged. He had been staring at the plate of uneaten food before him, and now he extended a forefinger and with a grimace pushed it away.

"Fancy set of wheels," he said. "Did you see it?—is it still there where she left it?"

"So your wife was driving," Strafford said.

He glanced at Dolan, who was standing beside the tiny fireplace with his notebook open on the mantelpiece. In the grate, three sods of turf leaned together in a tripod, sullenly smoldering.

"Oh, yes, she was driving," Armitage said with a chuckle. "No one was let near the wheel of that bloody car. She had a phobia about the driving seat, about other people sitting in it, sweating and farting." He glanced up with a thin little grin. "Pardon my French."

"And you were having an argument, you say? What about, if I may ask?"

Armitage threw up his hands.

"God knows," he said. "I can't remember. The price of potatoes. The Mau Mau rebellion. Any old excuse—she liked a scrap, did our Deirdre."

Strafford nodded slowly, his lips pursed. *Liked*, he thought. Past tense.

"She stopped the car, got out and—what?"

"Ran off down the field, toward the sea. I waited a minute, thinking she'd stop and come back. But she went on, and I lost sight of her. It was late, you know, it was getting dark."

"And then?"

"Well, I went after her, of course. I wasn't worried, yet. She's highly strung, she often does things like that, breaking plates, throwing food on the floor, running off. She does it to provoke me."

He took out a flat silver case, opened it with a click, selected a cigarette and lighted it.

"But tell me," Strafford said, "why did she drive into the field, onto someone else's property, in the first place?"

Armitage shook his head.

"You didn't know Deirdre. I'm telling you, it was the kind of thing she did. Impulsive isn't the word. Think of what's-her-name in *The Taming of the Shrew*." He shook his head ruefully. "No taming our Dee, mind you."

Dolan was hunched over his notebook and writing in it with schoolboyish concentration. Strafford leaned back on his chair, avoiding the smoke from Armitage's cigarette. He had not touched the mug of tea the publican had poured for

him. It had the look of bog water, dark brown with a floating of gray scum.

"So you followed her down through the grass," he said,
"onto the—what, onto the beach?"

"It's not much of a beach, down there, just a thin line of
sand with a mound of rocks at one end. I went out there, onto
the rocks. It would be like Dee to make things as difficult as
possible, for herself and for me when I came after her. Don't
know how she would have managed it—I nearly broke a leg."

There was a beat of silence. A heavy, wood-framed clock
on the mantelpiece chimed gratingly. The three men looked
at their watches.

"So you went after her, but you didn't find her," Strafford
said. "What did you think?"

"I was getting worried, I can tell you. It was almost dark,
and getting bloody cold. I shouted out her name, but there
was no answer. In the end, I gave up—what else could I do?—
and went back up to the field, and that fellow was there."

"Which fellow?"

"Wyams or Weems, some name like that."

"Did you know him?"

Armitage stared at him incredulously.

"Know him? How would I know a bloke I happened to
meet in a field in the half-dark in the middle of nowhere?"

"Why was he at your car?"

"Search me. Curiosity, I imagine. Or maybe he's keen on
swanky motors. The old Pagoda does turn a head, that's for
sure."

He tapped ash into the saucer before him on the table.
Strafford thought of Marguerite, sitting with him in Bewley's and stubbing out her cigarette in his saucer and telling

him not to make a fuss just because she had told him she wanted a divorce.

"Why are you asking me all these questions?" Armitage demanded, petulant suddenly. That excessively mobile mouth of his with its exposed upper lip had to Strafford's eye taken on the look of a rare species of mollusk. "Shouldn't you be out searching for my missus?"

"The Coast Guard were out all night. They're probably still at it. And there's a search party going along the shore on foot."

Armitage seemed impressed, though less by the persistence of the searchers, Strafford suspected, than by his wife's refusal to be traced.

"What was she wearing?" the detective asked.

He was baffled by Armitage's front of chipper, even amused, detachment. In his experience, people in this sort of situation were so distressed that it was difficult to get them to concentrate on anything other than their frantic forebodings. This man, however, seemed to regard the disappearance of his wife as little more than an inconvenience—a petty annoyance, even.

"What was she wearing?" Armitage repeated, looking at the floor. "Let me think." He inclined his head and pressed the fingertips of one hand to his forehead. "A green dress, silk, the crackly kind—taffeta, is it?—and a camel-hair coat. Flat heels, otherwise she wouldn't have been able to run in that field. And pearls, a single string of pearls—real ones, by the way, another gift from Daddy. No hat. She never wore a hat." He snickered. "Too vain of her auburn tresses to cover them up, don't you know."

McEntee put his large head in at the door.

"Can I offer you gentlemen a tincture of something stronger?" he asked.

"Christ, yes," Armitage said. "A drop of whiskey would hit the spot."

"You'd be a Scotch man, I'd say, sir?"

"Doesn't matter, whatever you have."

"The hair of any old dog, eh?" the publican said, and chuckled indulgently. He looked to Strafford. "What about you, Inspector?"

"Nothing, thank you," Strafford said.

Sergeant Dolan was ignored. McEntee withdrew his head. They heard him saunter into the bar, warbling the tune of "Mother Machree." Strafford was surprised to recognize it. It was not a song he would have heard sung around the turf fire of an evening when he was a lad. *Snob!* he told himself again.

"Did your wife ever—did she ever run off before?" he asked.

Armitage's mood was steadily darkening. It was as if this entire business, his wife's disappearance, these questions, even the hangover, constituted a personal affront. He picked vexedly at something invisible on the cuff of his blazer.

"She walked out on me in a restaurant once," he said.

"Which one?"

Armitage stared.

"Which restaurant? What the fuck does it matter?"

"It probably doesn't," Strafford said.

He was stumbling in the dark here.

McEntee returned with the glass of whiskey and set it on the table in front of Armitage. He glanced at the food congealing on the breakfast plate and pursed his lips and made a tut-tutting sound.

"Them vittles would have done you a power of good," he said to Armitage reprovingly. "What Madame McEntee will say I don't like to think."

He took up the plate, the cup and saucer and the cutlery, and went out, crooning softly to himself.

*"Sure, I love the dear silver
That shines in your hair—"*

"Have you children?" Strafford asked of Armitage.

The man shook his head.

"Dee wasn't keen," he said. He took a drink of the whiskey and smacked his lips. Then he mused for a moment, gazing into the amber depths in the glass. "She was a bit of a good-time girl, you know—is, I mean. She likes a party, and a sleep-in the morning after"—he leered—"if you know what I mean."

"She wasn't—isn't—Irish, I take it?"

Again, Armitage stared.

"Good God, no. Think I'd marry one of—?" He glanced at Sergeant Dolan by the fireplace. "Londoner, born and bred. Knightsbridge, Harrods, the Brompton Oratory—"

This time it was Strafford's turn to stare.

"She's Catholic?"

But Armitage shook his head and smiled with amused disdain.

"C of E, if anything. We don't go in much for the God stuff, she or I. You look at history and where's the evidence for divine intention?"

"Yes." Strafford paused. "Her parents are still living?"

"Oho yes," Armitage said, and did a sort of whistle, making a little funnel of his mouth and swiveling it to one side. "Alive and kicking."

There was a delivery boy in the village when Strafford was young who used to whistle like that, standing up on the pedals of his blunt heavy black bicycle and weaving from side to side as he sped along, the parcels joggling in the deep iron basket attached to the handlebars.

How, Strafford asked himself, how could it be that a woman who shopped in Harrods and visited the Brompton Oratory should think to marry a man such as Armitage?

"Have you contacted them, the parents?" he asked. "Have you phoned, or sent a telegram?"

To this, Armitage made no reply. He was gazing again pensively into the whiskey glass.

"What am I going to do with the car?" he wondered, addressing neither Strafford nor the notetaker at the fireplace.

"I'm sure there's a local garage that would tow it away for you," Strafford said.

"What?" Armitage looked at him dully. "I meant, what will I do with it long term? Can't keep it, that's for certain."

"Why not?"

"She'd never forgive me—swanning about in her precious motor and her gone in the sea? Blimey."

Strafford waited a moment, then said, "Tell me about the man you met in the field."

But Armitage had stopped listening. Slowly, quietly, almost absent-mindedly, he began to cry. The tears, unheeded, rolled down at both sides of his nose and around the stretched corners of his mouth.

"Bloody woman," he said, and gave a hiccupy, angry little sob. "*Bloody* woman."

Strafford was almost convinced.

10

Great sorrow cannot speak. It was a line that Quirke, still deep in mourning, often murmured over to himself. John Donne, yes, but where was it from, what poem, or sermon? Or was it in a letter, perhaps? No: a sermon, surely, commemorating the death of some eminent personage. It had the ring of a public utterance.

He was good at grief, was the dean. Hard to think of a more unlikely prelate, considering the love poems, unembarrassable in their lip-smacking eroticism, startling in their spiky, rocking rhythms. Did he keep on with the girls after he took to the pulpit? Crowds used to press into St. Paul's to hear him preach. Thrilling occasions they must have been. One thing he was wrong about, though. Every man *is* an island, lost in the world's vast waste of waters.

★ ★ ★

How many cinemas were there in Dublin? He thought he must have been to them all over the past year and a half, since the death of his wife. Mostly he went in the afternoons, when there was no one there but himself and a few other vague maimed solitary souls. It was a place to hide, in the rich, dusty darkness. He found it comforting, a little comforting, to sit back and rest in the flickering glow of the giant soot-and-silver images moving before him. He made little effort to keep up with the movie plots. When the opening credits rolled his mind relaxed, like a tensed muscle going slack.

Pictures in Technicolor he avoided. Monochrome was somehow more realistic than all that garish color. Or easier to look at, anyway. The actresses' skin had a wonderfully stark, chalky paleness, the stuff of their frocks flared and shimmered with an electric energy, and shed blood was black.

Often he didn't bother to look at the screen at all, but sat and leaned his head back on the rim of the seat and gazed at the projector's shivery beam above him, admiring the clouds of luminous silvery gray cigarette smoke that billowed through it constantly.

Afternoon moviegoers were an unacknowledged fellowship. Like him, most of them were alone. They had an odd, spectral quality, sitting there in isolation, stiffly upright, unnaturally still dim figures in raincoats or high-shouldered jackets. Some kept their hats on. Some smoked pipes, some ate sweets. Strange, how loud a noise the cellophane paper made as it was unwrapped.

No women, of course, not on their own. Courting couples kept to the back rows, from where now and then there would come the sound of a brief scuffle, and a huskily whispered *No!* or *Stop it!* followed by a giggle.

Once, a man left his seat at the back of the stalls and came down and sat behind him and leaned close to his shoulder and asked if he would care to join him for a drink after the show. Humid breath on his cheek, the soft words in his ear. He didn't answer, didn't turn his head, and the fellow stood up again and shuffled off along the row, until someone barked at him to sit the fuck down and he hurried away at a crouch.

Weekends were difficult. Hordes of school-age children came pouring in for the matinees, raucous and ungovernable. They filled the front rows, cheering on the hero and hissing the villain. Screen lovers in a clinch provoked a storm of hoots and whistles. Fistfights broke out. Things were thrown at the screen, apple cores, wadded fish-and-chip bags, still-smoldering cigarette ends. The taller youths would jump up and waggle their fingers in the light from the projector, throwing shadows across the feet of the prancing phantoms on the screen. The usherettes wielded the shining lances of their flashlights in vain. *Hey, miss, show us your titties!*

Sometimes, if it was still early, he would sit through two consecutive showings of the same picture. He did not want to leave until it was fully dark outside. Twilight, that liminal interval, he found hard to cope with, especially now that the autumn had settled in. Autumn, season of memory, where the past lives. Even winter would be preferable; he would welcome its unforgiving harshness.

Grief had turned out to be not at all as he would have expected. Not that he had given much thought to the matter, while Evelyn was alive. The abruptness of her going— she had been shot to death by mischance in a restaurant one sunny afternoon in Spain—had caught him unprepared. He had always assumed he would die before she did.

The first weeks of his bereavement had passed in a blur—

later on, he could recall almost nothing from that bleak time. True, certain disconnected moments would flare up in his memory as if lit by a spotlight, then would fade back slowly into the general murk. He supposed he should be glad of them, these briefly illumined fragments of lost time, but he wasn't, not really. They were a source more of discomfort than of consolation. Their intensity left him half-blinded, his mind groping for something to grasp and hold on to.

That was what surprised him most, that giddy sense of being groundless, of being helplessly at the mercy of the world and its random ways. His mind, reeling in anguish, would fix with sudden, awful clarity on the most unremarkable objects, the tinfoil lid of a milk bottle on a doorstep, a tin can glinting in a gutter, a spent match, a floating cloud—anything at all—and he would be pierced through by a shaft of acutest sorrow. Through these humble spyholes, each one a miniature Avernus, he would be afforded a glimpse, clear and breathtaking, straight down into the horror at the heart of things.

He felt as if he were falling slowly from a high place, and that the supports he clutched at desperately in the cliff face all came away in his hands, cutting his palms, or slicing his fingers, as the long blades of scutch grass did when he was a little boy playing in the ill-tended gardens behind the orphanage where he had spent the earliest years of his childhood.

Now, in these barren days of his middle age, there was no help for him, no comfort, no escape. He stayed away from people as much as possible. This was a loneliness company couldn't cure.

In the cinema he would suddenly burst into tears, silently, for no reason. The saddest scenes in a picture would leave him unmoved, then something, there was no accounting for it, some image, some bit of landscape, some trivial remark by one of the characters, would breach his defenses and the sluices would open, and he would have to sink down into the seat and cover his face with his hands. At such moments he felt ashamed, felt as silly and sad as a big soft jilted girl.

And yet, amazingly, things went on, the quotidian round kept spinning. Day followed night, night followed day, the sun shone, the clouds advanced across the sky like the smoke from distant battlefields. He ate, he slept, he woke, he ate, he shat, he shaved, he bathed, he went to work. His fingernails grew, his hair had to be taken to the barber. All as if nothing had happened. The blunt, unceasing continuity of things baffled him, affronted him. It was a scandal, the entire indifferent business of being alive.

He found some comfort in dreams. There the dead came back, more radiant than in life, yet at the same time distracted. It was as if they had lost something, had left something behind them, here, on this side, which they must search for, endlessly, though with scant hope of finding it.

In these flickering nocturnal pageants Evelyn herself made only the rarest appearances, and always in the guise of someone else, so that only he, the dreamer, knew who she was. Sometimes she was a vivid absence. In the dream world, he would be sitting with friends at dinner—what friends? where?—and one of them would suddenly point to the empty place beside him and say, accusingly, *But where is—?* and then stop, and everyone at the table would fall silent.

Sometimes he would be young, in his twenties or younger, with a girl at his side, Evelyn but also not-Evelyn, who would look at him with lips pressed tightly shut and eyebrows arched, as if she were trying not to laugh.

What was the joke? He was. He was the joke.

One image, a real image and not part of a dream, haunted

him. It was of Evelyn seated in a chair and starting forward, braced on her toes, her fingers grasping the arms at both sides and her face lifted up to him, eager and laughing. He could see her, he could see what she was wearing, a pale blue sweater she had knitted herself that from frequent washing had become a little too tight for her, a pair of loose corduroy trousers, once brown but faded to fawn, a pair of grubby sneakers, no socks. How young she looked, girlish almost, despite the strands of gray in her bangs exposed under a bright red headscarf tied not under her chin but at the back of her head. What had he done, what had he said, that had brought her surging up at him with such sudden animation, that sparked such a light in her eyes, that elicited such a smile?

So it went on, the long, the seemingly endless, bereavement. Then came that certain sleepless night after which everything was changed—no, not everything, but much, much.

He had gone to bed half-drunk as usual, but knew as soon as he switched off the bedside lamp that he would not sleep. He put the light on again, and got up and drank another brandy, then lay down and stared for a long time at the ceiling. He tried to read, but he couldn't concentrate. He listened to the wireless. He stood by the window in his dressing gown, looking down vacantly into the nighttime street. He thought of getting dressed and going for a walk along the canal, but couldn't bear the thought of being outside, alone, in the murmurous dark.

The hours passed, and nothing happened. He didn't really mind. On the contrary, he was suffused with a strange sense of elation, muted, mildly puzzling, seemingly causeless. At dawn he rose, and dressed, and sat at the kitchen table, smoking cigarette after cigarette. Then it came to him that he had completed the first part of his sentence, that his time in solitary confinement was over. And at once the image of Evelyn that had been with him since the day of her death, the image of her starting forward in the chair, was replaced by another. In this one, she was off in the middle distance, walking away, and stopping to look back at him over her shoulder, smiling a melancholy farewell.

It was a sad surprise to learn that even a partial recovery from loss must entail a further loss.

Evelyn. The tip of her nose was always cold. Her heart had a slightly irregular beat. She teased him for his incurable fear of spiders. And she was dead.

One night after the pictures when he came back to Phoebe's flat, he spotted a shadowy figure standing under the trees at the corner of Merrion Square. For a second, he was afraid. In the film he had been to, the hero had been shot and wounded on a city street like this, at night, against a backdrop of looming shadows. More than that, he had himself been badly beaten up around here one winter's evening not so very long ago.

Then the figure stepped forward into the sodium glow of a streetlamp, and he saw that it was Strafford.

"What are you doing here?" he asked truculently, when Strafford was still only halfway across the road. "Phoebe's not at home—she's out on the town with one of my old squeezes."

"Yes, Isabel Galloway—she told me they've become friends again. In fact, it's you I was waiting for."

This was not what Quirke wanted to hear. He was tired and out of sorts. But then, when was he in sorts, these days.

"You'd better come in, then," he said gruffly.

They entered by the doorway beside the pastry shop and

climbed the narrow stairs. As usual, the cloying aroma of vanilla lingered.

It was cold in the flat. They went into the front room and Quirke lit the gas fire, the element of which sputtered first and then fizzed. He went to the window and glanced down into the street, which he always did when he first came in. What did he expect to see down there? He didn't believe in ghosts, and anyway Evelyn wouldn't be so crass as to come back from wherever she might possibly be—she hadn't believed in an afterlife, and neither did he—and lurk in the shivery lamplight, among the twitching shadows of leaves.

He took Strafford's coat and hung it along with his own on a hook in the little hallway outside the kitchen, and came back rubbing his hands.

"Drink?"

"Not for me, thanks."

"You don't mind if I have one?"

He was being sarcastic, but of course Strafford didn't notice, or pretended not to.

"Please, go ahead," Strafford said, brushing back a lock of hair that had fallen limply over his forehead. It was a thing he did, all the time, and it never failed to irritate Quirke. Why didn't he get a shorter haircut, so the damned thing wouldn't keep flopping forward like that?

He went to the sideboard and poured himself a small measure of whiskey, then added another splash before he put the bottle away. A visit from Strafford called for stiff fortification. What was he doing here anyway, at nine o'clock on a weekday evening?

"Sit down," Quirke said, pulling a second armchair up to the fireplace. "What can I do for you?"

It was strange to be here, Strafford thought, without

Phoebe. As he sat down, he glanced at the sofa on the far
side of the room, the sofa on which they had made love one
memorable night when they arrived back here late after a
dinner at the Shelbourne. In the doorway of the flat he had
kissed her goodbye, as he thought, and was about to depart
when she seized the front of his shirt in one of her sinewy
little fists and pulled him hard against her. As they crossed
to the sofa, he somehow managed to shed his overcoat and
his jacket, but the rest of his clothes stayed on.

My God, he thought now, what would Quirke say if he
knew what I am thinking about at this moment?

"Did you come across a person called Armitage," he asked,
"in connection with the Rosa Jacobs business?"

Quirke thought for a moment.

"Armitage? No, I don't think so. Who is he?"

"Teaches at Trinity. Department of History. He's English."

The gas fire crackled again briefly. Dust falling on the element, Quirke thought. How the world goes intricately on,
in its secret ways.

"And?" he asked.

Strafford, sitting with his elbows resting on the arms of his
chair, tapped the tips of steepled fingers against his pursed lips.
Quirke looked away, asking himself yet again what it could
be his daughter saw in this cold-blooded long drink of water?

"Rosa Jacobs was Armitage's assistant. You remember
when we were investigating her death, I went to Trinity to
talk to him about her."

This was a delicate area. Quirke had carried on a brief affair with Rosa Jacobs's sister, Molly.

"And what did he have to say?"

Strafford shrugged.

"Nothing, or nothing that was of any use to us." He paused. "I saw him again, earlier today."

Quirke rose and crossed to the sideboard and poured another whiskey. Strafford drew in his elbows and leaned back in the armchair.

"Not about the Jacobs case, surely?" Quirke said over his shoulder.

"No. Chief Inspector Hackett sent me down to Wicklow to look into the disappearance of a woman there last night. It turned out to be this man Armitage's wife."

Quirke walked to the window with his glass. He pulled back the curtain at one side and again looked down into the deserted street. A wind had got up, and a torn page of newsprint slithered across the pavement and lodged in the gutter. Late one night he had seen a fox down there, trotting unconcernedly along the middle of the road.

Metempsychosis.

He closed his eyes for a moment, and let the curtain fall back. *My missing woman, where are you?* Foolish, foolish. *She is not anywhere.*

Behind him, Strafford was speaking again.

"At first, when I heard the name, I didn't make the connection. Then when I met him, I remembered."

"You didn't think he had anything to do with Rosa Jacobs's death, did you, at the time?"

"No, no. At that stage we had no idea who was responsible. I was just trying to fill in the background. He was one of the people in her circle, so to speak."

So to speak, Quirke thought, with an inward sneer. He came back to the fireplace with his whiskey and sat down again.

"When did this wife of his go missing?"

"Wednesday evening. They were driving in the countryside, by the sea."

"Where were they going?"

"Nowhere, I think. The weather was fine, they were out for a drive. So he said."

"So he said?"

"He didn't seem to me the kind of person who would go out for drives. And his wife didn't sound like it either. Anyway, the outing didn't go well. They had a row, apparently, and she stopped the car in the middle of a field—she was driving—and jumped out and ran off in the direction of the shore. That was the last he saw of her."

"Has her body been found?"

"No. They searched all night and half of the next day. Not a trace."

Quirke glanced at him.

"What do you think? Is she dead?"

Again, Strafford joined his fingers at the tips and touched them to his lower lip. Quirke looked away. He was finding Strafford's mannerisms particularly irritating this evening. After a moment, Strafford said, "I don't know what I think. Armitage's behavior was very peculiar when I spoke to him. Admittedly, he had a hangover—"

"Had he and the wife been drinking?"

"No, I don't believe so. He went for help to a house near where the car was stopped, and the people there gave him whiskey. It seems he drank half the bottle, more than half. He was in a bad way this morning when I went down there to interview him. Even so, he just didn't seem as upset as a man should be, whose wife had vanished the previous evening."

Quirke chuckled.

"Maybe he was happy to be rid of her." He paused. "Do you think he might have done away with her himself?"

"I don't know."

They were silent for some moments.

"Coincidence, though," Quirke said thoughtfully. "Rosa Jacobs and this fellow's wife—two cars, two women, the same man." He sipped his drink. Rosa Jacobs had been left unconscious in her car and poisoned with exhaust fumes. "Do you want me to talk to him?"

"What reason would you give? It would seem a bit odd, a pathologist asking to meet a person while his wife's body is still missing. Anyway, there may not be a body. It's possible she's not dead. He said himself she might have run off—'It would be just like her,' he told me."

Quirke was nodding to himself.

"It must have been some fight they were having, if she ran out on him and hasn't come back yet. Even if they hate each other."

"Why do you say that?"

"What?"

"That they might hate each other."

"Well, I don't know," Quirke said, and shrugged. "From what you say, they don't seem to have been love's young dream, the pair of them."

This time, there was a longer silence. Then Strafford said, "There was another person in the house."

"Which house?"

"The one Armitage went to, looking for help. A holiday place, rented by people called Ruddock. A couple, and their child. I went to school with him."

"With Armitage?"

"No—Ruddock."

Quirke, confused, was frowning.

"And who was this other person, then?"

"Fellow called Wymes. W-y-m-e-s. He was passing by, he said, and saw the car abandoned in the field. He went with Armitage up to the house, where the Ruddocks were, but left later."

"Did you speak to him?"

"Not yet," Strafford said. "He'd left by the time I got there."

He drew back his legs from the heat of the gas fire. His trousers were giving off a faint smell of scorched cloth. He thought again of himself and Phoebe on the sofa that night. The fire had been on then, too, doing its best to warm the chill air in the big room. After their lovemaking they had sat cross-legged in front of it, Strafford drinking tea while Phoebe, sated, smiling, catlike, sipped a glass of tepid Liebfraumilch and watched the dancing gas flame. Strafford, in his turn watching her, had felt a twinge of disquiet. He was not sure what to make of this hungry, almost rapacious version of herself that Phoebe had revealed to him on that sofa. He was not sure he liked it. He was not sure he was not a little afraid of it.

He realized with a start that Quirke was speaking to him.

"Sorry—what?"

"I said, where is he, where does he live, this other fellow?"

"In a caravan along the coast. I'll go down and see if I can find him. The local Guards are pretty useless. Fellow called Crowley."

"What is he?"

"Sergeant. I checked on him. A rough diamond. Not young, past retirement age. Drinks, gets into trouble, has been transferred around the country I don't know how many times."

Quirke turned the glass in his hand. The whiskey in it swirled and glittered, dark gold and brazen.

"There's definitely something odd about the whole thing," Strafford said. "I can't quite—"

He broke off. A key was turning in the lock in the door of the flat. Phoebe came in, bringing with her a waft of the chill air of outside. Seeing the two of them, she stopped and frowned and then smiled.

"Well," she said, "look who's here."

She was blushing, Strafford saw. In that moment it came to him, with some force, that despite everything—despite what everything?—it seemed that he did love her. Perhaps he was even *in* love with her.

Always a surprise, life, he thought. Always. Then he sneezed.

11

Denton Wymes had always hated his name, both parts of it. He had been christened Denton after a legendarily rich relative on his mother's side. His mother was supposed to have been Uncle Denton's favorite niece, but when the will was read her name wasn't in it. Which was a grave disappointment, for the Wymeses were as poor as church mice, and had been banking on inheriting at least a few thousand from the old skinflint.

They lived in the house where Wymes's father was born, as had been the many generations of fathers before him. It was a decent-sized manor house on a couple of hundred acres. The land was poor, however, poor certainly for Wicklow, the so-called Garden of Ireland, and besides, Mr. Wymes had no head for farming. His son remembered him as kindly, vague and ineffectual. In his younger days, he had sought to make his mark as a poet—he knew Arthur Waley, and had been published in *The Yellow Book*—and played, of all things, the spinet. His wife was large and loud-voiced, and bred Pomeranians. Even in a milieu of unlikely alliances, the Wymeses turned out to be extravagantly mismatched.

The name of the house was Wychwood. It dated from the 1740s. It stood in gloomy seclusion at the end of a wooded lane off the main road, roughly halfway between Arklow and Gorey. The family had been in residence at Wychwood since its beginnings. The first Wymes, one Sir Peregrine, had fought with George II against the French at Dettingen, and afterward there had been settled upon him a goodly tranche of Wicklow land. Here he built a home for himself and Lady Wymes and their steadily increasing brood of square-faced sons and gawky daughters—half a dozen family portraits, dark brown and glazed with age, leaned out menacingly from the walls in the drawing room at Wychwood.

The Wymeses had money then, but over the centuries their fortunes had steadily declined. It was a common-enough trajectory for many of the lesser families of the Protestant Ascendancy, and even for one or two of the great ones.

Mrs. Wymes had been an Ireton-Clinch, of the Carlow Ireton-Clinches, a fact she missed no opportunity of mentioning.

Denton's father had been obsessed with Wychwood, especially the roof, which was chronically in a bad way. It was said of all the landed families that one could judge unerringly the health of their fortunes by the state of their roof. Mr. Wymes had expended much energy and all his ingenuity on ways of finding the money to keep the warmth in and the rain out, with little success. Three days after his death, a storm took off a good half of the slates, as if to mark his passing.

When the old man was gone, the son straightaway sold the house and what was left of the land for a pittance to a local farmer. By then, his mother was in a nursing home. Her mind was gone, which, however sad a thing, had one benefit, in that she never knew of her son's arrest, trial and imprisonment. Had her mind been sound and she heard of his public disgrace, the shock would surely have killed her. A son of one of the Carlow Ireton-Clinches in jail for interfering with scores of little girls and almost as many little boys—the very thought!

Scamp was scratching at the door of the caravan to be let in.

The weather today was fine again—the Indian summer could last till Christmas, so the wiseacres said. It was the end of October and still the sun shone from morn till dusk, and the grass in the fields was so dry it crackled underfoot.

He let the dog in, and stood for a while in the narrow doorway, looking across the dunes to the sea. The air was bright, gold-tinted; the morning breeze was soft. A couple of riders were out, wading their horses through the shallows on the near side of the sandbank that lay fifty yards offshore, like the humped back of a tawny whale. This long, improbable spit of hard sand held an odd fascination for him. In the years since he had settled here, it had appeared and disappeared and then appeared again many times. The currents were strong along this stretch of coast. One summer, a young mother and her child had been caught in the undertow and swept out past the tip of the sandbank and drowned. It was three days before their bodies were found.

A shiver went through him, as he stood there in the doorway. He was wondering if the Englishman's wife had turned up yet, or if she was lost forever to the deep.

Behind him, the dog sat back on his haunches and barked at him.

"What's the matter?" he said, turning. "You've had your breakfast." The dog barked again, making a sharp yipping sound. He'd talk if he could, his master thought. And if he did, it would be all about food, most likely. "You want to go for a run, is that it?"

He looked out at the beach again. He did not want to venture out there, with the woman not yet found. Imagine coming upon her corpse, flopping to and fro at the edge of the waves. No, they could go instead through the dunes and along the sandy burrow out beside the road. But the dog didn't like the burrow—probably the tough grass that grew there hurt his paws. For a working breed, he thought, collies were remarkably sensitive.

He put a hand to his forehead, assailed suddenly by the past. A boy running barefoot over grass as short and prickly as the nap of a carpet, and the man standing by the lupins, with sweets in his pocket.

"Denton? What sort of a name is that, for Pete's sake? Do you live around here? Are your mammy and daddy with you? No? Have a sweet. Scots Clan—do you like Scots Clan? I have Liquorice Allsorts, too. Here—take your pick."

In among the lupin bushes, his hands, his greedy mouth, the smell of camphor and tobacco on his breath.

"You'll tell no one, now, will you, Denton? Here's half a crown. Come again tomorrow and I'll give you five bob."

Five shillings! A fortune!

But it wasn't for the money that he returned, day after day, running with pounding heart over the stubbly grass toward the patch of lupins, and the man waiting.

That was the start, the beginning of it all. But of course, it would have happened anyway, sooner or later. He had been waiting, without knowing it, waiting for the revelation.

He told no one. He kept their secret, his and the man's. The money he buried in a hole in the sandy ground underneath the wooden steps that led up to the door of the chalet. At night, in bed, he would think of it, the magical silver hoard, hidden out there. His talismans, he would have said, if he had known the word. He was only nine.

On the last day of the holiday, with their things packed and Dinny Molloy on his way down from Wychwood to collect them in the pony and trap, he cried and cried. His father, puzzled, tried to comfort him, pleading with him to stop, but on he sobbed. Later, lying on his stomach on the floor behind the old chintz sofa with his wet cheek resting on his folded arms, he heard his parents in the next room talking about him.

"Is he coming down with something, do you think?" That was his father, in a worried voice. "Such tears—it's not natural, even if he has to go back to school."

"He's neurotic," his mother said shortly, with unchecked contempt. "Like all the Wymeses."

On the way home he would not be consoled, even when old Dinny let him sit up at the front with him and take the reins and drive the trap along a straight stretch of road. All he could think of was the scent of the lupins, and the sweets soft from being in the man's pocket, and the man's breath warm on his belly, and the swoony feeling at the end, and then the silence all around, and the sense of peace descending, light as silk, and the breeze against his burning forehead, soft like the breeze today, and the grass blades between his bare toes, and the gulls squawking.

Now, standing at the door of the dingy trailer, he closed

his eyes, letting his mind rest for a moment in inner darkness. Then he took up the Malacca cane that had belonged to his father. The dog, seeing it, whined excitedly and danced on his hind legs, pawing the air.

"Come on, boy, we'll go down the beach."

It would be all right. If there was a body, the riders would have found it already.

By the time he came down through the dunes, however, the riders were gone and the long stretch of sand was deserted. He turned away from the stony patch under the low cliff and set off northward. Behind him was the archbishop's summer home. McQuaid. A cold fish. There were rumors about him among the local people.

Oh, bejasus now, you wouldn't want to let the youngsters go near that fellow, I'll tell you that for nothing.

And then the low chuckle, the wink, the nudge.

Wymes derived a certain doleful amusement from the thought that this all-powerful prince of the Church should be, like himself, a common-or-garden child molester.

Do they know about me, round here? he wondered. He kept himself to himself as much as possible. But some things were unavoidable. Once a week, on Saturdays, he had to cycle over to the village shop to fetch provisions. If there were customers in, the talk would cease the moment he appeared on the threshold.

The shopkeeper, Mulrooney, was a little weasel of a fellow with a leery eye and a few greasy strands of hair combed over a shiny pink bald scalp. It was plain to see the contempt in which he held the world in general, and his customers in particular, though he sought to hide it behind a mask of oily obsequiousness.

Good morning to you, sir, isn't the weather keeping grand, for the time of year.

And that eye, moist as the skin of a soft-boiled egg, looking up from under an ash-white brow. Yes, an unsavory type, hushed, furtive, always on the watch. What were *his* secrets? He had no wife. That crooked, cautiously suggestive smile, the yellow tips of the side teeth showing. He recalled the evening, a Sunday it was, when he met him walking along the road, dressed up in a shabby suit and a spotted slime-green tie.

Where was he off to? The road ended at the archbishop's gate.

Now, what would they have to say to each other, the shifty shopkeeper and His Grace the Archbishop of Dublin?

Scamp ran ahead, stopping now to sniff at a piece of driftwood, now to pee against a stone. My companion and comfort, like Pangur Bán, the old monk's cat. *Pangur, white Pangur, how happy we two.*

My father at the spinet, his long pale fingers sleepwalking over the keys.

Gulls swooped, uttering their coarse cries. The smell of lupins. The sticky sweets. His hands.

Loneliness, he thought, loneliness is a kind of cancer, eating away at one in secret.

Scamp had halted, and stood aquiver with one paw lifted. A girl was approaching, walking barefoot at the water's edge, the small waves washing over her toes. Narrow white feet, almost prehensile, with that exquisite curve on the inner sides.

What was she? Fourteen. He was good at guessing their ages. Long practice.

As she passed by, she glanced at him sidelong with a narrow-eyed smile, sly and saucy, biting the flesh of her upper lip at one side.

Was she not nervous, to be encountering a solitary stranger
out here like this? The beach was empty in both directions.

Neither spoke. In a moment she was gone. When he turned
to look after her, she too was looking back, still with that
smile.

He went on. There would have been no need for her to
worry. At fourteen, she was, for him, already too old. They
all became old, at the first hint of maidenhair.

Low in the sky over the sea there floated a small white
cloud, soft-looking, like a scrap of cotton wool. He stopped
to gaze at it. Scamp came and sat on the sand beside him. Was
the animal too looking at the cloud? What would his dog's
mind make of it? Nothing, probably. For Scamp, surely, the
world was the world, was all that is, without rhyme or reason and with no need of either.

When it came out, when all the filth came spewing out,
the school had to let him go, of course. It should have been
known long before what he had been up to. One of the boys
had told his parents and wasn't believed, but then two of the
girls told theirs, and that was that.

He had expected the sky to fall on him, but it didn't, not
then, not yet. Perkins, the headmaster, though embarrassed
and furious, had managed to express regret at his going,
and even wished him well for the future. No handshake,
of course, and no meeting his eye. The staff too were kind,
remarkably so, in the circumstances. Margaret Trilling, a
soft-faced spinster who had once invited him to her home
for sherry, approached him in the staff cloakroom, where he
was putting on his overcoat, and presented him shyly with
a fountain pen, a Parker Duofold, the box wrapped in tissue
paper and tied with a scrap of red silk ribbon. She had bought
it specially, she said, "as a keepsake."

He had a little money in the bank, what was left from the sale of Wychwood and its remaining few acres of ancestral land. Also, the school board, albeit grudgingly, had granted him a small pension. He had enough funds, then, to keep him going, if he was careful, to keep him going to the end. He had never been extravagant, except in his illicit desires.

He thought he had got away with it, more or less, until the evening when a detective accompanied by a Garda in uniform appeared at the lodging house where he was staying, asking for him. One of the girls had begun to suffer from bouts of hysteria, and her parents had gone to the Guards and lodged a formal complaint against him.

When he came out of Mountjoy Prison, his first cousin, nice Minnie Banks, whom he used to play with when they were little, let him have the old trailer for nothing. It had been parked in a corner of her garden since a disastrous, rained-out and quarrelsome trip she and her husband, Bill, had been foolish enough to undertake one summer when they had driven down to Tramore and stayed there for a few days, and which they had vowed never to repeat.

Bill pumped air into the camper's tires, hitched it to the Land Rover and towed it down to Kilpatrick beach. However, he flatly refused to let its new owner and his burden of disgrace travel in the car with him. So Wymes had taken the train to Arklow and hired a taxi, at frightening expense, to drive him over to the beach, and his new home, such as it was.

He had chosen Kilpatrick because it was there he had spent that momentous summer when he was nine, the summer of the sweets and the half crowns and the sweaty games amid the lupins.

The lupins were gone now, and so was the chalet his parents had rented for that month of August. He couldn't remember, now, if John Charles McQuaid or his house had been here in those days. The Wymeses, being Church of Ireland, would have been careful to avoid the archbishop, if he had been in residence.

They never returned to Kilpatrick. His tears on the last day of the holiday had not been forgotten; they hung over the memory of the whole holiday like a rain cloud.

A sea gull swept low across the beach and out to sea, skimming the wavelets, and the dog ran after it, barking, and plunged into the water and swam out a good way, until he was called back. When he came out of the water, he stopped and stood splay-legged on the sand and shook himself, giving the man an indignant scowl—he had extraordinarily expressive features, for a dog. The gull, far-off now, sent back a chattering call; it floated to them across the water like a peal of mocking laughter.

"Come on, old chap, let's go home."

Man and dog turned and started back the way they had come.

The white cloud had dissolved, or drifted away, somewhere out of sight.

Home, he thought. The most melancholy word in the language.

12

One evening, Phoebe suggested to Strafford that they should take advantage of the continuing unseasonably fine weather and go for a picnic. Next day was a Saturday, and Strafford would be on his day off. In the morning she would make a trip to Smyth's on the Green and buy crackers and cheese and fruit, and a nice bottle of wine.

Strafford, under Phoebe's tutelage, was becoming a wine drinker, though in a very modest way. Phoebe knew her wines, thanks to the weekly dinners at Jammet's or the Russell Hotel her father used to treat her to in the old days, and still did, occasionally. Strafford practiced diligently, but he was never likely to be an oenophile. Phoebe would instruct him to roll a mouthful of wine around his tongue and teeth before swallowing, and to hold the glass up to the light to judge the "legs" of the vintage. But in truth, it all tasted, and looked, much the same to him. The only distinction he made with any confidence was between white and red, though he suspected if he were to be blindfolded and both kinds were served to him at room temperature, he wouldn't be able to tell one from the other.

They sat in the front room of Phoebe's flat—Quirke was out, of course, or Strafford would not have been there—toasting bread at the gas fire and discussing where they might go for their picnic. For a quarter of an hour, as dusk came on and the city went quiet, they were childishly happy.

Strafford confessed that in fact he had never been on a picnic before. Phoebe stared at him and laughed.

"What, not even when you were a child, with your family?"

"We didn't go in for that kind of thing. A rather cheerless lot, the Straffords, I'm afraid. As you will have guessed."

She leaned her shoulder against his and gave him an affectionate shove.

"Oh, go on—you love running down your family."

"Do I?"

He was genuinely surprised.

"Not in a serious way. Just to make people feel sorry for you and press on you the treats you missed out on when you were little."

The gas fire hissed. Why, Phoebe asked, does bread never smell as good as it does when it's being toasted? Strafford looked at her fondly and smiled.

"I have no idea," he said. "I'm sure there's a scientific reason."

"Oh, no doubt there is, Professor," she said, teasing him.

She rose and went to the table and came back with a plate and they put their slices of toast on it. He fetched the butter from the kitchen. She told him to hurry up, while the toast was still warm.

"That's another thing," she said, "hot buttered toast is delicious, but it's oogey when it's cold."

He smiled again, again indulgently. *Oogey.*

In the end, they decided they would go to Sandycove for their picnic. They could take the Dún Laoghaire bus and get off at Sandycove Avenue and walk down to the harbor and the beach.

They finished their toast and tea.

"Come round at eleven," Phoebe said.

By this, Strafford understood that he would not be invited to stay. This night, there would be no lovemaking. He was disappointed, but only a little. He would enjoy walking home along the canal, under the pale night sky, where bats flitted and now and then there would be the tiny flare of a shooting star. Among the stands of dry sedge, the moorhens would fluff themselves up and twitter indignantly as he passed by.

At heart, he told himself, he was a solitary.

She went down with him to the front door, and they exchanged a chaste kiss—no one kissed as Phoebe did, with a kind of melting reluctance—and he buttoned his overcoat and walked off into the night.

At Mount Street Bridge, a prostitute accosted him. She was dressed entirely in black, with black stockings and a crooked black dress and a funny little black hat cocked at a jaunty angle and stuck with a pearl pin. She might have been out of the last century, one of the Monto girls who figured in ballads and dirty jokes. She could not have been more than fifteen, he judged. He mumbled a word of apology and stepped past her.

"Aw, mister," she called after him, "give us a cig, at least, will you?"

He stopped and patted his pockets with large gestures to show her that he had no cigarettes, and hurried on. Such encounters always left him flustered and slightly ashamed. He really didn't know quite how to deal with women, of whatever type.

The bats were indeed out. They looked, he thought, like scraps of charred paper flying up from a fire. Had he read that somewhere, that simile? In a novel, he thought, yes. It seemed to him their leathery wings made tiny flickering sounds in the calm and darkly luminous air.

Next morning, he called for Phoebe at the flat as agreed. They embraced quickly at the door, and she brushed a few flakes of dandruff from the shoulders of his coat and stepped back.

"Honestly," she said, "you're like a child, the way you refuse to look after yourself."

They went along to the bus stop at Holles Street Hospital. The weather had held, though the air was not quite as balmy as it had been of late. Phoebe wore a tartan skirt and a white blouse and a light raincoat. The picnic things she carried in a straw basket with leather handles that she had brought back from a trip to Provence the previous summer. Strafford carried a bulging string bag, containing a blanket.

"Aren't we ridiculous?" she said happily. The mood of the previous evening had persisted. "I feel like a child."

Yes, Strafford thought, she had the look, bright and fearless and fragile, of a girl in a fairy tale, Goldilocks, say, or Snow White. They too carried baskets on their arms, and wore their hair bobbed, and probably were slightly pigeon-toed, as she was. Phoebe and Marguerite: he could not imagine two women more unlike each other. But were they so different? He suspected men always sought out the same type, without realizing it.

In the bus, they went up the steps to the top deck and sat in the front seat on the left. Mount Street rolled past, then Northumberland Road with its venerable trees. She had said something to him about this road the first time they had— what was the term?—*stepped out* together. What was it? Something about the name, about her liking it. Northumberland.

"I got a bottle of Chablis," she said. "Not cheap, but this *is* your first picnic."

"Let me pay for it."

"Certainly not. It's my treat."

"Then I'll pay for our fares."

The conductor was approaching behind them along the aisle, with his ticket machine and his flat black money bag, the flap of which was worn to a rich deep shine.

"All right, I'll allow you to do that much," she said, and leaned her head briefly on his shoulder.

Since it was Saturday morning, there was hardly any traffic. There were not many passengers on the bus, either, and it was flagged down only at every third or fourth stop. At Booterstown, the stand of dead water between the road and the railway line gave off a rank smell. Strafford's spirits drooped a little. Would he be restless, at the beach? A picnic, he suspected, could be trying, especially if it went on for long. One of the very few things he shared with Phoebe's father was a deep dread of boredom.

Phoebe seemed to sense his lapse in mood, for she said, "I hope you don't think this is a waste of your Saturday."

"Not at all," he said, with forced conviction. "I'm looking forward to it."

"Mm." She peered down into the basket at her feet, squinting a little. He wondered, not for the first time, if she might be shortsighted. "I put the wine in a bag with a handful of ice cubes, but I think they've melted already."

This is your life, a jaded voice in Strafford's head told him. This is all our lives.

"Marguerite," he heard himself say, "has asked for a divorce."

Good God, he thought, what has come over me, to be blurting out a thing like that?

"Oh, yes?" Phoebe responded, looking straight ahead through the big square window in front of them. "Marguerite."

"My wife."

"Yes, I gathered that. You didn't mention her name before."

"Didn't I? Sorry."

"No need."

A terrible silence rose up between them, like some swollen, mushroomy thing growing out of the floor. Strafford cursed himself. He had intended to tell her of Marguerite's visit and what had transpired between him and his wife, but not in the way that he had done just now, as casually if he were remarking on the weather.

"I mean, I'm sorry I mentioned it," he said, floundering, "without any warning."

She laughed shortly.

"In what way, exactly, would you go about warning me that you were about to tell me your wife has asked you for a divorce?"

"Oh, God," he said, letting his hands go limp in his lap, "I'm such a duffer."

"You're not. Well, you are, but—"

"But?"

"I think it's one of the reasons I—I like you."

Like. There were things they were still not ready to say to each other, declarations they were not yet prepared to make.

They had passed through Blackrock, and now here was Monkstown, with its peculiar church that looked like the palace of a Mughal emperor—or at least what Phoebe thought the palace of a Mughal emperor would look like—with its big square central tower and its many curlicued turrets. Someone had told her once that the architect who built it had got his plans mixed up and this was the building that had been meant for somewhere in India. In which case, somewhere in India would have a church meant for Monkstown.

"Yes," Strafford said, "I heard that too."

"Lutyens, I think was the architect."

"No, not Lutyens. Anyway, it's a myth, one of those stories that stick in people's imaginations."

She turned her head and gazed at him with round-eyed, feigned surprise.

"You looked into it, did you?" she said. "You investigated the matter, and found there was no case to be answered?"

He didn't respond to this, only smiled a little, sheepishly. Oddly, her amused raillery was just what he had needed to elevate his sunken spirits. The humors, he thought: no accounting for them.

When they got off the bus, they found that the sun was cloaked in sea mist and the air had a distinct damp chill.

"We are mad," Phoebe said, "going for a picnic on a beach at Halloween."

Strafford held up the string bag.

"I brought a blanket," he said, "for us to sit on."

"Or lie under."

She made a face and blushed. What was she thinking of, she wondered, to say something so risqué, if not downright crude? But she knew, of course. "Marguerite" was what she was thinking of.

The little crescent-shaped beach was empty, except for an elderly woman walking on the hard sand down by the waves with a fat dachshund wallowing at her heels.

Phoebe looked at Strafford's brogues.

"You should have brought galoshes," she said.

He gave her a sideways glance. Was she making fun of him again? What did it matter, if she was?

They chose a spot beside the concrete slipway that slanted down from the road. Strafford, with an effort, untangled the blanket from the string bag and spread it on the sand. Phoebe knelt and unpacked the picnic basket. Carr's Water Biscuits, Gorgonzola cheese, apples, two bananas, a packet of choco-late biscuits, the wine in its bag of melted ice. She sighed.

"Not exactly a feast, I'm afraid."

"It's splendid," Strafford said gallantly.

But she had already noted the hint of desperation in his manner. Who was it she had heard it said of that he stood at a slight angle to the world? The observation could be applied perfectly to St. John Strafford. Even his name was awkward.

She handed him the bottle of wine and a folding corkscrew.

"Here, open the booze and we'll get drunk."

She had brought two wineglasses. He knelt beside her and struggled with the cork, which at last came out with such suddenness that he almost fell over. She took the bottle from him and poured the wine.

"Cheers."

"Cheers."

"Oh, God."

"What's the matter?"

She groaned.

"This was a terrible idea."

"Why?"

"Look at us, out here in the mist. And it's freezing."

"Well, the wine is warm."

She laughed, despite herself.

Far out at sea, a white sail tilted over at a sharp angle and shone suddenly in the damp sunlight.

"So," Phoebe said, "will you give your wife the divorce she's asking for?"

They were sitting side by side on the blanket with their wineglasses and paper plates. He had not noticed before how knobbly her knees were. They reminded him of a child's clenched fists. Something rose up in him, a warm wave of something. Fondness? Tenderness? Or even—?

"No wonder you're cold," he said. "You've got no stockings on."

And no knickers either, she thought of saying, but didn't— it wouldn't be true, anyway. But she was annoyed. What business was it of his, what she wore or didn't wear? She knew, of course, that her indignation was entirely artificial.

They ate the cheese and crackers, they drank the wine. The mist cleared a little and the sun broke through, and everything became gauzy and bright. They might be in a watercolor, Strafford thought, by—what was the French painter's name? Dufy? Yes, Raoul Dufy. How had he remembered it? So much lies dormant in the memory, awaiting its cue.

Phoebe was watching him over the rim of her glass.

"It was you who mentioned it," she said. "Divorce, I mean. It doesn't matter if you don't want to talk about it."

She saw again the dull fretful light in his eyes. He looks like a trapped animal, she thought, and swore at herself for bringing him here, on this ridiculous outing.

"I don't know what there is to say," he said. "I just wanted you to know. But of course I bungled it. I'm sorry to be so clumsy."

He bit off a fragment of cracker and munched on it disconsolately. He disliked crackers. In one's mouth, they had a way of turning into a sticky paste that was almost impossible to swallow. He took a drink of wine from his glass. It really might be red, he thought, so far as he could judge.

"What will you do?" Phoebe asked.

"I'll have to go to London, it seems."

"For what?"

"There's a set procedure, apparently."

"A procedure? You make it sound like an operation—like having your varicose veins removed."

"Yes, it'll be a bit like that, I imagine. I'm to go to a sleazy hotel with a tart."

"Really? To do what? Or need I ask?"

"I won't *do* anything. It's just a formula."

She considered this for a moment, then laughed.

"You poor thing," she said, still laughing. "Will you have to stay the night at this sleazy hotel?"

"It seems we have to make a point of registering, and then be discovered together in the morning."

"Oh, my." She paused to picture the thing, smiling in mischievous delight. "It sounds like the best fun."

"Not to me, it doesn't," he said gloomily.

"Maybe you should make the most of it. I mean, you're going to have to pay the tart anyway, aren't you? So you may as well get your money's worth."

"Phoebe!"

"Do they let you have your choice of tart? I'm sure there are some nice ones, in London. Or will you have to bring her over with you?"

"Phoebe!"

"What? You have to be practical about these things. There you'll be, like someone in the *News of the World*, in your vest and socks, goggle-eyed in front of the flashbulbs. And there will be Polly, or Molly, or whoever, sitting up in a four-poster bed, bold as brass, with a glass of Babycham in one hand and a cig in the other, grinning and winking for the camera. What a lark."

She stopped, and suddenly, to her surprise and deep dismay, she felt two fat hot tears squeezing onto her eyelids and spilling over onto her cheeks. She brushed them away angrily, and turned aside and rummaged in the basket so that Strafford would not see that she was crying. But he had seen.

"I'm sorry," he said, not knowing exactly what it was he was apologizing for.

But perhaps he wasn't apologizing. Or perhaps he was apologizing not for what was happening here but for things in general. He almost always felt it must be he who was to blame when matters became difficult, whatever the circumstances.

He said, "Marguerite, of course, claims not to understand why I'm making such a fuss—not that I am." He thought for a moment. "In fact, I'm being very reasonable—" it sounded prissy, even to his own ears "—very reasonable indeed."

Phoebe had found a paper napkin in the basket and was using it to blow her nose. There was a tickle in Strafford's sinuses too—traces of that damned cold persisted still.

"Yes, well, I imagine she's feeling a bit awkward," Phoebe

said. "Some women tend to get snappy when they're in the wrong."

They both thought about this, while down the beach the woman's little dog barked, and the small waves plashed, and that far sail righted itself and went from glowing white back to dull gray.

"I'm not sure she is in the wrong," Strafford said carefully. "That is, I'm not sure she thinks so. In fact, I'm sure she doesn't. The marriage is over—has been, for a long time. She's only being practical, I suppose. The thing has to be done, and the law says I must be caught—"

"—with your pants down," she finished for him, more sourly than she had intended.

"Yes," Strafford said, with a mournful little laugh, "caught trouserless, as men so often are in their dreams. But this won't be a dream."

The woman had walked the length of the little beach three times, back and forth, and now she was departing. She wore a green rainproof jacket and a woolen hat with a pom-pom. As she passed by, she gave them, for some reason, an indignant stare. The dachshund waddled over to them and inserted its long snout delicately into the basket.

"Tristan!" its owner called out crossly. "Come!"

The dog lifted its head out of the basket, looked at the two picnickers with its fixed, cheerless grin, and trotted away. Its hind half swayed independently of its front half, as if it were jointed in the middle.

"Did I hear her right?" Phoebe asked. "Did she really call that creature Tristan?"

"Good thing it's not a bitch," Strafford said. He mimicked the woman's high sharp voice. "'Come, Isolde!'"

"Or Brünnhilde."

They watched the pair, woman and dog, as they made their way up the slipway, the woman leaning forward as if battling against a gale.

Phoebe reached into the pocket of her raincoat and brought out a packet of cigarettes and a metal lighter.

"Balkan Sobranie!" Strafford exclaimed.

"After Smyth's, I went down to Fox's. Very decadent."

"But you don't smoke."

"I buy these now and then. I like the look of them—I like the look of myself, with them in my hand. They make me feel as if I'm on the *Orient Express*." She was worried that she might start crying again. "The Grand Duchess Olga," she went on quickly, "last living relative of the last czar, in her sables and her diamonds and a big fur hat."

She flicked the lighter, but the breeze kept snuffing out the flame. Strafford took it from her and cupped it in his hands, and she leaned forward with the cigarette in her fingers. She lifted her head and blew out a stream of smoke that wobbled an instant before the breeze snatched it away sideways, like a magician's handkerchief.

He gave her back the lighter, and she pocketed it and gazed out to sea, one eye narrowed against the smoke. The unpracticed way she held the cigarette made her seem suddenly much younger than she was. Strafford felt again that bubble of affection, or whatever it was, swelling behind his breastbone.

"I was in Wicklow, the other day," he said. "A woman had been reported missing. Do you know who she was?"

"Who?"

"Remember that fellow in Trinity, that professor, Armitage? Rosa Jacobs's boss."

She shook her head.

"Do I know him?"

"I mentioned him to you, at the time."

"Did you? I suppose I might have met him with Rosa—I don't remember." She turned to look at him squarely, confident there would be no more tears to surprise and shame her, not today. "Is his wife the one who's missing?"

"Yes."

They were both frowning.

"What happened?" she asked. He told her. She listened, looking out to sea again. When he had finished, she nodded. "And she hasn't been found?"

"No. She hasn't been found."

The mist had drifted all the way out to sea and the sun was free again to assert its warmth. Phoebe refilled their glasses. She saw to her surprise that they had drunk three-quarters of the bottle. She didn't feel the least bit tipsy, which she knew she should—she hardly ever drank in the middle of the day, and certainly not this much. Perhaps the sea air, the ozone, or whatever it's called, was canceling the effect of the alcohol.

She looked all about now, at the narrow mouth of the harbor, at the little stone jetty, at the famous architect's white wedding cake of a house up behind the beach, and at the Martello tower, Joyce's *omphalos*, off to the side of it. *Entelechy*. What did that word mean? In the book, Stephen Dedalus talked of *entelechy*. His creator showing off, as usual. She must look it up.

And then she thought, I can put it off no longer.

Strafford was gazing out toward the no longer visible horizon. She examined his profile. Was he handsome, or not? The jawline was strong, but not the chin, though it wasn't weak, definitely not weak.

The sail was gone now. What had happened to it, where had it gone to? Must be the mist. Lost in the mist.

Entelechy. Is it *key* or *chee?*

She picked up a handful of sand and made a funnel of her fist and let it pour out, back to its own. *Sllt.* Then a last trickle. So dry, everything so dry, the sand, the grass—when had it rained last?

"I had an ulterior motive in suggesting this," she said.

He did not look at her.

"In suggesting what?"

"This—the picnic."

"Ah."

There was no end to the inflections, all of them uninterpretable, with which he could color that word.

"You can almost see it in capital letters, can't you," she said. "An Ulterior Motive."

He went on looking steadily out to sea. He did not like the sound of this. Some primordial instinct, of warning and alarm, was stirring within him.

"And what was it, this ulterior motive?" he asked.

She sighed, impatiently, it seemed.

"I'm pregnant," she said.

If he says Ah *again, I'll hit him,* she told herself.

But he said nothing. He was thinking, *Quirke: What will Quirke say, what will he do?*

There was the sail, it had appeared again, out of the mist. It was all he could see of the vessel. Strange to think that it was attached to a yacht with people on it, pulling at ropes, turning the tiller, doing the things that sailing folk do. He had never seen the point of it, cruising around within sight of shore, gliding about in long slow loops and going nowhere.

At last, he spoke.

"Three times," he said tonelessly, "we've only slept together three times."

"Once, is all it takes," she responded drily.

He retreated into silence again. She watched him. He was shocked, of course—perhaps he was even *in* shock. Men, she knew, were always astonished to be presented with the fact that the sexual act could have a certain and highly significant consequence. It was funny, in a way. Women were supposed to be the flighty ones, but when matters turn serious, men revert to being little boys.

"How long?" he asked.

He had still not looked at her. What could be so interesting, she wondered crossly, out there on the sea? That silly bloody sail?

"Not long," she said. *Of course, he suspects I'm only telling him now because of the divorce,* she thought. "I had to be sure, before I said anything. I got the test result the other day."

"I see."

Oh, do you? she thought.

He drank the wine that was in his glass and held it out to her for more. There was only a little of it left in the bottle. He was as surprised as she had been that they had drunk so much, so quickly. He had not enough experience of alcohol to know how he should feel. There was a faint buzzing in his head, just behind his forehead. It was not pleasant, but not bad, either. Didn't people drink to be relaxed and happy? He felt neither. Well, he hardly would, in the circumstances.

"What will you do?" he asked.

"What do you want me to do?"

He pondered this.

"I don't know," he said.

He really didn't. His thoughts, if they could be called thoughts, were moving at a helpless, sluggish pace. Was that because of what she had told him, or was it the wine? Both, probably.

She picked up another handful of sand and watched again as it poured out of her fist.

"I imagine I'll get rid of it," she said. She gave a sort of moaning laugh. "We can go over together on the mailboat, the two of us, and take the choo-choo to Paddington. You can go to your sleazy hotel with your tart, and I'll find a back-street abortionist." She gave him a level look, her lips a thin pale line. "Am I shocking you?"

He shook his head unhappily.

"I don't know what to say to you. I didn't expect..." He let his voice trail off. After a moment, he tried again. "It's so—it's so soon."

"Soon?"

"We've only known each other for, what—?"

"Long enough, obviously, as I've said."

"Yes, but we only—"

Once more, his voice lapsed.

"We only recently started fucking," she said. "Is that what you mean? Why do you keep harping on that?—why are you so surprised? I told you, it doesn't require time and dedication for a girl to find herself in the family way. It's easy-peasy. Those little tadpoles race along like lightning."

"I'm sorry," he said yet again, feebly.

"For what? For yourself, or for the fact that I'm knocked up?"

He made a grimace of distaste. Being coarse like this didn't suit her—was it the effect of her having taken up again with Isabel Galloway?—and besides, it wasn't convincing. She was crying again, in anger this time, he could see. He tried to take her hand, but she snatched it away.

"Listen, Pheebs—" he began.

"Pheebs?" she almost shouted, laughing through her tears. "Since when did I become *Pheebs?*"

He didn't know, but then did.

"I had a cousin, when I was young," he said. "Phoebe Butler-Bryan."

"What a name."

"She and I used to go bird's-nesting together. She was Pheebs, that's what everyone called her. I haven't thought of her in I don't know how long." He paused. "Does your father know?"

"Christ," she breathed in disgust, shaking her head. "I'm surprised you waited so long to ask."

"Does he?"

"It's none of your business." Abruptly, she got to her knees and then pushed herself to her feet, brushing the sand from the folds of her raincoat. "I'm going home," she said.

He rose too, but more slowly than she had, and with an effort. He looked at his shoes. She was right, he should have worn galoshes. *Galoshes:* what a ridiculous word. All at once he felt old, old and infirm. Besides Quirke, there was Marguerite to think of. He would have to tell her of the pregnancy, sooner or later. Somehow, this thought made the prospect of the London trip more ghastly than ever.

"I'll go up out to the main road and see if I can hail a taxi," he said.

"No." She was tossing the remains of the picnic back into the basket. "I'll go home on my own. You stay here and— and gaze out at the horizon and think deep thoughts."

He touched her arm, but again she drew away from him sharply.

Entelechy.

She would, she'd look it up the minute she got in the door.

13

As the date of Hackett's retirement loomed ever closer, he and Quirke had got into the habit of meeting for a drink at noon on Saturdays. They went to the Palace Bar in Fleet Street, or Neary's or McDaid's, both off Grafton Street. Sometimes they ventured farther afield, to Searson's on Upper Baggot Street, or along the river to the Brazen Head, which claimed to be the city's oldest pub, there since the first of the Normans had settled in Ireland. But mostly they kept to the old, familiar haunts.

Quirke was surprised then, on that Friday evening, when he received a message from Hackett through the switchboard at the hospital, suggesting that next day they might skip the drink and pay a visit to St. Stephen's Green instead. The detective would be waiting for him at the central fountain at noon. In the unlikely event that the fine weather should break, they could stroll across to the Shelbourne Hotel and find shelter there.

Quirke at once had a sense of foreboding, he could not have said why.

At lunchtime these days the city's streets and parks were thronged with people enjoying, if in a wistful way, what could well be the last weeks, if not the last days, of the long Indian summer—it had to end sooner or later. Hackett hailed from the Midlands, and though he had spent all his working life in Dublin, he was still at heart a countryman—or so he liked to claim—and often bemoaned the long hours he was compelled to spend cooped up in his office in the Pearse Street Garda station. It was hardly remarkable that he should want to pass a fine Saturday noontide in the Green, basking in the sunlight of late autumn, listening to the sound of water playing in the fountain and watching the countless tiny rainbows flickering in the curving jets as they rose and fell, unceasingly.

Yet Quirke couldn't shake off that nameless unease. It wasn't like Hackett, not only to suggest a change to their usual routine, but to send the suggestion by way of a phone message. Hackett was nervous of the telephone, and resorted to it with the greatest reluctance.

On the following day, when Quirke arrived, the detective was sitting on one of the benches that ringed the paved circle where the fountain stood. He was leaning back with one leg crossed on the knee of the other, and his arms stretched out along the bench on either side. His hat was pushed to the back of his head, and his old raincoat was unbuttoned, and so was the jacket of his blue suit, which was shiny from age. It was the pose of a man at peace with himself and the world, yet something was amiss. He seemed, to Quirke's eye, a size smaller than he had been the last time they met. Probably, Quirke thought, this was just the effect of his sitting there alone in the broad expanses of blued air and parched grass and graying foliage. Quirke was accustomed to finding him squatting froglike on a bar stool, or on a three-legged stool in a dim snug, half-hidden in a cloud of cigarette smoke.

"There you are!" Hackett said by way of greeting. "Isn't it a grand day altogether?"

He was in his country bumpkin mode, Quirke did not fail to note, his Midlands accent as broad as his grin and his hobnail boots as dusty as if he had just come from overseeing the saving of the hay. His fat and greasy tie reached hardly halfway down his chest, and, to the eye of Quirke the pathologist, suggested the protruding dark blue tongue of a strangulation victim.

As usual, they let the first minute or so of their encounter pass by in companionable silence. Quirke watched the approach of a black-clad nursemaid wheeling a high black pram. She smiled at him, shyly, and blushed a little, too, if he was not mistaken. Extraordinary, he thought, what a few weeks of fine weather will do to even the most timid denizens of this poor little dusty city.

Evelyn, he recalled, had treated a girl who, when she first came up from the country, had found a job looking after a child, a little girl, hardly more than a toddler. In her care, the child one afternoon fell by accident into the Grand Canal and was drowned. The parents, decent folk, forgave the distraught nanny, but she could not forgive herself. He couldn't remember what had become of her. Evelyn tended not to speak of the *lost ones*, as she called those patients who proved to be beyond her help, and beyond all help, in some cases. This reticence on his wife's part was not due to guilt or a heavy sense of responsibility, Quirke knew. It was intended only to shield him, her death-haunted husband, from the incurable sorrows of others. Now that she was gone, he had his own seemingly incurable sorrow, and could be counted, he supposed, among the lost ones.

There was real heat in the sunshine, for all its autumnal thinness. First he took off his hat, then put it on again, when his forehead began to sting. The nursemaid, he saw, had paused on the little humpback bridge over the duck pond. She had taken the baby from the pram and was holding it aloft to see the ducks. *Be careful!* he thought, recalling again the drowned little girl and her unfortunate nurse.

From this distance, the woman on the bridge bore a faint resemblance to Phoebe, who mostly dressed in black, and wore her hair tied back severely. When she was a child—so pensive, so grave—he used to think of her, when he thought of her, as *the little nun.*

Thoughts of Phoebe turned his mind inevitably to her— her what? Boyfriend? Lover, God help us? The lanky-looking galoot in the gabardine raincoat.

"Your man, Strafford," he said now, "how is he doing?"

Hackett glanced at him, startled by the harshness of his tone.

"He's doing grand," he said, "he's doing all right. Stubborn as a donkey, of course, and stuck-up, like the rest of them."

Like all his coreligionists, was what he meant. Unlike Quirke, the detective had spoken mildly. He had nothing against Protestants, had, indeed, a high regard for them, for their diffidence, their probity, their all-round soundness. The southern kind, that is, he would have said. Northern Protestants were a different breed, with a sense at once of privilege and a smoldering resentment that was all their own.

"He told me," Quirke said, and squinted at the dazzling waters of the fountain, "about this fellow whose wife seems to have disappeared, down in Wicklow somewhere."

"Oh, did he," Hackett responded vaguely. "Armitage. Professor of something or other—history, I believe—at Trinity."

"Did you come across him when you were investigating the Rosa Jacobs case?"

Hackett shook his head. When he did so, his lower jaw wobbled from side to side. A couple of years previously, a quack dentist had fitted him with a defective set of false teeth. Lately he had taken to letting the top set come loose and fall on the lower with a small, skeletal clatter.

"Strafford went over to Trinity to talk to him that time, but he was no help. She worked with your man, right enough, poor Rosa did, but that was as far as it went. Strafford didn't say so, but I had the impression Armitage wouldn't hold the sons of Abraham in high regard, or the daughters, either."

Quirke nodded. The nursemaid was returning the way she had gone. This time she kept her eyes lowered as she went past, the big pram squeaking on its springs. She had delicate ankles, shapely calves, and her neck was long and pale. These days he noticed such things almost clinically, with only the faintest after-echo of interest, much less desire. All that was dead in him. He had fallen into a something or other with Rosa Jacobs's sister, Molly, but it had not lasted, and Molly had gone back to her job as a journalist on the *Daily Express* in London. Odd to think of that bullish and bigoted paper appointing a woman, and a Jewish woman at that, to a top position as a feature writer.

Molly Jacobs. The image of her came to him from off to the side, swiftly, wingingly, and made him start back and catch his breath. Molly and Rosa, Rosa and Molly, mismatched siblings. Rose of Sharon. *What shall we do for our sister in the day when she shall be spoken for?* Molly had offered him love, but he had been too much caught up in mourning for his wife to accept it, and that was that.

What shall we do for our sister—

"I've told him to go down and talk to this other fellow," Hackett said.

Quirke frowned.

"What other fellow?"

Hackett was lighting up a cigarette.

"It seems there was somebody passing by, a fisherman I believe, when Armitage's missus disappeared. He spotted the car, the fisherman did, the car stuck in the middle of the field, and stopped to have a look."

"Yes," Quirke said, "he mentioned him. Some sort of odd name."

"Wymes. Useless, probably, for Strafford to go down there, but you never know."

Quirke caught something in the detective's tone.

"Is there more to this than meets the eye?"

"Mm. Isn't there always? Anyway, let's see what Strafford can find out." There was a pause. "Did someone tell me himself and your daughter are in a friendly way together?"

Quirke set his jaw and glared at the fountain's monotonous busyness.

"He takes her out now and then," he said, in a tight, neutral voice. "Dinner, or the pictures, that kind of thing."

"Ah. Right. Dinner, or the pictures."

Maybe, Quirke thought, maybe I should ask him to transfer Strafford to somewhere conveniently far-off, the Aran Islands, say, or out at the end of the Dingle Peninsula. That would settle his hash. No more cozy dinners then, or evenings at the cinema or the theater. It would be just Phoebe and himself, then, the two of them, together, as before.

Wishful thinking, of course. By rights, it was he who should be making himself scarce. But he thought of the mews house where he and Evelyn had lived for the brief span of their time together, and his heart quailed. He couldn't go back there, not yet—not ever, probably. Probably he would sell it, and send the proceeds to the ancient aunt, one of the few of her family to survive the Nazis, that Evelyn had once told him about.

But how would he trace the old woman? All he knew was that she was living somewhere in Paris, in the seventh arrondissement, was it? What was her name? Something short and blunt—Bloc, that was it. Geneviève Bloc. Maybe he could ask Molly Jacobs to help him find her. Oh, sure. *Dear Molly, sorry for the long silence. I wonder if—?*

Suddenly, Hackett leaned far forward on the bench and began to cough. Drawn-out, soupy squelching sounds came up from deep within his chest, as if instead of lungs there were a faulty suction pump wheezingly at work in there. His hat had fallen off, and Quirke leaned down and picked it up and offered it to him. The detective, his shoulders shaking, waved him weakly away. Still he coughed, and coughed. Quirke watched him, horribly fascinated. Would there be blood? Would something inside him sunder, sending purplish slivers of flesh shooting out of the poor man's open, funnel-shaped mouth?

At last the spasm passed, and he flopped back, exhausted, against the bench.

"Holy God," he gasped. "Holy divine Jesus." He flung the half-smoked cigarette onto the ground and trod on it violently with the toe of his boot, grinding it into the gravel. "It's them blasted things that have me in ribbons."

"That's a dreadful cough," Quirke said. "You should have yourself looked at."

Hackett emitted a low, rasping sound that it took Quirke a moment to identify as laughter.

"I'm going to keep myself out of the hands of the sawbones for as long as I'm able," the old man said, "saving your presence." He sat back again, his hands, palms up, resting limply at either side of him on the bench. Quirke looked at his little round potbelly shallowly heaving. "I'm ruined, is what I am, Doc. Ruined."

Quirke was unsure how to take this grim declaration. The detective had a way with irony that was as flat as his accent.

"Are you..." he hesitated "...are you sick?"

"Aye, sick. *Sick* is the word."

They were silent. Before them, the unceasing jets of water splashed and sparkled, and from over at the duck pond came the sound of children at play. Quirke was thinking, with what he knew to be unpardonable selfishness, *I can't lose another one, not yet!* Another what? Another loved one? That would be to put his dead wife, in all her tragic grandeur, alongside this unlovely little man with his ill-fitting dentures, his shabby blue suit and hobnail boots and that awful, damaged pump laboring wetly inside him.

"How bad is it?" he asked.

"You're the medical man," Hackett said, with another rattly chuckle, "have a guess."

To this, Quirke made no reply. What could he say? It would be less than tactful to point out that as a pathologist he did not deal with the living.

After a moment, he asked, "Will you keep on working?"

He winced. This was no less clumsy than what he had prevented himself from saying. However, Hackett's thoughts were elsewhere.

"The missus wants me to throw in the towel and the two of us to move up to Leitrim," he said. "We have a place there."

"Yes, you told me."

Hackett chuckled again.

"Did I? Ah, I'm forgetting everything, these days. First the noggin goes, then the rest follows in short order."

"I'm sorry," Quirke said.

He wondered how many times in his life he had uttered those two simple words, on which hung so much, or on which so much was meant to hang.

"Aye, well, we're all sorry, half the time, and the other half we don't give a damn."

Was he being rebuked? Quirke wondered. But there had been no bitterness in the detective's voice. Probably, in his present predicament, he was beyond caring what was said to him. By the sound of him, he had already taken the first, unwilling steps into the realm of the dead.

"I should go," Quirke said. "I have a meeting, at the hospital."

Hackett was not listening.

"Isn't it a queer clever yoke," he said, indicating the fountain and its lavish sprays of water, "the way it keeps on, hour after hour, day after day. I've always wondered how it works." He paused, nodding. "Hour after hour, day after day."

He lighted another cigarette.

"Listen," Quirke blurted, not quite knowing what he intended to say, "I'll cancel the damn meeting. It's only the ways and means committee. Let's go and have a drink."

There's a nice piece of moral sleight of hand, he thought,

to seek to cancel a heartless falsehood with a kindlier one. For he had lied, there had been no meeting for him to cancel. Hackett gave him a queer sly lopsided look.

"Ah sure, why not?" he said. "The folk waiting for you won't be going anywhere."

He hadn't lost his ear for a lie, then. He had always been a shrewd old bugger, Quirke thought ruefully, and was so still. *Country cute*—wasn't that the saying?

They rose and strolled over to the taxi stand opposite the Shelbourne. Only one car was there, an old-fashioned Ford with a high, rounded rear end, like the bustle of a nineteenth-century lady's gown. The driver, an oldster in a cloth cap, was asleep in his seat. He woke with a wide-eyed start when Quirke rapped with his ring finger on the window.

"How about Ryan's of Parkgate Street?" Hackett said. "That's a sound house."

On the quays, they tried not to smell the river's yeasty stench. Hadn't someone, Quirke remarked, some politician or other, come up with a grand scheme to stop the factories and the farmers throwing filth into the Liffey's upper reaches, so the salmon could come back?

"That'll be the day," Hackett said, with grim relish.

He had no time for politicians and their grand schemes.

They got out at Kingsbridge station. Quirke paid the fare. He was still putting his wallet away when the driver leaned his head out at the window and hawked and spat at his feet, then rolled up the window and drove away, the old motor trailing a derisive burble of exhaust smoke in its wake.

Hackett moved along with a dodderer's shuffle, sighing to himself. Quirke wondered guiltily how it was he hadn't noticed before now how much his old friend had deteriorated physically. When had he last bothered to notice him? Too much engrossed in his own troubles, astray in a fog of sorrow for his lost wife.

The pub, as they approached it, had an overbright, unreal aspect, the paint of its facade aglitter in the sunlight and its slate roof shining. Pubs, no matter how sound, Quirke was thinking, always looked slightly uncomfortable, slightly shamefaced, in broad daylight.

As if he had read his thoughts, Hackett said, "Do you know what, I've never been in Ryan's in the daytime before."

"Neither have I."

Inside, the place was empty, and the floor was streaked with long shafts of smoky sunlight. Tall Mr. Ryan in his tubular white apron stood behind the bar lost in thought, leaning forward on the heels of his hands. He straightened smartly and gravely greeted them.

"Good day, gents."

He pulled on a string that ran along the back wall, above the ranked row of bottles, and they heard the latch of the snug at the far end of the room click open. The publican had a bad hip, and the contrivance with the string saved him a walk.

Quirke had gone halfway down the bar before he realized he was on his own. He turned. Hackett was standing just inside the doorway, gazing at the floor and frowning vaguely. He hadn't taken off his hat. He seemed not himself, suddenly. He looked, Quirke thought, like someone's aged father, lost in his dotage.

Mr. Ryan gave Quirke a quick, inquiring glance, then turned to Hackett.

"What'll you have, Chief Inspector?" he asked loudly.

He knew all his customers and their proper titles. Hackett lifted his head and gazed at him vacantly.

"What's that?"

"A drink, sir," the publican said, more loudly still. "Will you take a ball of malt, or is the hour a bit early?"

Quirke retraced his steps. Hackett looked at him. He seemed baffled and alarmed, as if he had forgotten where he was. A thin shaft of sunlight was coming in through a gap above the double swing doors behind him.

"I think," he said, "I think I'll go home."

Again, Quirke and the publican exchanged a glance.

"We've just got here," Quirke said.

"Right, right," Hackett murmured, casting about the familiar room and seeming not to know it. He looked at Quirke again, falteringly, then turned to address the publican. "May will have the dinner ready," he said. May was his wife. Again, he looked about with empty eyes. "I might sit down," he said. "Just for a minute."

Quirke brought forward a high stool, and took the old man's arm, shockingly frail inside the sleeve of his raincoat. Some words from a poem came to his mind. *In every old man I see my father.* He had mangled the line, but the gist was there.

"Take your time," he said, guiding Hackett toward the stool. "Take your time, now, there's no rush."

Mr. Ryan, his long gray face professionally impassive, fetched a rag from behind the cash register and wiped the bar with broad slow circular strokes.

"A grand day now," he said.

Hackett sat on the stool, his toes not touching the floor. He pushed his hat to the back of his head, looked at his hands, and heaved a fluttering sigh.

"Take your time," Quirke said again, as the thought came to him: *he's dying.*

14

Strafford, having seen quite enough of Garda Dolan in recent days, decided not to request a squad car, and instead took the midmorning Wexford train from Westland Row, and got off at Arklow.

He had not been here in a long time. It was still a pleasant little town, neat and respectable. He walked along the narrow, sinuous main street, his hands in his pockets. Even yet the weather held, autumn still masquerading as summer. But there was none of summer's languorous vibrancy, only a great pale blue stillness, the air shot through with glints of old gold. All was misted, pensive, tinged with melancholy.

My time of the waning year, he told himself. He sighed. He was thinking of Phoebe, carrying his child. It was fantastical—his child! An impossibility, surely. What would

he be doing with a child? What would he do with its mother?
Had she broken the news to Quirke yet? Quirke. Oh, God.

He stopped at the Royal Hotel, halfway up the town. He
recalled that he had stayed here once, with Marguerite. They
had been on their way to Rosslare to take the mailboat to
Fishguard and on to London to visit one of Marguerite's un-
cles, and for some reason had decided to break the Irish part
of the journey halfway. Someone had told Marguerite that
Arklow was a Protestant town. In that case, she reasoned,
they would be guaranteed a decent room with clean sheets
and a lavatory that worked, and civilized fellow guests.

"How do you mean, civilized?" Strafford had asked her,
genuinely curious.

"Oh, you know. Solicitors. A doctor or two. Our sort."
However, when they came down to the bar before dinner,
she stopped on the threshold and looked about with tightened lips. There was an agricultural show on in the town,
and the room was full of farmers, flushed of face and loud
of voice. "Oh, God," she had said under her breath, "it's the
bloody bog."

Now, on the same threshold, Strafford paused and looked
about. But was it the same? It wasn't as he remembered it.
Had it been another hotel they had stayed at, in another town,
Wicklow, perhaps, or Enniscorthy? Well, what did it matter.
One country town was much like another, even if this one
supposedly contained more of Marguerite's sort.

He ordered a glass of Smithwick's ale and sat down at a
small table by the window. He watched the people passing
by in the street, housewives doing the morning shopping,
satcheled schoolchildren going home for their lunch, old cod-
gers with walking sticks tap-tapping along the sidewalk in
the grainy sunlight.

Again, his thoughts turned to Phoebe and her baby—hers and his. He must be calm, he must be reasonable. He wished to help her, to be a support, but he didn't know what to do, what to say. And then there was Marguerite. Should he tell her that his "bit of fluff," as she had scornfully referred to Phoebe, was pregnant by him? But owning up to his wife was a prospect too dreadful to contemplate.

All the same, confessing, making a clean breast of it, might save him the trip to London and the humiliation of being pounced on in a supposedly compromising situation in some ghastly hotel bedroom smelling of stale flower-water and carbolic soap.

Supposedly? There was nothing supposed about the predicament in which he had landed himself, even if he had not meant to. Getting a girl half his age pregnant was a serious matter, and no supposing about it.

He felt sorry for himself, profoundly so, he couldn't help it. It wasn't as if the thing were all his doing. Phoebe should have warned him that she wasn't taking precautions. Men didn't know about these things, or certainly he didn't. And always, of course, behind it all, there slithered the worm of doubt, of suspicion. Had she let it happen deliberately, to trap him? No, no, she wouldn't be capable of playing such a base trick. She wouldn't, surely. He trod on the squirming worm, and tried to turn his thoughts to other things.

But dear God, such a mess. Such a truly awful mess.

What he felt most strongly was a peculiar kind of deep sadness, through the gloom of which, however, there struck a sharp little radiant beam of—what? It seemed to be, of all things, pride. If nothing intervened to prevent it, he was going to be a father. He smiled, though shamefacedly, to think of it, while a horrible little voice that he could not ignore piped up inside his head, *That'll be one in the eye for Marguerite.*

There was of course an absurd, a comical, aspect to the impossible position into which he had been so unceremoniously pitched. Try as he might, he could not see himself dandling a baby on his knee, changing its diaper, taking it in its carriage for walks in the park, and presenting it—Christ almighty!—to his father.

No, he didn't want a child, really he didn't, no matter how much it would infuriate Marguerite. Children in general he regarded as profoundly disabled adults who in time would be more or less cured of their condition.

He wondered how Phoebe felt. After the debacle on the beach they had returned to the city separately, in silence. The pregnancy would have been as much of a surprise to her as it was to him. Or so he assumed, despite that unworthy niggle of suspicion as to the circumstances of her getting into the condition in the first place. But perhaps women had some inbuilt system that alerted them, even subconsciously, to the momentous process that had started up inside them. Wouldn't that be one of the functions of what people called the maternal instinct? An instinct that, he knew well, was entirely lacking in his wife.

And so his mind had circled back yet again to Marguerite. Now there were two poles to his existence, Phoebe and his wife, his wife and Phoebe. There was ice at both of those extremes.

After half an hour of these troubled ruminations he abandoned most of the glass of ale, which by now was tepid anyway, and went out to the reception desk. The young woman there smiled and said yes, of course she would call a taxi for him. It struck him, not for the first time, how readily, how radiantly, how unselfconsciously, women smiled. Even Marguerite did, in her good moods.

It was one o'clock, and the hotel had its lunchtime smell of cabbage and boiled bacon.

While the receptionist was telephoning the cab, he went and stood by the window and looked again idly out into the street. How would it be, to live here? He had studied law once, but gave it up to become, of all things, a policeman. What if he had kept on, and set up practice as a solicitor in some small, unassuming town such as this one? Instead of Marguerite he would probably have married a local girl, like the one before him speaking on the phone, with permed hair and freckles. He would have bought a fine old Victorian house on the market square, and set up his office in a front room on the ground floor, and his clients would smile at the sound of children playing upstairs.

Children. Ah, yes.

So strange, he thought, that we should be allowed only one life, one humdrum destiny.

The receptionist came from behind her desk and tapped him on the arm, recalling him from his reverie.

"The taxi car is here, sir," she said. And smiled.

"Ah. That was quick. Thank you so much."

The young woman colored, a faintest pink flush, and lowered her eyes. It must be his accent, he thought. It often made people behave oddly. And that added-on *so much*, that was a real giveaway. *A Prod*, she would be thinking, *look at that waistcoat, look at those shoes.* If he told her what his job was, she wouldn't believe him.

The driver turned out to be a woman. When she rolled down the window to ask Strafford where he wanted her to take him, she saw his look of surprise, indeed of mild con-

sternation, and cocked her head at him pertly. Her father—
"the da"—owned the car, she said, but he was sick, and she
was standing in for him. Was that all right?

She was tiny, blonde and bright-eyed. Her name was
Billie—"like the singer." *Which singer?* he wondered. She saw
him wondering. "Billie Holiday," she said. "Jazz, and that."

Billie Holiday. What was it they called her, what nickname? He couldn't remember.

The car was an antiquated model, a big black humpbacked
beast with dented head lamps and a rubber-lined running
board. It put Strafford in mind of a creature of the deep, a
battle-scarred sea elephant, say, or a giant manatee. The seats
were high-sprung and squashy, and again he thought of the
sea. A garishly colored Sacred Heart medal dangled on a ribbon from the driving mirror.

He settled himself in the back seat. They drove out of town
along the winding coast road. Billie wasn't sure exactly where
Kilpatrick beach was.

"But we'll get you there, don't worry."

Some miles passed in silence. Sunlight dazzled the windscreen, the greenery flashed blurredly by. Here and there a
tree had turned into an eruption of gold and umber foliage.
Strafford's eye kept veering back to the image of the Sacred
Heart, all gore and sacred flame, with its crucifix and spear,
swinging on its bit of ribbon like a runaway pendulum.

They came to a crossroads and Strafford recognized
McEntee's Bar and Lounge. Billie brought the car to a wallowing stop and went into the pub to ask for directions. In a
minute she came back and perched herself once more on the
front edge of the driving seat. The top of the steering wheel
was level with her chin.

"It's just down the road a few miles along," she said. "I

should have remembered, since I used to go for swims there when I was little."

She asked who it was he was visiting.

"Person by the name of Wymes," he said. "Denton Wymes. I'm told he's staying in a trailer at the beach. English, I believe. I haven't met him." As he was speaking, he sensed a shift in the atmosphere in the car. He stopped, but Billie did not respond. Something had happened, some connection, unwelcome, had been made. "Do you know him?" he asked.

Again, the little woman was silent. He looked at her tiny fists gripping the enormous steering wheel. Her father must have attached wooden blocks to the pedals, so that she could reach them. At last, she spoke.

"I've heard tell of that fellow all right." Her tone had darkened. "He's not English."

"I see. Is he a local? I thought, from the name—"

"No, he's from round here. Big house, up the coast. Wychwood. It's spelled funny, like his own name, with a *y*."

Strafford looked out at hedgerows of tangled briar, thorn bushes, down-sweeping branches. *Linden Lea.* For a second, he saw his mother in the drawing room at Roslea, the one at the back of the house, with the bow window that looked out on the lawn. She was arranging flowers—*sweet pea, look!*—and singing to herself.

To where, for me, the—something—tree
Do lean down low in Linden Lea.

Her favorite song, probably the only one she knew, for she had never been musical. He thought of her long-drawn-out dying, in that same green-shadowed ground-floor room, the lawn outside the window stretching to the margin of the beech wood. Deer used to come here, she told him, they would walk right up to the window, trying to see in. I remember them, their black snouts, the streaks under their eyes as if they had been crying ever since they were born. All gone now, all gone. And then she too was gone.

The apple tree—that was it.

To where, for me, the apple tree
Do lean down low in Linden Lea.

All gone.

"Can you tell me something about him?" he asked. "Mr. Wymes?"

Again, time passed before she spoke.

"The local people, they steer clear of him."

"Yes? Why is that?"

They were ascending a steep hill and she had to change to a lower gear, the engine whining.

"He's peculiar, they say. Bit of a hermit. It's just him and the dog. They're a pair—you never see the one without the other."

They crested the hill and the sea came into view, beyond a ragged line of sand dunes, a band of white near in and then a sweep of purplish-blue bounded by the horizon. Strafford leaned forward with his hands on the back of the passenger seat in front of him. He saw the trailer, squatting on its two flat tires. It was tiny, with a narrow door and a single, small square window. The roof sloped at both ends. There would hardly be room to stand upright inside it.

He asked Billie if she would wait and bring him back to Arklow when he had finished with the outcast Mr. Wymes.

She said she would go over to McEntee's and get "Mr. Mac" to make a cup of coffee.

"If I come back in an hour, say?"

"Yes, that should be fine," Strafford said.

For some reason, he couldn't bring himself to address her by her name. Odd, these little social restrictions.

Lady Day! That was what they used to call her, Billie Holiday, her nickname, her love-name. How did he know that? He wasn't even sure he had ever heard her sing.

Your heart is full of song and singers, today, St. John old boy. He smiled bleakly to himself. It was all just an attempt to duck out from under the shadow of the thing that loomed over all his thoughts, which was, of course, Phoebe and the blasted baby.

Oh, God.

He recalled a story Quirke had told him, about a one-time girlfriend of his—that actress, he supposed, Isabel Galloway, Phoebe's friend—who had rung up Waltons shop and ordered the sheet music for a Victorian ditty, the name of which was "Could I But Express in Song." When she went into the shop the next day to collect her purchase, the young woman behind the counter told her they had searched all the catalogs, but were unable to find Kodály's "Buttock-Pressing Song." Could it be true? Hardly.

Billie the driver drove away along the sandy track, the car's suspension rattling.

When he knocked on the door of the caravan, the dog inside began to bark shrilly. He stepped back. He had always been nervous of dogs—it was another of the many timidities his father mocked him for.

A voice spoke within the camper, soothingly, and the dog

fell silent. Then the door opened and the animal, a collie, bounded out at him, whining excitedly and wagging his tail. Man's best friend.

Wymes, tall and gaunt, was neither young nor old. He had thinning pale hair and a large nose, his cheeks sagged, and his heavy eyelids drooped at the outer corners. He wore a faded checked shirt unbuttoned at the neck, and a moth-eaten gray pullover. His once-brown corduroy trousers were faded to beige, and had a dull shine at the knees.

"Mr. Wymes? Detective Inspector Strafford." His eye was distracted by the shabby pair of slippers the man was wearing. They were a shade of faded pink, with, on the toes, large pink pom-poms that had once been fluffy. "Might I have a word?"

Wymes looked at him in silence for a moment in wary surmise. It was a look Strafford knew well. No one welcomed a visit from the police.

"It's not about the dog license again, is it?" Wymes said on a wearily plaintive note. "I told Sergeant Crowley that I have got one. It's here somewhere, I just can't put my hand on it."

Strafford registered the accent and recognized it at once, the blazon of their shared class. It was mild, round-voweled, diffident, yet underpinned by a certain cool assurance that even the pink slippers could not dent. It came to him that he had known a Wymes at school, though not this one. Can't be many families with that name, though.

The man in his turn had registered Strafford's accent, and was surprised, with good reason. How did a son of the Protestant Ascendancy, as Strafford patently was, get to be a detective in the Republic's almost exclusively Roman Catholic police force?

That was twice in the space of an hour, Strafford gloomily mused, that he had been recognized for what he was—

first Billie, now Wymes, each surprised by him, each from a different perspective.

"No, it's not about a dog license," Strafford said. "I'm looking into the case of the woman who went missing."

"Ah, yes," Wymes said, relieved for a moment but then suspicious again. "What about her?"

Strafford smiled his professional smile.

"Do you think I could come in? I won't keep you long. It's just"—the never-failing cliché—"routine."

The trailer inside was cramped, with the low ceiling that sloped downward at front and back, and sure enough, both men, though not particularly tall, had to stoop under it. There was a narrow bunk bed, a sink, and a couple of plywood presses. A Primus stove stood on a square of linoleum on a rickety makeshift table with folding legs. The air was stale, and smelled, not unpleasantly, of dog. There was only one chair, made of bleached wood, with a canvas back, like the chairs in which Hollywood directors sit, with their names printed on the back. Wymes ceded it to Strafford, and sat himself on the edge of the bunk. The dog settled at his feet, watchful, proprietorial, and boundlessly excited by the presence of a stranger.

"I'm told you were there when Professor Armitage went to the house looking for help," Strafford said. He paused. "What are the people called, again?"

"What people?"

"At the house."

"Ruddock."

"That's right. Ruddock. Did you know them? I mean, before that night?"

Wymes shook his head.

"No, I'd never met them before. They don't live there, at the house, they're only renting."

"Yes, they said. They come every year, it seems, at this time, Halloween."

Then a silence. The dog lowered his head and set his muzzle between his front paws and looked up first at Strafford, then at his master, then at Strafford again.

"What's his name?" Strafford asked.

"Scamp."

Hearing his name spoken, the dog lifted his head expectantly, and Wymes reached down and patted him, ruffling his fur.

"Good company, a dog," Strafford said.

"Yes," Wymes responded coolly, as if to say *Don't try getting round me by way of my pet.*

Strafford looked away. He felt awkward. He rarely encountered one of his own class and kind, in the course of his working day. They were, himself and Wymes, like a pair of former prisoners who long ago had shared a prison cell, and who now, meeting up by chance all these years later, didn't know how they should comport themselves. The old codes didn't work, out here in the world.

"There really isn't much I can tell you, Inspector," Wymes said at last, with a touch of impatience. "I'd been down at the shore, fishing, and was passing by the gate when I looked in and saw the car stopped in the field. It was an odd sight. I thought there might have been an accident. Then this man came along and said his wife had drowned herself, or at least had disappeared." He coughed, and made a constricted, humming sound at the back of his throat. "Did you say he's a professor?"

"Yes. Teaches history at Trinity College."

"Didn't seem the professor type to me. Sounded English."

"He is English," Strafford said. "From the north, some-where, Manchester, Birmingham, somewhere like that."

"I wouldn't have taken him for a northerner, either."

"No."

They both looked at the floor. A hole seemed to have opened in the air between them. The tension was no lon-ger to do with class or background, Strafford thought, nor with the matter of Armitage and his missing wife. There was something else.

Wymes coughed again, and again made that sound in his throat. It was like the buzzing of a fly against a window-pane. He put his hand on the dog's head, and the dog too made a low sound. Was it a mode of communication between them, the solitary man and his canine companion, buzzing at each other?

Then Wymes stirred, squaring his shoulders.

"You do know who I am," he said, "don't you?"

He fixed the detective with a curiously defiant stare.

"The Ruddocks told me your name," Strafford said, puz-zled. "What else should I know?"

"How did you find me?"

"I spoke to the Garda station in Wicklow."

"Oh," Wymes said flatly. "Crowley, I suppose."

"Yes. Sergeant Crowley. He told me you were here at— what's it called, again?"

"Kilpatrick. That's the name of the townland. The beach is Kilpatrick beach."

There was another silence. The dog gazed up inquiringly at his master. Dogs become uneasy when humans go quiet like this; Strafford had often noticed it. There were always dogs around the place, when he was a boy. They did not take to him. There was something about him that made them as wary of him as he was of them.

"I thought," Wymes said, "you would have checked up on me. There must be a file."

Strafford was smiling, he didn't know why.

"What kind of a file?" he asked.

Wymes stood up and went to the sink, the dog slinking at his heels, in the sly and watchful way that collies do, his head low and his belly almost brushing the floor.

"Cup of tea?" Wymes asked over his shoulder.

He was filling a kettle from the tap. Strafford wondered where the water was stored. Tank on the roof, to catch the rain, a mesh over it to keep the birds off. How the mind strays, like a restive child, he thought.

"Tea, yes," he said. "That would be good." He paused, then asked again, "What kind of a file?"

Wymes might not have heard. He had put down the kettle and was engaged in the intricate business of lighting the Primus stove. He poured methylated spirit into the little round trough under the burner and put a match to it. It flickered spectral blue. Then he pumped the plunger and after some seconds the quick flame caught with a soft *whoomph*. He stood for a long moment gazing at the seething corona, then set the kettle on the trivet and stepped back.

"I was in jail," he said, not looking Strafford. "Arbour Hill, special wing."

"Ah," Strafford said softly. "I see."

Wymes turned to him, a glint of what seemed amusement—could it be?—in his no-color eyes.

"Do you?" he said. He returned to the bunk and sat down, and again the dog settled itself Sphinxlike at his feet. "I was arrested on a charge of interfering with children." He added, "I was a teacher, you see."

"The children were your pupils?"

"Yes. And there were others, too, besides." He looked at Strafford with his head to one side. "I'm an addict, you might say. Have been, for as long as I can remember, right back to my own childhood." The brittle grass, the lupins, the gleaming coins too precious ever to be spent. "So I imagine—" a bleak smile "—there would be a file."

Strafford clasped his hands together and gazed at them, frowning.

"It must be very difficult."

"Yes," Wymes said tonelessly. "It is."

All was still. The dog gave a whimper, so faint it was barely audible. Then Strafford stirred, and cleared his throat.

"But that's not my concern, here," he said, and again had to clear his throat. "I just need you to tell me all you know about Professor Armitage, about his wife, about the night she disappeared. Anything at all that struck you as significant."

Wymes stood up from the bunk again. The kettle on the little stove was coming to the boil, the water rumbling in its depths. He took down a teapot from a shelf, and spooned tea into it from a dented Bewley's tin.

"I don't know what I can tell you," he said. "This fellow, Armitage, he was behaving very peculiarly, I thought. Mind you, how would he not, in the circumstances."

"Peculiar in what way?"

Wymes lifted down two mugs and handed one to Strafford. "I'm afraid there's no milk," he said.

"It's no matter," Strafford said, "I take it black."

He didn't—the polite lie was as natural to him as breathing. Wymes hovered before him, stooped and gaunt. There were ancient stains on the front of his pullover. What age was he? Strafford wondered. Fifty? Sixty?

He supposed he should check up on the poor fellow—he was right, there would be a file, of course—and find out how serious his crimes had been, and how long a sentence he had served. Most likely he wouldn't bother, though. What would be the point? His past sins were hardly relevant to the present.

The man's anguish was palpable. He looked crushed, as if something, a boulder, or the side of a cliff, had come loose and fallen on him. Yet he shouldn't allow himself to feel sorry for him, Strafford knew. There were the children, they had to be considered. They in their turn would be trapped under their burdens, as weighty as his, perhaps weightier. All the same, none of this was germane to the matter in hand.

"Tell me about that evening, will you? What did you think was peculiar about Armitage's behavior?"

Wymes had sat down again on the edge of the bunk. He gazed before him, stirring a spoon slowly round and round in his tea.

"It was twilight, nearly dark. As I said, I was just passing by, with my fishing gear. I saw the car. I don't know what made me go in and take a look at it. I'm not naturally inquisitive." Saying this, he pursed his lips and raised his eyebrows in what seemed prim self-righteousness. "I had the feeling something was wrong—the engine was running, the driver's door was wide-open—but also that, well, that I shouldn't be there."

"How do you mean?"

Wymes looked down and cast about him on the floor, as if vaguely in search of something he had dropped there.

"I don't know," he said. "But I knew I had stumbled on something that was no business of mine. I was about to turn and leave when the man appeared, coming up the field from

the direction of the sea and waving his arm above his head."
He paused, seeing the scene again. "It was odd. He said at first
his wife had drowned. Then he rambled on for a bit. Then he
said maybe she hadn't drowned but had just run off. A light
came on in the house at the top of the slope. I suggested he
should go up and ask the people there to phone for help. He
said he would, but insisted I go with him."

He fell silent, and sipped his tea.

"And then?" Strafford urged.

Wymes, with a start, came back from that remembered
twilit shore, and blinked rapidly. The dog at his feet was still
watching him, motionless.

"That was odd too."

"What was?"

"At the house…" He paused again, then went on hesitantly, like a traveler feeling his way over uncertain terrain.
"It seemed to me that the people in the house, the Ruddocks,
it seemed they knew Armitage, or knew of him, in some
way—or that at least he did, the man, I mean, Ruddock."
He paused. "He wasn't surprised enough."

"What do you mean?"

"Well, you know, here was this fellow turning up at the
door out of the blue, saying wild things about his wife having
drowned, and all the rest of it. And Ruddock, he—he didn't
ask the right questions. He seemed all the time to be thinking about something else, speculating, calculating. I had the
impression he was worried about something—not the missing
woman, but something to do with himself." He rose again
from the bunk and poured himself another mug of tea from
the pot. "And then there was the phone."

"The phone?"

"Ruddock should have called for help, but he didn't. I

would have been on to the Guards, or the lifeboat, or something, straightaway. His wife kept urging him to call someone, but in the end she had to go out to the phone herself. The husband just sat there at the table, plying this fellow with whiskey. And watching him. All the time watching him."

"Watching him how?"

"As if he was suspicious of him, or even—well, nervous of him, not of the man himself but nervous of what he might do or say." He took another sip of his tea. "I think he didn't believe him about his wife. I think he thought he had made up the story as an excuse to get into the house. And Armitage, he kept looking round, you know, as if it was a place he had heard about and now was getting to see at last."

"So you thought he had known them already?"

"The Ruddocks?" He considered this. "I had the feeling there was something between them, yes, between the three of them, though don't ask me what it might be. The woman, Ruddock's wife, she seemed to be angry about something. At first, she was fine. Just puzzled by the situation. But then— then she seemed to start to understand something." He shook his head and sighed. "Probably I was just imagining things. But it was all so—so odd."

Strafford thought about this for a while, then rose, taking up his hat.

"How will I contact you, if I need to?" he asked.

"Contact me?" Wymes looked suddenly alarmed. "Why?"

The dog, still resting by the bunk, watched them both, his ears twitching.

"If I have more questions," Strafford said. "There might be something you've forgotten, or didn't think was important at the time."

Wymes was gazing at him as if mesmerized.

"Did they find the woman's body?" he asked.

"No," Strafford said, turning the hat in his fingers. "They found nothing, not the Coast Guard nor the search party. She seems to have disappeared without a trace. If, that is—" he shrugged "—she was there in the first place."

"So you think he may have been—Armitage—you think he may have been lying?"

Strafford permitted himself a wan smile. *Everyone lies*, he might have said, *everyone*.

15

Hackett's doctor sent him to hospital for tests, to try to determine the cause of his nagging cough, as well as the bouts of forgetfulness and the dizzy spells he had been experiencing lately, with increasing frequency. He was brought into St. James's. Quirke was relieved it wasn't the Holy Family. He would have been expected to pop up daily from the pathology lab and call in on the old boy and engage him in encouraging chats. The tests, he feared, would not produce a good result. Though he worked only with the dead, Quirke was familiar enough with the living to know that Hackett was a sick man. The question was, how sick.

He would have to pay him a visit, that went without saying. He had known Hackett for a long time, and was fond of him, in a way. All the same, he dreaded seeing him, dreaded seeing anyone, in a hospital bed. He never knew how to behave on such occasions. Dealing with cadavers, one didn't need to put on a bedside manner.

The thing to do was to get someone to go with him. He thought of asking Phoebe—Hackett had always had a soft spot for Quirke's daughter—but didn't think it would be fair on her. He brooded for some time, then all at once he hit on the perfect candidate.

"Hello," he said into the phone, "Quirke here."

From his office he could hear the steady buzzing of the big ceiling lights out in the dissecting room.

"Oh, yes," Strafford replied, sounding even more wary than usual. Quirke knew the detective was afraid of him.

"You know Hackett is in hospital," he said. "I'm going over there this morning to see how he's doing. I thought you might want to come along."

Want to: he liked that touch.

A pause. There was a buzzing on the phone line that was the same frequency as the buzzing from the lights.

"I'm at work," Strafford said flatly. Quirke did not think this required a response. After another pause, the detective asked, "What time are you thinking of going?"

"Eleven, say? Visiting hours are ten until noon."

Quirke, impatient, fiddled with the papers on his desk. He was always eager, once he was on the phone, to get off it as quickly as possible.

"Yes, all right," Strafford said glumly. "I'll get a taxi. Do you want me to call for you on the way?"

"No, I'll walk over. Stretch the legs."

"I'll see you there, then."

It was plain that Strafford was not only reluctant, but annoyed. He would be no more eager than Quirke to pay a visit to his boss in hospital, and certainly not with Quirke.

All the same, he couldn't get out of it now. Quirke hung up the phone.

Heh heh.

Although he had steeled himself, still Quirke was shocked when he saw the state of Hackett. He seemed even more shrunken than he had in Ryan's. He was sitting up in a big white bed like a lone survivor on a raft. He was wearing a pair of faded calico pajamas with a blue stripe. A paper identity bracelet was fixed around his left wrist. His little shriveled face had a chalky pallor, and the pink of his skull was visible through thin lank hair. When his visitors entered, Quirke first and Strafford after him, hats in their hands and preceded by a nurse, he looked at them as if he had no idea who they were. Perhaps he didn't, Quirke thought.

"Here's a nice surprise," the nurse said, brightly but too loud. "Dr. Quinn and Mr. Stafford, come to see you."

He ignored her. He was watching the two men with what seemed a kind of baffled desperation. His eyes were bloodshot, his mouth was sunken—the set of ill-made dentures, grayish-white and pale pink, the color of marshmallows, grinned in a glass of water standing on the cupboard beside the bed. The papery skin in the hollows under his eyes was bruise-brown and shiny.

"That's grand," he said vaguely, picking at the turned-down sheet.

Quirke took in a sharp breath and stepped forward boldly. Hackett drew back, as if he thought he was being attacked.

The nurse, large and no longer young, smiled at everyone, showing her teeth and managing to meet no one's eye, and departed in a swirl of starched linen. The door gave a forbearing sigh as it closed behind her.

"How are you doing?" Quirke said to the man in the bed. He, like the nurse, had spoken too loudly. Abashed, he lowered his voice. "You're looking well."

Which he most certainly was not.

Strafford came to the bed in his accustomed sideways fashion—Quirke thought it accustomed—with a hand extended. Hackett looked at it as if he had never seen a hand before.

"That's grand," he said again, defensively, looking up at the younger man and blinking rapidly. He could only mumble out of that collapsed, dentureless mouth.

Quirke brought forward a chair and sat down. Strafford withdrew his unnoticed hand and drifted to the window. There were three other beds in the room, all unoccupied. Someone must have pulled strings to ensure Hackett would have a private ward.

Below the window there was a large empty flagstone square that must once have been an exercise yard for the military—this building, he thought he remembered reading somewhere, had been a barracks originally. Farther off, there was a jumble of undistinguished brick buildings, their roofs dully agleam under a flat gray sky.

"May was in earlier," Hackett said, abruptly and with some force, as if he expected to be contradicted. Strafford thought he meant the month, then remembered that May was the name of the old man's wife. The legendary wife, whom no one at the station had met or even had a glimpse of, except Quirke, once, long ago, but he could hardly remember what she looked like. "She brought them yokes. Do you want some?"

The old man indicated a soggy-looking brown paper bag of grapes on top of the bedside cupboard, beside the glass with the submerged, grinning dentures. There was also a banana, and a half-peeled orange.

"Thanks, no," Quirke said.

"And young Jenkins, he looked in too," the old man said, with his crooked smile, nodding. "A good lad."

Quirke and Strafford glanced at each other quickly, frowning.

Garda Sergeant Jenkins, poor Ambie Jenkins, had died a year or two past at a place called Raven Point, his remarkably flat skull stove in by three blows of a hammer, any one of which would have been enough to kill him.

"Are they looking after you?" Quirke asked, in a voice even louder than before.

He and Strafford had wordlessly agreed to pass over in silence Jenkins's imagined visit.

Hackett frowned, struggling to comprehend what had been asked of him. Then he smiled, showing the ridge of his lower gums, jelly-bean pink and glistening.

"That one—" nodding toward the door where the nurse had gone out "—is from Leitrim. Dennehy. Something Dennehy. Louise, or Laura, something like that." He paused, his remembering frown directed upward. "I knew a Dennehy. Had a place outside Ballinamore. Pigs, I think. Or sheep, maybe." He sat forward suddenly, his hands on his raised knees under the covers. He had turned his eyes toward Strafford, who was still by the window with his back to the room. "What about that woman that got drowned?"

Strafford turned.

"The woman that—?"

"That disappeared. The wife of the fellow from Trinity."

"Ah." Strafford glanced at Quirke again. "No trace of her, as yet."

The atmosphere in the room had become less tense—it seemed to both the visitors that they had been holding their breath up to now. They both drew back their shoulders and turned their necks this way and that inside their shirt collars. So the old boy wasn't entirely gaga.

Quirke brought out his cigarette case, hesitated, made to put it away.

"Go ahead, go ahead," Hackett said, gesturing with a claw-like hand. "Have a smoke, go on—I'll be glad of a whiff, at least. They took my packet of Gold Flake off me." His lungs responded to the prompt and he began to cough, his shoulders heaving. When the spasm had passed, he fell back against the standing bank of pillows behind him, his hands lying limp on the sheet. "Jesus God almighty," he wheezed, "one of these days that cough will turn me inside out."

Strafford had come back from the window and was standing by the side of the bed with his hands in the pockets of his gabardine raincoat. He looked down on the old man with what to Quirke seemed a heartlessly dispassionate eye.

"Have they done the tests yet?" he asked, in a tone almost brutal.

Quirke looked at him sharply, frowning a rebuke. Then he went on watching him, sidelong, for a long moment. There was something different in his demeanor today; Quirke had noticed it the moment they met down at the reception desk on the ground floor. He had a furtive, anxious air, and his eyes kept sliding away to fix on neutral things, the doorknob, the locker beside the bed, the mild light of day in the window. What was the matter with him? What had become of his much-vaunted detachment, his languid self-assurance? He had—yes—he had a guilty look about him. Why was that? Quirke was reminded of certain of his fellow orphans at

Carricklea, when he was a captive there, as a little boy. There was a handful of them, set apart from the rest by a mysterious, unexpressed but absolute interdiction. Skinny pale creatures they were, knock-kneed, with long necks and sticklike wrists and anxious, red-rimmed eyes. They were known to all, even to themselves, as the crawlers.

They were frightened of everything, the crawlers, all of them, all the time. Yet they made no effort to shield themselves from the violence and general abuse to which they were subjected. On the contrary, they courted danger, always hanging around the worst bullies and the most brutish among the Christian Brothers, gazing up at them mutely with a kind of fearful longing. They seemed to yearn to be set upon. In their anguished loneliness, they would endure anything, from having their ears boxed to being raped in the back of the storeroom where the hurley sticks and shorts and jerseys were stored—the spot most favored by the Brothers with a taste for that kind of thing, which was a goodly number of them.

To be touched, to be fondled, to be beaten, to be buggered—in a word, to be overborne—they would put up with it all, in a state of abject gratitude, simply because it was contact. For it was contact, just contact, whatever pain and humiliation it inevitably entailed, that the crawlers most miserably craved.

But no, Quirke thought, reining himself in, no no, Strafford wasn't a crawler, he wasn't the type. No son of the Ascendancy would let himself stoop so low. Yet how to explain that air he gave off today, of foreboding and dire expectancy?

Something was up, Quirke told himself darkly. Some limit had been crossed, some compact had been violated. He needed watching, this stealthy interloper from a privileged domain, with his floppy forelock and bony white fingers and pale, disdainful gaze.

Was it something to do with Phoebe? Had he broken up with her, had he left her in the lurch? It baffled him that his daughter should care for the fellow at all, but that she should care so deeply that his dumping her would break her heart, *that* he would not accept. She had suffered worse things, much worse things, in her short life, than being jilted by this limp-wristed shirker.

Hackett was speaking of one of the doctors, a cancer specialist, to whom he had taken a strong aversion.

"Fennelly is his name," he said. He looked to Quirke. "Do you know him?" Quirke shook his head. He supposed that to Hackett, all doctors would be members of one grand, all-powerful fraternity. "Little sandy-haired fellow with a mustache," Hackett went on. "Sergeant-Major type. ''Tenshun, you man there in the bed!' Holds the X-rays up to the light and squints at them with one eye shut, like he was taking aim along the barrel of a Lee-Enfield. A right martinet." He paused, and then smiled, gently, almost wistfully. "I've a notion he knows I'm a goner, only he won't say."

Quirke shifted on the chair and blew a stream of cigarette smoke in the direction of the ceiling.

"Has he said anything definite?" he asked, but in a gentler tone than Strafford's when a minute ago he had asked the same question in different words.

Hackett only shrugged and looked away with unfocused eyes. Strafford paced slowly back to the window. This time he did not look out, but stayed facing the room, leaning his hip against the sill, watching the man in the bed. Who said now, "I keep thinking about that poor young one that died in the car." He glanced from Strafford to Quirke and back again. "Do you think it was really the German fellow that did her in?"

Quirke had to think for a moment. Rosa Jacobs: of course.

"You mean the Kesslers?" he asked. "The father or the son?"

"Either one." The old man shifted on his haunches, grimacing. "God love us, but I'd give my eyeteeth for a cig." When he spoke, he smacked his lips.

Quirke rose, walked to the other side of the bed and stubbed out his cigarette in an ashtray on the bedside cabinet. He caught the cloying, sugary smell of the grapes in the paper bag. That orange: who had given up peeling it halfway through, and why? He returned to sit down again on the chair.

"How is it she's on your mind still," he said, "Rosa Jacobs?"

"I can't shake off the notion that there was something queer about that case."

"Queer in what way?" asked Strafford at the window.

He hasn't met my eye, not once, since we arrived here at the hospital, Quirke thought. Yes, Phoebe—something to do with Phoebe. If he had done something to her, caused her pain or sorrow, he would break the fellow's neck.

"I don't know in what way," Hackett was saying. "Only I feel it in my water." He turned again to Quirke. "What about you, Doc?"

Quirke was thinking of the day he and Strafford had gone down to Wicklow, at Hackett's behest, to talk to the wealthy horse-breeder Wolfgang Kessler, in his country mansion. A cool customer he was, with his pinched yet easy smile. Quirke had wondered at the time how the man had made his money. The war wasn't over all that long, and the whereabouts of all the riches the Nazis had plundered was still a matter of speculation. It had turned out eventually that Kessler had a murky past and an even murkier present. He was a man who wouldn't hesitate to eliminate a troublesome Jew, as Rosa Jacobs had made it her business to be. She had stirred up trouble for him in Israel, where she got a newspaper friend to investigate his business affairs. It was Kessler's son, at Kessler's directive, who had locked Rosa in her car and fed a rubber hose from the exhaust pipe through the window and gassed her to death. Kessler knew all about gassing people.

Hackett's instincts had always been sound—but were they sound still? He thought of him again in Ryan's that day, forgetting where he was or what he was about. And then there was the imagined visit today by poor dead Ambie Jenkins.

"Kessler had an interest in seeing Rosa Jacobs gone," Quirke said, hefting the cigarette case in his hand and thinking again of Nazi gold. "And the son was unhinged, as it proved."

He was looking at Strafford, who still would not sustain his gaze. Kessler's son, Frank, had shot himself in Strafford's presence one night on the towpath by the Grand Canal. A bloody business, the whole thing, first the murdered girl, next the son killing his own father, and then himself. And now Hackett was wondering if the case should be revisited. If it were, would the old man live to know how it turned out?

Quirke stood up, looking at his watch.

"Must go," he said.

He turned again to Strafford, but Strafford gave his head a quick shake, looking at the floor.

"I'll hang on," he muttered.

For a moment, Quirke hesitated—what *was* the matter with the flop-haired long drink of water?—then shrugged and turned to go.

"Right, then," he said to the old man sitting marooned in the wide expanse of the hospital bed. "I'll come again another day."

"See you, so," Hackett said, his crabbed hands folded on the sheet over his lap. "If I'm still here."

16

Strafford had run out of things to say to the old man. He had only stayed behind in order to be rid of Quirke. Now he too took his leave. "Goodbye, Chief," he said. Hackett seemed not to hear, or notice. He was lying back against the pillows and gazing distractedly at the ceiling, his twiglike fingers clasped together over the mound of his little potbelly.

Strafford turned away. The door clicked as it opened before him, and drew shut behind him, emitting its curiously intimate little sigh.

As he descended the stairs, he thought again about the Kesslers and Rosa Jacobs. He didn't share Quirke's high opinion of Hackett's hunches. Kessler and his son between them had destroyed that young woman, and then had destroyed and been destroyed themselves. The case was closed.

He walked across the hospital's dim and echoing reception hall. The place hadn't changed much, he supposed, since the turn of the century. The air smelled at once sharp and stale—new medicines, old dust. He went out through the front door and stopped in the little stone porch, under a hanging lamp that looked like a storm lantern, and maybe was, or had been. He pictured horse-drawn carriages pulling up here and depositing pale shivering patients, and other carriages departing, bearing away the dead. The lacquered boards, the steel-rimmed wheels, the horses' nodding plumes. They were in thrall to death, back then, in their silk hats and bombazine, and now they were all dead themselves.

Hurriedly, he stepped out into the light. Cleave to the living, while he could.

Marguerite came unbidden to his mind. He wondered where she was, at this moment, and what she was doing. *I've met someone.* What was his name? Teddy? Tommy? No: Tom, Thomas. One of the Spencers, with a *c.* He would have a mustache, surely, and be of a military bearing. Had she said what he was, what he did? Nothing, probably. Tommy Spencer: once, like Strafford, a son of the Big House, and now—what? Living off his wits and what he could get out of married women the likes of Marguerite. Or so Strafford preferred to think.

The day was cold and bright. The cobalt sky was fringed with little fluffy white clouds, like tufts of hair around an old man's bald pate. He stood a moment, glooming into himself. Marguerite vanished, giving way to Phoebe. These days, his every second thought was of Phoebe. Yet he hadn't phoned her, not once, since that miserable day at Sandycove: the waves, the distant yacht, the woman with the sausage dog, and Phoebe letting the sand run out of the funnel of her fist.

He should have called her, really he should. Was he being

cowardly? Marguerite would say he was. But Marguerite would have many things to say, many worse things, if she knew the reason that Phoebe was so much on his mind.

In chill sunlight he walked along James Street, past Guinness's brewery with its reek of roasting hops, along by the Liberties and then left down Lower Bridge Street onto the river. He could have taken a taxi but decided to walk to Pearse Street instead. He liked to walk. It slowed his racing thoughts, forced them to match his measured pace.

She hadn't told her father yet about the pregnancy, of that much he could be certain. If she had, Quirke would have come after him by now. Violence had been done to Quirke, and surely he would not hesitate to do violence in his turn, knowing his daughter dishonored. One night when he was drunk he had tried to attack Strafford as he was leaving Phoebe's flat, but Phoebe had prevented his blundering assault. Next time, if there were to be a next time—there was a part of him that wished he might never see her again—she would most likely fold her arms and stand back and let her boozed-up progenitor have at the father of the tiny madman—madwoman?—steadily burgeoning inside her.

It wasn't a fight that Strafford dreaded, but the embarrassment of the thing—two grown men tussling over a wrong done to a daughter. Honestly. Like something in Dickens, or Mrs. Humphry Ward.

He walked on along the quays in watery sunlight. Winetavern Street, Fishamble, the tumbledown frontage of Temple Bar, the Ha'penny Bridge. The cooling air of autumn had suppressed the river's greenish stink. A Guinness dray went past, drawn by a mighty Clydesdale with a flying mane and fur-rimmed hooves. The stacked wooden barrels joggled, the driver lazily flicked his whip. Strafford envied him. He almost envied the horse.

Yes yes, he must call her—he must. But to say what? He didn't know what to think, so what could he find to say? The thing was impossible—to be a father, at this stage of his life! He would probably have to resign from the force, charged with moral turpitude. If, that is, Quirke didn't kill him first.

Oh, God. It would be laughable if it weren't all so ghastly.

In Fleet Street he thought of stopping at the Palace Bar, then drew up short, surprised at himself. When had it ever crossed his mind to enter a public house, on his own, at lunchtime, without a sound reason? What next? Was he going to take to the drink, and find himself stumbling along the sidewalks morose and truculent, and snarling at people and picking fights, just like Quirke?

Quirke: his prospective father-in-law!

He would laugh, really he would, if he didn't feel so much like screaming.

He had climbed three flights of stairs—the smell of old cigarette smoke was seeping from behind the door of Hackett's deserted office—and had just arrived in his own cubbyhole when the telephone rang. It was the desk sergeant, calling up from downstairs. There was a person below asking to speak to him. Name of Ruddock.

He made his way back down the three flights, and at the bottom lifted the counter flap, expecting, with awful misgiving, to find Charles Ruddock waiting for him. However, the only person in the day room was a woman. She was standing at the noticeboard with her back turned to him. He glanced inquiringly at the desk sergeant, who nodded toward the woman. Strafford looked again, and recognized Charles Ruddock's wife.

She had the child with her, the strange little boy, sitting up in a high carriage that was much too small for him—Strafford thought of a cuckoo squatting on a linnet's nest—dressed in a girlish little coat and a red skullcap with a tassel.

"Mrs. Ruddock?"

She turned.

"Hello."

He saw at once that she was nervous. Why was that? And more to the point, why was she here?

They shook hands, the woman leaning back with a long arm extended toward him, as if she thought he might try to embrace her. She wore a woolen jacket with toggles for buttons, and a black beret. The green irises of her wide-spaced eyes were flecked with tiny splinters of gold. He was struck by the prominent jut of her large, wide, shapely mouth. It gave her an oddly pugnacious aspect. He pictured himself kissing her, and was startled.

"I'm sorry," she said haltingly, "I was passing by and I—"

She stopped, half in a panic by now. He could see her telling herself that she had been a fool to come here, unsummoned and unannounced. He was equally nonplussed. What could she want from him? He didn't know what to do. There was no question of his asking her up to his office.

The child in the carriage was watching him with placid curiosity out of enormous shining dark eyes.

Charlotte Ruddock withdrew her hand—slim, cool, slightly damp—and took a half step backward. Strafford felt himself floundering.

"Perhaps we should," he began, "perhaps we should go for a—"

"No," she said quickly, her pale forehead flushing. "I'm sorry, I don't know what I was thinking of. I mean coming here, like this. You're in the middle of your working day."

"Well," he said, managing a smile of sorts, "even I get time off at this hour."

He stopped. Christ, she would think he was asking her to lunch. However, she gave her head an angry shake and turned abruptly and strode out into the street, driving the carriage before her. He told himself to let her go, but instead he hurried after her. Of course he did.

She was at the traffic lights, waiting to cross over to College Green. Wan November sunlight gleamed on her thick dark hair.

"Mrs. Ruddock," he called.

She pretended not to hear. She had reached the far sidewalk and now turned and set off resolutely with long swift strides toward the front gates of Trinity College.

He called after her again, louder this time, sounding an odd note of entreaty. Like a lovesick swain, he thought, left standing by his headstrong lass.

Yet on she went. He had to let a bus pass by, then sprinted across the road and soon caught up with her, and set a hand on her elbow. She turned to him but drew her arm away, her eyes glittering.

"I'm sorry," he stammered. "I was rude, I should have—"

"It's nothing," she said quickly, and looked along the street. "I just wanted to ask—I just wanted to—"

"Yes," he said, smiling, and laid his hand again on her arm. "Yes." It was as if they had both lost, for now, the ability to utter more than the simplest monosyllable. "It's all right."

They passed by the gates of Trinity and walked together up Grafton Street. She had some trouble negotiating the carriage through the lunchtime crowds. Neither spoke until they had reached the top of the street and passed under the stone arch into St. Stephen's Green.

Strafford asked, "Did you drive up?"

"What?" She looked at him, and it seemed as if she might laugh, at what, he couldn't think. "No, no—I came on the train, from Wicklow. Charles drove me to the station. I had things to do. Shopping."

The child was crooning to himself. He had risen to his knees, and was facing forward and bouncing up and down, making the carriage wallow on its springs.

"Stop that!" his mother told him sharply.

He turned his head slowly and looked at her with a thin smile, letting his eyelids turn down at the corners. What an uncanny creature, Strafford thought yet again.

They came to the duck pond.

"Shall we sit for a moment?" Strafford asked.

He led her to an unoccupied bench under the drooping fronds of a weeping willow.

"Did you have your lunch?" she asked of Strafford suddenly, gazing at him with uncalled-for concern.

He waved the question aside.

"If you came to ask for news of Mrs. Armitage," he said, "I'm afraid there is none."

She was still gazing at him, and now a small knot formed between her eyebrows.

"Oh, no," she said, "no, I wasn't—I didn't—" She lowered her eyes. "We hadn't heard anything either, so I assumed—I assumed she must have turned up."

"No, no, she hasn't. It's entirely a mystery, I'm afraid."

"Isn't that your job, solving mysteries?"

It seemed not a rebuke but a real question. Strafford gave a small laugh, and he too looked down.

"Yes, I suppose it is. Though, most of the things we deal with are not mysterious at all." He looked at her again. "A policeman's lot is not a thrilling one," he said, putting on a wry smile.

And now she too smiled, lifting her eyes to his, and it was as if a curtain had been drawn back from her face.

For a time they did not speak, then she said, "That man, Armitage."

"Yes?"

She was watching the ducks on the pond. The child lay on his side in the carriage in his little buttoned-up coat with his knees pressed against his chest, sucking his thumb and gazing before him, vacant and drowsy.

"My husband," she said, "I think he knows him."

"Armitage? Your husband knows Armitage? You mean, knew him before the night he came to the house asking for help?"

She nodded.

"In fact, I'm sure he does." She paused. "Or that he knows his wife, at any rate."

She had narrowed her eyes against the sharp little sparkle of reflected sunlight striking up from the surface of the water. People passed to and fro before them like flickering shadows. She had undone the toggles of her coat. Underneath, she wore a loose white blouse and loose gray slacks. Her shoes, he thought, must be Italian, and expensive.

"How would he—?" he began, but she interrupted him, still with her eyes on the water.

"I'm very unhappy," she said. Her tone was so flat and matter-of-fact that it took Strafford a moment to grapple with the abrupt change of subject. "He thinks he's God's gift to women," she went on. "Maybe he is." She gave a bitter laugh. "I haven't had many gifts from him in recent times."

Strafford sat frowning, hardly daring to breathe. The woman went on gazing at the water with its busy ducks. Despite her words, she seemed quite calm, almost detached. The only sign of inner tension he could see was in the white-knuckled hand with which she clutched the handle of the carriage, rocking it swiftly back and forth. The child, who had fallen into sleep, slept on.

"I'm sorry," Strafford said.

She turned her head and looked at him with interest.

"Are you?"

"I'm sorry that you're unhappy."

"Oh. Right. I didn't know what you meant." She lapsed again into apathetic staring. "Kind of you," she murmured.

Strafford could feel the muffled beating of his heart. Everything suddenly seemed to have taken on a heightened significance, the light on the water, the leaning tree above them, her tensed knuckles on the handle of the carriage. She stirred herself and looked at him, or almost did, her gaze shyly faltering.

"My sister has offered to mind the child tonight," she said. The child. "We could meet, you and I. Later. We could—do something. Maybe?"

She had turned her eyes back to the water, as if there were some promise, some sign of sustenance, to be gleaned from it.

"You mean, to meet for a drink, or something?" Strafford said. "Is that it?"

"Yes, whatever." She paused. "Or you could come to the house."

He thought about this.

"I shouldn't."

But he would. A line came to his mind from a poem he had read some time in the past. *Life's nonsense pierces us with strange*—what? with strange what?

They rose then and walked along under the trees.

"Where does your sister live?" Strafford asked.

She laughed, and gave her head an almost girlish toss.

"I haven't got a sister. Well, I have, but she lives in Rhodesia. Married a rancher. Dreadful man—bullies her. I warned her he would." She turned her head to look at him. "Will you come this evening? I wish you would. The child will be asleep. We can drink gin and tell each other our life stories." She laughed again, with forced gaiety. "Wouldn't that be fun?"

I know nothing about her, he thought—*I don't even know what age she is.*

"Look, I must go back to the station," he said.

She stared.

"The station? Are you going somewhere?"

"The Garda station. Pearse Street—where you were, earlier. Where my office is."

"Ah, I see." She nodded. "Yes, you have to work, of course. What do you do, exactly? I know you're a detective, but what do detectives do? Search for clues, and so on, like in the movies?"

"It's desk work, mostly. Not at all like the pictures."

They had paused on the humpback bridge under a canopy of ancient trees. A breath of wind rattled the dry autumnal leaves still clinging to the boughs.

"Have you ever had to kill someone?" Charlotte Ruddock asked.

"Yes. Twice."

"I suppose you don't want to talk about it."

"Not particularly."

She turned to him again quickly and put a hand on his arm. The pressure of her fingers was electric, even through the sleeve of his coat, through the sleeve of his shirt, through his skin.

"Please come," she whispered. "I need to—" She stopped, and cast about her, scanning the trees, the stones of the bridge, the glittering pond below them, as if in desperate search of what to say and how to say it. Then she let her shoulders droop and gave a sort of helpless, hollow-chested shrug. "I would like to see you. I would like to—to talk to you."

Relation, he thought—that was the word. *Life's nonsense pierces us with strange relation.*

Oh, yes, he would go to her. He would.

17

It was evening, the evening of the same day.

The house on Vesey Place was a fine Regency dwelling of two stories over a basement, with a flight of shallow granite steps leading up to a stone porch and a front door painted red. It would be bigger inside than it looked from outside, Strafford knew—he was familiar with such houses, he had grown up in such surroundings.

The daylight was fading fast; the sky had turned a shade of deep violet. A bat flittered around the still-pale light of a streetlamp.

At the gate, he hesitated. Everything on the way here, every single step taken, had been fraught with awful consequence. He might try to reassure himself—a woman was missing, he was following up information on her disappearance, that was all—but it wouldn't work. He knew very well why he was here, why she had asked him to come.

When she opened the door, she was still wearing the white blouse from earlier but had changed from trousers into a calf-length pleated skirt. This he took as a sign of something, though he wasn't sure what. Perhaps she did just want to talk to him. Women were always eager to talk, it was a thing he liked about them, being overly reticent himself.

"Well, good evening," she said, as if his being here were a grand surprise. "Come in, come in."

The hall was tiled in black and white, the walls were painted cream. There was a shallow table of gleaming mahogany, a big gilt mirror, a large Chinese vase of pink and blue chrysanthemums. They must be her favorite flower. She led him into a drawing room. He admired her smooth calves, slim as he remembered them.

Here was a sofa, red like the front door, here were matching armchairs, three identical standing lamps, two small tables, a glass-fronted bookcase with shadowy volumes bound in leather. A faint lemony scent hung in the air—hers, her perfume?

"I was joking about the gin," she said, "but we can have some, if you like." She took up a silver box from one of the tables and opened the lid and offered it to him. "Cigarette?"

She was being somebody—Lauren Bacall, he thought.

"No, thanks."

"Then I won't, either."

She put the box back on the table, excused herself and went out, leaving the door ajar behind her.

In the sudden quiet, he went and stood at the window and looked down into the front garden. Grass, flower beds, some kind of shrub with delicate white blossoms. The light from the streetlamp was stronger now, made brighter by the advancing night. He was aware of a faint, continuous hum inside him, just behind his breastbone. He didn't know what to expect. Or rather, he did, but didn't know in what form it would be manifest.

When she returned, she was carrying a tray with bottles and glasses, and had to push the door closed behind her with her hip. There was the usual expectant hush while she poured the drinks. She handed him his.

"Chin-chin," she said, her eyes smiling at him over the rim of her glass.

Now she was someone brightly English. Kay Kendall? Jean Simmons? He was impressed by her repertoire.

"The little boy," Strafford said, "is he—?"

"I managed to farm him out for the night after all. Neighbors' girl, three doors up. He likes her, she's very kind to him. Good job somebody is." She pushed back her hair at one side and tucked it deftly behind her ear. "He's a hemophiliac. Charles calls him *our little bleeder.*" She made a wry mouth. "He's such a wit, my husband."

She moved to the sofa. He admired the way in which, prior to sitting down, she smoothed her skirt under her bottom with a quick sweep of her left hand. He often thought it was his lack of experience with women that made them seem so remote and fascinating. His secret belief was that they were from some other place than the place where men came from, a lighter and yet more serious, more substantial, realm. How else to account for how different they were?

He was gazing ruminatively into his glass—he did not care for the taste of gin, and not much for that of tonic water, either—when suddenly she rose and stepped forward, draped one of her long arms around his shoulders, clasped her hand to the back of his head and pulled him against her and kissed him fiercely on the mouth.

It was exactly as he had imagined it would be.

To his surprise, and no little consternation, she took him upstairs to the child's room and there, among a litter of toys and fluffy animals, drew him down with her onto the little narrow bed that was hardly more than a cot.

It occurred to him that every adulterous couple, since the invention of marriage, must imagine, as they take their first rapturous bite of the forbidden fruit, that they are a new Adam and Eve, whom presently a wrathful God in the cool of the day will cast out of the paradisal garden—presently, but not yet.

Already a towel had been laid over the sheet, an act of precautionary forethought on her part which he found almost as deflating as the surroundings in which they lay.

Her skin was smooth and cool and slightly waxen to the touch. He liked her slim hips and trim behind, her breasts that were hardly bigger than apples and not much softer, and that he did not think could ever have suckled a child. She wrapped her arms and her long legs around him and made not a sound, no sigh or cry, except that once she spoke a word, a quick monosyllable that he could not make out. There was a dimple like a shallow little cup at the base of her spine. Her hair smelled faintly of fresh-baked bread, or it did to him, anyway.

The tiny room was hushed around them, as if it were holding its scandalized breath. The hot water coursed in the radiator under the window with a low continuous rustle incongruously suggestive of a hidden woodland stream. At the climax she bared her large white teeth, and two quick tears, one at each side, ran down her temples.

Afterward, they sat facing each other at either end of the bed, since it was too narrow for them to lie on side by side. The air in the room was not warm, and Charlotte— he would not think of her as Charlie—draped the coverlet over her shoulders, while he wrapped himself in his raincoat. Surrounded by so many childhood objects, they might be preparing to play a children's game. What would it be? Consequences, say, or truth or dare?

She told him something of herself. Her parents were English, though she, their only child, was brought up in Ireland. Her father had been a medical consultant, a specialist in pulmonary diseases, with a practice at the Mater Hospital. Her mother had died when she was young. On his retirement, her father and his second wife, Charlotte's stepmother—"quite a jolly soul, against expectations"—had emigrated to Cape Town. She supposed she would not see them again, for she had no intention of traveling to South Africa and they were unlikely to return for a visit, due to age and other considerations.

These nuggets of information he absorbed without comment, only nodding now and then. He felt like a bored employer conducting a job interview. It was hard to credit that ten minutes previously they had been rolling in each other's arms, flesh against damply clinging flesh.

"Charles and I met at a party. Yes, banal, I know. I can hardly say I was swept off my feet. But I liked his swagger, his self-confidence. Didn't see it for the arrogance it was until later on, and by then of course it was too late."

He nodded again, frowning in what he hoped would seem a show of interest and warmth. What he wanted to say was

Yes, that's all very well, but why me? He thought it probable that he was no more than a brief diversion, a short stop along the path of a marriage that had gone wrong, or had not been right in the first place.

Yet she had deliberately sought him out, though he had given her no sign of interest that he was aware of. Had she felt the heat of his attraction to her, that first day when he went down to Wicklow to talk to her and her husband? "Women have an antenna for that sort of thing," Marguerite used to say, with a dismissive sniff. She found the business of amorous pursuit more or less ridiculous.

Charlotte rose from the bed now and put on her clothes, excused herself, and went off, to the bathroom, as he supposed. He sat on for a while, his mind idling. He could faintly hear the dog—what was it called, Ruffles? Raggles?—down in the back garden, barking. Then he rose and got dressed. His mood had turned to melancholy. He was trying not to think of Phoebe. He *must* call her.

Then Charlotte came back, smoking a cigarette.

"I should go," Strafford said.

He was sitting on the side of the bed, tying his shoelaces. A ragged teddy bear sat slumped in a high chair, regarding him coldly out of one remaining, vindictive shiny black eye.

"Want me to call you a taxi?" Charlotte asked.

Her manner was cool, offhand, slightly distracted. Or at least, that was how she appeared. She was hard to interpret. Would she ask to see him again? It would not be easy. He had explained to her his living arrangements in the house on Mespil Road, had spoken of the two ever-vigilant sisters and even mentioned Mr. Singh. There was no question of the Claridges countenancing a clandestine affair being carried on under their respectable roof.

Dressed, he recalled himself to duty.

"You say your husband knew Armitage's wife?"

She was standing in the doorway, leaning against the jamb with her ankles crossed, an elbow propped in a palm and one eye narrowed against the smoke from her cigarette.

"That was just an excuse to come to where you worked," she said.

Her pursed, prominent mouth and slightly concave cheeks made it seem as if she was sucking on something slightly too big and slightly too sour. It gave her a look of being about to say something withering. She worried at the cigarette, taking rapid little drags and shooting out thin streams of uninhaled smoke. She was brittle, impatient, discontent. He had known other women unhappily married, and one in particular, and he recognized the signs.

They went back downstairs, to the drawing room. The ice had all melted by now in their glasses of unfinished gin and tonic. Charlotte picked up hers and drank it up in one go, and grimaced. She put the glass back on the table.

"All the same," she said, gazing vague-eyed at the floor, "there was something odd about that night. I know the woman had gone missing and so on, but it was more than that. The fellow, Armitage, he kept grinning, and looking about the place, as if—I don't know. As if he had heard about us, or about the house, as if someone had told him things, and he was checking to see if everything matched what had been described to him." She paused, then went on again. "He seemed angry, too. Pent-up, the way people get when they're furious but have to keep it covered up. That's why he was smirking—you know that kind of smirk that's full of anger and frustration."

"Well, he would hardly have been himself, given that he believed his wife had drowned herself."

She looked at him.

"Did he? I didn't believe he did, not really. There was something else, something—I don't know—something worse." She gave a cold little laugh. "That's why I thought Charles might be involved in some way—the usual way."

"What way is that?" For answer, she glanced up at the ceiling, in the direction of the room where they had lately been. "Oh," Strafford said. "I see. You think your husband and Armitage's wife were—"

He didn't finish. She shrugged.

"God knows, it wouldn't be Charles's first time—" she twisted up her mouth at one side "—or the last."

Revenge, Strafford suddenly thought—that's why she brought me up there, to the child's room. Revenge and defilement. Could it be? Had he been her weapon, the hammer with which she had struck a blow at all the awfulness of her life, at her errant husband, her poisoned marriage, her sickly child? He would not come here again. He should not have come in the first place.

Defilement.

"You think," he said slowly, "that Armitage had gone down to Wicklow purposely, to confront your husband, and then changed his mind?"

Again she shrugged. The thing, she seemed to say, was just another in a long line of things she had to cope with.

"It's what men do, isn't it," she said simply, without rancor. *"You've been screwing my wife, now I'm here to have it out with you."*

The crudity of verb she used had made Strafford blink.

"Except he didn't have it out, did he," he said. "He just got drunk, on your husband's whiskey, and went off to stay in that pub, and next day, or the day after, he returned to Dublin."

"Without his wife. Yes."

They stood in the middle of the room, looking away from each other. It had begun to rain, absent-mindedly, as it seemed, the insubstantial drops whispering against the windowpanes.

"I should talk to them both again," Strafford said. "Armitage, and your husband."

She laughed. She had taken another cigarette from the silver box on the table and was lighting it.

"Good luck," she said. "Armitage is a slippery customer, from what I saw of him. And if Charles has been up to something, he'll just deny it. He's a great denier." She mimicked her husband's rugby player's voice, puffing out her cheeks. *"What, me? I never laid a finger on that woman—wouldn't touch her with a ten-foot-pole."*

Strafford put on his raincoat. It seemed all the more implausible that a short while ago he and this woman had gone to bed together, and that something of his was still inside her.

He turned to the door. She went ahead of him, out to the hall. On the front step, she threw her unfinished cigarette into the shrubbery.

"Goodbye," he said, ducking away from her in a sudden excess of awkwardness, of barren regret.

She did not suggest that they should meet again, and neither did he.

As he descended the granite steps, he felt like the residue of himself, the real he having already left, a long, an impossibly long, time ago.

18

Next morning, he ventured up to St. James's to talk to Hackett again. He didn't know what he could hope for, given how yesterday's visit had turned out, but he had to do something. Of course, he could simply give up and walk away. Deirdre Armitage was not the first woman to disappear in mysterious circumstances, and Armitage himself seemed not overly concerned at the loss of her. But that was the point: the man's heartless and jaunty indifference was the most striking aspect of the entire affair.

At the door of the old man's room Strafford hesitated, his resolve wavering. But he couldn't turn back now. He knocked twice, and went in.

Overnight, the chief had sunk to yet another level of decrepitude. He was perched at the top end of the bed like an ancient child, with frightened eyes and his crooked mouth hanging slack. Over his pajama top he wore a brown woolen garment that might be a woman's cardigan—perhaps his wife had brought him one of hers. It added an extra note of pathos to the scene of general ruin.

The room had a different smell, too, warmish and rankly sweet.

At first the old man took Strafford for a doctor, and plied him with a series of gnomic questions—"Is the bellows in sound order, Doc?"—that would have made no sense even if Strafford had been a doctor. It was all awful, and horribly embarrassing—the shrunken frame, the raggedy woolen jacket, the deluded interrogation—and not five minutes had elapsed before Strafford rose, squeezed the old man's tiny, withered hand, and fled, as he had fled the last time, afflicted by shame and ignominy.

In the corridor, he spied a young nurse with rust-red hair and pellucid green eyes. For some reason she made him think of his wife. There was not the slightest resemblance to Marguerite, yet he glimpsed the shadow of a memory—from where, from when? He stopped her, and inquired about the patient in room seven. She too seemed to take him for a doctor, called in perhaps to give a second opinion. There must be something about him—his dark suit, his grave demeanor?—that led them to think him what he was not.

"Ah, he's in a bad way, the poor man," the nurse said confidingly, as one professional to another. "It's in the lungs, you know, and maybe the liver, too—they did the tests, now they're waiting for the results. But from the look and the sound of him, I'd say it's a foregone conclusion."

He thanked her, and went on.

In the taxi he thought at first to return to Pearse Street and his office, but then he changed his mind and told the driver to take him to the Hospital of the Holy Family. The vehicle pulled away from the rank, and he fell back slackly against the seat, surprised at himself. Since Phoebe's momentous announcement he had made every effort to avoid Quirke, yet here he was, of his own volition, on the way to Bluebeard's castle.

He was directed to the cafeteria, where he found Quirke sitting at a corner window above the parking lot. He had been at work down in the lab and was still in his white tunic and shapeless white cotton trousers, a green surgeon's cap pushed to the back of his head. There was a mug of tea before him on the table, and he was smoking a cigarette. He was slumped and haggard. He had done five postmortems in a row.

"The last one was a child," he said, blinking slowly with swollen, reddened eyelids. "Playing in the street, ran smack into a bus." He tapped his cigarette and an inch of ash tumbled silently to the floor. "No matter how many you do, it's always the children that stay with you. Or with me, anyway." He picked up the mug, then put it down again. "Tea," he said grimly. "Jesus."

He had not asked Strafford why he was here. Now the detective said, "I spoke to that woman, Ruddock's wife." Quirke looked at him blankly out of exhausted eyes. "About the woman that went missing—you know? Hackett mentioned her yesterday."

"She was found, then?"

"No, no. The woman who's missing is Armitage the Trinity fellow's wife. The Ruddocks are the people he went to that night for help."

"Oh. Right."

Quirke turned to the window and watched a nurse walking across the parking lot. She had on her nurse's winged hat, and had pulled on a raincoat over her uniform. She had red hair, Strafford saw, and he thought she must be the one he had spoken to earlier, until he remembered he was in a different hospital. There was no scarcity, in this country, of redheaded nurses. Then he realized what it was about the other one that had struck an echo of Marguerite: the slight upward tilt at the tip of her nose. He marveled, as he did so often, at the mind's unblinking eye for detail.

"She came to see me, Mrs. Ruddock, at the station," he said, trying to contain his impatience.

"Did she?" Quirke was still watching the nurse, who by now had reached the gate of the car park. "What about?"

"She said—" Strafford began, then paused. His hat was in his lap; he fingered the brim of it. He had heard again, quite clearly, that smudged, incomprehensible word Charlotte had uttered as she writhed in his arms in the child's narrow bed. "She said she thought her husband and Armitage knew each other. Or that Armitage knew of him, at least, of the husband, in some way."

Quirke had turned back from the window, and was frowning, struggling to concentrate.

"In what way?" he asked.

Again, Strafford hesitated.

"She said she thought her husband might be having—well, that he might be having an affair with Armitage's wife. First she said it, then denied it. Though not exactly."

Quirke looked at the table, at the cigarette case resting on it.

"Not exactly what?"

"She didn't exactly deny it," Strafford said. "Only—" He was still fidgeting with the hat brim, his eyes lowered. He hoped he wasn't blushing, but suspected he was. He was remembering the one-eyed teddy bear's malevolent, accusatory regard. "She seemed to think that something was up, that something was—was not right."

"So she came to see you," Quirke said slowly, his voice wearied, dragging.

Strafford nodded, but did not look up. He should not have come here, as he should not have gone to see the chief. He knew Quirke to be truculent and vengeful, but he was no fool. Somewhere inside that alcohol-insulted system of his there was crouched an altogether other version of the man, watchful and sharp of instinct. He could sense things, this other Quirke, he could nose things out, the hidden fears of others, their secrets, their sins. That was what Hackett had used him for, as his second set of eyes and ears, as his second sentinel.

"She came to me because she—I don't know. Because she was worried, or puzzled, or something."

"Worried about what? Her hubby having it off with this other woman?"

Strafford had begun to sweat, he could feel the dampness on his shoulder blades, in the creases in the palms of his hands. He thought again of Phoebe on the beach, sitting on the blanket with her bare legs stretched out before her, making a funnel of her fist and letting the sand pour out in a thin swift trickle. The mouse-gray sand with tiny mica glints. His fate in her hand, trickling away.

"It seems that when Armitage came up to the house, saying his wife had drowned herself, there was something in his manner that struck her as—as odd. Her husband too was acting strangely, she said. It was as if they knew each other, or knew of each other, and that Armitage had come there to have a look at Charles Ruddock, and that the story about his wife was just an excuse, a story he had made up."

Quirke was lighting another cigarette. He took off the green cap and dropped it on the table and scratched the back of his head vigorously.

"Some story," he said. "'Right, so you're this chap Ruddock I've been hearing about—my missus has drowned herself, by the way.'"

"Yes, I know. It doesn't seem to make sense. And yet—"

They sat in silence for a while, looking away from each other. Around them, hospital visitors came and went, carrying trays, handbags, rolled-up newspapers, some drably worried, others putting on a brave front, all feeling out of place by not being sick themselves, yet.

Quirke stirred, and rapped his knuckles on the table.

"Come on," he said, "let's go for a drink."

Strafford stared—when was the last time Quirke had issued such an invitation?—then nodded. A truce, then, partial and no doubt temporary, but a truce all the same.

They were silent again in the taxi. A fine drizzle was drifting down from a gray and depthless sky. The windshield wipers dragged themselves back and forth, back and forth, squeaking. They could have gone to a pub close by the hospital, but Quirke wanted to be out of the vicinity. No doubt he's thinking of the child, Strafford thought, the child who had gone under the bus, and then under the dissecting knife.

Along the quays, the traffic was light. The river was high and fast-running, a rain-stippled surge, tin-colored, frothing against the slimed, gray-green granite embankments on either side.

They stopped at the Ormond Hotel. In the bar, as they

settled themselves on high stools, Quirke said, "What are they like, these people, the Ruddocks?"

Strafford pondered the question for some moments.

"Rich," he said, "or well-off, at least. He's a solicitor, in Daddy's firm. I doubt he spends much time there. Rugby type, sure of himself, but—"

"But?"

"There's something about him, something edgy. He's worried about something."

"About Armitage, and his missing wife?"

"Yes, I think so."

Quirke pondered for a moment.

"You knew him in school, you said?"

"I wouldn't say I knew him. We were there at the same time. He was the sporty type, I wasn't."

Quirke nodded, smiling to himself. *He's trying to imagine me then,* Strafford thought, *in my blazer and baggy gray slacks and clumpy shoes. St. John Strafford, the Milksop of Greyfriars.*

The barman came, and Quirke ordered a Jameson. Strafford asked for coffee. Quirke was lighting yet another cigarette. The hand that held the match was not quite steady. He gave off a faint odor, of sweat and something else, hard to identify—misery, perhaps. He looked weary still, and his eyelids kept closing slowly, as if it were an effort to keep them open. He had the hunched and pummeled look of a boxer resting after a hard and punishing ten-round bout. Strafford realized, to his surprise, that he felt sorry for him. In other circumstances, in another life, they might have been friends. They had in common the fact that they both dealt with human beings at their furthest extremes, as criminals, as corpses.

Quirke's whiskey arrived. He sat gazing dully at the glass

for a full minute before lifting it to his lips. Strafford only had to look at the coffee the barman had set before him to know it would taste like tar water with a drop of wormwood added. He pushed the cup away with a fingertip.

"Why are you keeping on at this?" Quirke asked.

Strafford had to think about that.

"I suppose, for the same reason you keep on doing post-mortems. It's my job."

"Yes," Quirke said. He was silent a moment, then went on. "I suppose they're not unalike, your job and mine." He chuckled. "We have one thing in common, at least."

"What's that?"

"Death."

"You more than I."

Quirke was examining the tip of his cigarette.

"Do you ever find yourself wondering how you ended up a detective?"

"Frequently."

"Do you come up with an answer?"

"Never."

This was, Strafford reflected, the nearest they had ever come to speaking to each other without rancor on Quirke's side and defensiveness on his. He was glad of it. Oh, of course you are, a sardonic little voice said from deep within him, and you had better take advantage of the moment and build on it, since one day soon you may find yourself his son-in-law.

After a time, Quirke asked, "Where was the school you and what's-his-name went to?"

"Kilkenny. The New School."

"Quakers, right?"

"The school was Quaker, yes, but Ruddock wasn't, and neither was I."

Quirke nodded, those leaden eyelids drooping. It occurred to Strafford that he had not appreciated how hard Quirke worked, or how much wear and tear the job inflicted on him. He sat there hunched and spent, a St. Christopher arrived on the far bank of the river only to discover the child on his shoulders had been dead before the toe of his sandal had even touched the water.

"I went to see the chief again this morning," Strafford said. "How is he?"

"Poorly. I spoke to a nurse. She said it's in his lungs."

"That's hardly news," Quirke said harshly. "You only have to hear that cough."

"And it may have spread to the liver."

"Very chatty, that nurse."

"I think she thought I was a doctor."

Quirke looked him up and down with a humorously disparaging eye.

"Aye, you have the look of it, all right." He rolled his shoulders, stiff and weary from the dead weight they had been carrying for so long. "Could I pass for a detective, do you think?"

I should tell him, Strafford thought, *I should tell him about Phoebe. Don't I owe it to him? No*, the inner voice piped up, *you don't owe him anything—and besides, if anyone is to tell him, it should be his daughter.*

"I don't believe Armitage about his wife," he heard himself saying in a rush, "I think he's lying. I think she wasn't with him in the first place. I think he went down there to Wicklow to accuse Ruddock of having an affair with her and lost his nerve at the last minute."

Quirke drank off the last of the whiskey and signaled to the barman for another. He glanced at Strafford's cup.

"You're not drinking your coffee," he said, and for some reason laughed. Then he sighed, letting his shoulders slump back as before, and gazed at the ranks of bottles behind the bar. "If he didn't do her in, where is she?"

"That's what I intend to find out," Strafford said.

Quirke shot him an ironic, sideways glance.

"Go to it, Sherlock."

And he laughed again, from the back of his throat. Strafford knew from that laugh that they were back to where they had always been. The temporary truce had been called off.

19

When Phoebe spotted the man for the second time, she wondered if he was following her. The odd thing was that yesterday, at his first appearance, she noticed him because she thought she had encountered him before somewhere, though she couldn't think when, or in what circumstances. But he did seem familiar.

Just now she had been walking down Grafton Street, and was passing by Switzer's when she remembered that she had meant to buy coffee in Bewley's. She stopped and turned and there he was again, coming along behind her. He veered aside at once, halted at Weir's the jewelers and pretended to be examining a display of fancy watches in the window. As she drew level with him, she caught his eye where it was reflected in the glass. He glanced away quickly.

Men could be so idiotic, pretending they weren't looking at you when plainly they were, their eyes out on stalks.

Yesterday she had been in Fred Hanna's in Nassau Street, in the basement, browsing among the secondhand books, when her attention was caught by the tall skinny man in a blue blazer. He was standing some way off, leaning against a bookcase with his ankles crossed, his nose deep in a quarto volume bound in green cloth.

What struck her was the studied way in which he was ignoring her. She was convinced he had been watching her, and had managed to drop his eyes a second before she lifted hers. That was when she thought he looked familiar.

He was in his forties, she guessed. She took him in at a glance—sharp nose, lips thin and moistly pink, oiled black hair combed straight back from a narrow forehead—then turned back to the wooden barrows of old books.

She was used to having men's eyes on her. She knew she wasn't beautiful, but there must be something about her that caught their attention, their interest. Or perhaps it was just that all men were always looking at all women, if they were acceptably young and not hopelessly plain. When she looked back at them, as she made a point of doing, they usually turned away, putting on a vague, bland expression, mouths pursed and eyebrows lifted, like little boys caught out in something naughty. Mostly she felt sorry for them. They were so self-conscious, so furtive, so needy. Even the bully-boys, all brawn and bluster, couldn't quite suppress the flaw of uncertainty in their bold stares.

This one was different, though. He was cautious, yes, and watchful, but she had the impression he knew exactly what he was about. And what might that be?

He wasn't looking for what the rest of them were after. He

was not going to accost her in the way the others wanted to do, only they couldn't work up the nerve. She didn't know how she knew this about this man, but she did know. He was after something else.

She passed him by where he stood at the shop window pretending to be absorbed in the watches, and went on up to Bewley's and bought her pound of coffee. When she came back, he had gone. She glanced about the street, but he was nowhere to be seen. She went on. Just some married man, she told herself, eyeing up a single girl. But she didn't believe it.

When she reached the bottom of the street and the stony bulk of Trinity College came into view, all at once she experienced one of those almost-memories that stir a moment in the mind and then lapse, like a person in bed turning over and settling back to sleep again. Something about someone she had known. Something sad. What was it? No. Gone. The bedclothes were still again, the sleeper slept on.

As she crossed Wicklow Street she glanced over her shoulder, scanning the crowd. He still wasn't there. Or if he was, she couldn't see him. But why would he hide from her? She reached the far footpath. It was just a coincidence, she thought, nothing more. Dublin was a small city, it was hardly remarkable that she should encounter a particular person twice within two days.

Then, when she was passing by Kapp & Peterson's, a voice spoke behind her.

"Excuse me." She turned. She fixed again on those thin, mobile lips, moist and shiny and faintly reptilian. "Excuse me," he said again, advancing a step. "Aren't you—aren't you Phoebe Griffin?"

She waited a beat.

"That's me, yes. Do we know each other?"

A newsboy farther down the street was calling out the names of the morning papers in a shrill, repeated and incomprehensible warble.

"We met, last year," the man said, with an odd smile, at once insinuating and apologetic. English accent, the posh part of it put-on. "I knew your friend, Rosa Jacobs. My name is Armitage. Would you like to have a coffee, or something?"

Afterward, she was surprised that she should have consented to go along with him. He suggested the café above the Grafton Cinema, and they walked back up the way they had come. He told her he was a professor at Trinity, in the history department, and that Rosa had been his assistant.

Armitage. Armitage. Someone had mentioned that name to her recently. The Trinity professor who had known Rosa Jacobs. She tried to remember, but couldn't.

"It was with her that I met you," he said. "You won't remember, of course—it was just for a moment. She and I ran into you as we were crossing Front Square one wet evening and she stopped to say hello. I'm not sure she even introduced me. But I—" he lowered his eyes, those wet lips snaking up at one side in another sinuous half smile "—I remembered you."

"Yes," Phoebe said drily, "you even remembered my name."

He drew open the glass door of the cinema and stood back and she passed through into the foyer. As she climbed the curving stairs ahead of him, she could feel his eyes on her. It meant nothing. Men, she knew, always fix on women's behinds, it was as instinctive with them as blinking.

Try as she might, she couldn't recall that twilight encounter between herself and poor Rosa Jacobs and this man. But it must have occurred, and that was why she had felt she had

met him somewhere before. How was it he had remembered
her after just that one brief meeting?

They sat down at one of the little tables on the balcony,
beside the wrought iron railing. He ordered their coffees.
She studied him sidelong. He wasn't quite genuine. He made
her think of card sharps, and the men who keep stalls at fair-
grounds. Or he might be the loose-limbed cad in one of those
Ealing comedies—he had the blazer and the sharp shoes, all
he lacked was a silk cravat and a pencil-stroke mustache.

"Did you know Rosa well?" he asked.

"I'm not sure anyone knew Rosa well."

He nodded, gazing at her but thinking of something else,
she could see, remembering something. He brought out a
packet of Capstan cigarettes and offered her one, which she
declined.

"Grand girl, though," he said, lighting his cigarette from a
trembling match flame. "Fine researcher, too, a fine scholar.
She could have made a career."

He lifted his head and made a funnel of his lips and blew
three perfect smoke rings, each one a size bigger than the last.
She could see him down the pub, the King's Arms or the Red
Lion, smoking cigarettes and knocking back gin and tonics
or half-pints of bitter, and cracking jokes with his chums, all
of them like him, more or less, all petty criminals. Could he
really be a professor?

"And what about you," Phoebe asked, "how well did you
know her?"

He glanced at her sharply, then relaxed. He shrugged.

"Didn't see much of her outside college," he said. "She was
the private type, kept to herself. As you know."

She watched him again. He was lying, she thought. He
had seen Rosa outside the lecture hall and the library. He

had seen a great deal of her, she was sure of it. That, some-how, was why he was here, and why she was here, with him.

And just then, suddenly, she recalled that encounter in Front Square. It was as if a door had blown open on the scene, the lowering November sky with a livid rent in the clouds down behind the trees, the rained-on cobbles gleam-ing, a student passing by on a bike, the tires slipping in the wet, and Rosa stopping.

"Oh, Phoebe," in that offhand, sulky way of hers, "haven't seen you in ages."

And the tall thin man looming at her side, with that smile. Something different about him, though—what was it? Rosa had behaved as if he weren't there. She had no hat, and had pulled her coat up over her head, so that her shoulders were level with her ears. A couple of wiry black curls had escaped from under the collar. Her dark eyes, her dark, throwaway voice. That was Rosa.

"I met her through a friend," she said.

He gave her a look, having caught a sharper edge to her tone, she supposed. She had turned wary.

"Yes?" he said easily. "Who was that?"

This time, he swiveled his mouth to the side and blew a straight stream of smoke out past the railing. That's it, she thought, that's the difference: he had worn a mustache then, of exactly the kind she had thought of earlier, a narrow black line drawn just above his upper lip. He had been wise to shave it off.

"A doctor, David Sinclair. He went to Israel." She paused. "In fact, I thought he and I were going out together—I mean, we were, but then I discovered that he and Rosa—" She let her voice trail off, and gave a sour little shrug. "At least, I believed they were. I might have been wrong."

Armitage watched her again. He was thinking again, again remembering. What did he want from her, what use did he think she could be to him? For it wasn't she he was interested in. Rosa, then? But what about Rosa?

"Went to Israel, this fellow?"

"Yes. But he's back now. Works in Cork, in a hospital down there."

"Jew, is he, like her?"

She nodded.

"I didn't think it mattered much to him, until he announced he'd got a job in Haifa and would be off in the morning."

"In the morning?"

"As good as. I thought he was tired of me, but maybe it was Rosa he had to get away from." She gave a cold laugh. "Maybe it wasn't me he was jilting at all." She looked at him with an eye merrily aglitter, bit her lower lip at one side. She hoped she wasn't going to cry. Why on earth was she telling him these intimate things, as if they had known each other forever? "I ask again, how well did *you* know her?"

He lowered his gaze. It was, she suspected, the first time he had taken his eyes off her since they had sat down.

"Well, we were colleagues," he said. "Even though I was her boss, I still thought of her that way. But you know what she was like. As far as Rosa was concerned, no one was superior to her. I didn't mind." He toyed with the cigarette pack on the table. "Spirited girl, I admired that in her."

Ah, yes, yes, that was it: she had been his mistress. Though he would hardly have been her type. Did Rosa have a type? She had once confided to Phoebe, or rather had casually remarked, that she would sleep with any man who asked her often enough. How often is enough? Phoebe had inquired. Rosa only laughed. Rosa was like that.

"She should never have got involved with those Krauts. I knew that would go badly—mind you, I didn't know how badly."

"The Krauts?"

"That young fellow, what's-his-name, Kessler—he was sweet on her, wasn't he?"

Again she considered him. She tried to picture Rosa in his arms, and couldn't. But didn't most couples seem the unlikeliest match? She couldn't imagine Rosa with David Sinclair, either. Rosa was always Rosa, the singular being, no matter where she was or what she did or whom she was with.

It came to Phoebe that she had always been jealous of her friend, even before the question arose of her having stolen David away from her—if he had ever been hers to steal.

She realized that Armitage was waiting for her to speak. What had he asked her? About Frank Kessler, yes, about him and Rosa.

"Frank Kessler wasn't much interested in girls," she said quietly, looking at her hands.

Armitage grinned lopsidedly, baring a glistening eyetooth.

"Gay, was he?" he said, with a happy little whoop, and gave the tabletop a slap with the four fingers of his right hand. "Like half the Jerry army, in the war."

She looked at him with unconcealed distaste.

"I don't know what he was," she said. "He was always very nice, to me."

Now Armitage leaned forward with a conspiratorial air.

"He wasn't very nice when he stuffed a hankie soaked in knock-out juice into poor Rosa's mouth and left her in her own car in that storage garage with the engine running, now was he?"

This man really was objectionable, she thought. She should stand up at once and leave. But she didn't. What held her was a horrible fascination. This, she thought, must be what Eve felt like when the serpent came slithering out of the leaves of the forbidden tree and offered her an apple.

"You're very sure it was Frank who did it," she said.

"He went and killed himself, didn't he?"

"He had just killed his father."

"So they say," Armitage muttered, and gave a sniff.

It was hard to credit, even yet, the man Kessler, a war criminal hiding in plain sight in Wicklow, shot to death on his doorstep by his own son, and then the son shooting himself. There had been a great sensation, of course, the story and its ramifications splashed all over the newspapers for weeks. The police maintained that Frank Kessler had murdered Rosa Jacobs at his father's bidding, and then, in an excess of guilt no doubt, had turned the gun on himself. Case closed. But Phoebe had never been able to believe that Frank would have murdered Rosa, his friend and frequent confidante. Was he so much in the power of his dreadful father? It didn't ring true. She had said so to Strafford, but Strafford, glad to be shot of the whole affair, balked at delving into it anew.

"Mind you," Armitage said, "that's the Krauts for you, mad for blood and mayhem."

"I wish you'd stop saying that word."

"What?—Krauts? That's what everyone called them, back then."

She was angry at him now, and at herself that she should have allowed him to bring her here. She pictured herself leaning across the table and slapping his face.

"Poor Frank," she said, "he just didn't fit in."

"Didn't fit in? I could make a risqué joke out of that, but I won't, as I'm in the company of a lady."

It was time to change the subject.

"You were in the war, you say?"

"Signals Corps. Crete, the Ardennes, and lots of other screwups in between."

She was sure he was lying. He may have been in the Signals Corps, but he was no battle-scarred warrior, of that she was certain. She could see him in uniform, all ears and wrists, a cigarette stuck in a corner of his mouth.

"And then you landed in Trinity College," she said.

He did his charming smirk, those glistening lips, pink as a popsicle, sliding up at one side. She noted how his accent kept slipping.

"Got married, you see," he said. "I'd hardly put my foot down in civilian life before I found myself doing the dead march up the aisle in a tailcoat."

His wife—that was it. He was the one Strafford had spoken of on the beach that day, just before she broke her bit of bad news to him. Something had happened—his wife had gone missing, was that it? She must be back by now, for he showed no sign of grief or regret, sitting here chipper as you like, in the Grafton Cinema café at half past eleven on a Thursday morning.

"Someone spoke to me about you recently," she said. "Mentioned your wife. Is everything all right now?"

It was some moments before he replied. He picked up the cigarette pack between a finger and thumb and turned it end over end on the tabletop.

"I lost her," he said, "my wife."

"You lost her?"

"Threw herself in the sea. Body hasn't been found yet."

Phoebe put a hand to her mouth.

"I'm so sorry."

He made a movement with his shoulders that could have been a shrug.

"Yes, well."

Phoebe knew she was blushing.

"I wouldn't have mentioned it, only I assumed she must— that you must have found her—I mean, that she must have come back."

"No. She hasn't come back."

"But this was quite recent, wasn't it? When she disappeared?"

"Seems like centuries to me."

She didn't know what to say, and sat aghast, gazing at him, as he rotted the cardboard pack on its corners. And yet it was strange—she couldn't feel the weight of the moment. There was a fraught stillness, yes, but it was stillness as in a theater when a vital turn of the plot has been revealed.

"I'm sorry," she managed to say again. "It must be terrible for you."

He glanced at her quickly and then away.

"Yes, bloody awful. I must be in shock—it hasn't really hit me yet. I keep expecting her to walk in the door and ask me why I'm looking so glum." He paused, then a frown wrinkled his forehead. "You said someone mentioned me?"

"Yes, um—a detective."

"Ah. Tall bloke, lock of hair falling over his forehead?"

"Yes. His name is Strafford—St. John Strafford."

"That's right. He came down the day after Deirdre took off, asked me a lot of questions. I wasn't impressed."

"No, I imagine not."

The sense of theatricality was growing stronger by the moment. Suddenly, everything around her seemed a stage prop, the little round table, the dainty chairs they were sitting on, the gilded railing in front of them. Why was she here? And more to the point, why was he here? What did he want from her? She had a strong desire to get up and walk away from him, now, this second, never to see or hear of him again. And yet she couldn't.

"Do you want to talk about it?" she said hesitantly. "Would you like to tell me what happened?"

Please say no, she prayed.

He was watching the filmgoers passing in and out below them in the foyer. There was a Jane Wyman movie showing this week. A weepie. For a mad moment, it seemed to Phoebe that she might burst out in laughter. They were talking about the disappearance and possible death of a woman, a real person, not a character in a Hollywood extravaganza. Yet it all seemed a travesty.

Armitage was speaking of those twilit minutes in the meadow in Wicklow.

"Drove in through this gate, middle of a field, stopped the car, jumped out and was gone. Last I saw of her." He sat in silence for some moments, blinking. "We'd been having a fight, of course, but it was nothing out of the ordinary." He lifted his shoulders high and let them fall again. "Don't know what came over her. Temporary insanity, maybe."

He might have been speaking of a stranger whose misfortunes he had read about in the papers. Suddenly, before she knew it, she found she had somehow got herself on her feet.

"I'm very sorry," she said hurriedly, "really, I am—but I must go." She made a show of looking at her watch. "I just remembered I have to meet someone." She was pulling on her gloves. "I hope things get better for you, soon." *Shut up, you idiot.* "I mean, I know you'll be in mourning, but it may not be"—*stop*—"it may not be as bad as you expect."

He was gazing up at her with a puzzled expression, half smiling. She put out her hand for him to shake.

"How do you know him?" he asked.

"What? Who?"

"The detective. Stafford, or Strafford, or whatever he's called. How do you come to know him?"

20

At that moment, Strafford was in his office, seated at his desk, with the phone to his ear, being screamed at by Charlotte Ruddock. She was already speaking when he picked up the receiver, her voice shaking. He could hardly understand what she was saying. Something about the child, about Bunny.

"He's gone!" she shrieked. "We've looked everywhere!"

"Please, Char—please, Mrs. Ruddock, try to be calm."

"Calm? *Calm?*"

"Stop for a moment, close your eyes, take a deep breath. Now. Tell me."

"Oh, Christ!"

He waited. Her voice receded as she turned away from the phone and shouted something at someone in the room with her. She was sobbing now. She banged the receiver against something, then there was a loud honking sound as she blew her nose. When she spoke into the phone again, all the energy had drained from her voice.

"It's been hours," she said, stifling a sob. "We can't find him anywhere. He's gone."

Strafford waited.

"Go on, please," he said. She was silent. He could hear a buzz of voices behind her, seeming to come from an adjoining room. "You're in Wicklow still, yes?"

"That Guard is here, what's his name—Cowley."

"Sergeant Crowley?"

"Crowley, yes, whatever. I think he's drunk. He certainly smells of drink."

With two fingers, Strafford tapped a rapid little rhythm on the desk.

"Tell me what happened," he said.

An icy dread was spreading its tentacles inside him.

"I don't *know* what happened!" she cried. "He's gone. The child is gone."

He thought for a moment.

"Let me speak to Crowley."

"He's not here. He just left. He's going to organize a search party." She made a guttural sound that might be a laugh, but surely wasn't. "It's grotesque. First that woman disappeared, now Bunny."

She took the phone from her ear again and made a banshee wail.

"Mrs. Ruddock," he called into the mouthpiece. "Mrs. Ruddock, please!"

Then she hung up.

The driver on duty was a Garda Dineen. Strafford had seen him about but had not traveled with him before today. He was a large, somber young man with enormous hands. He spoke when spoken to, otherwise he was silent. He smiled to himself now and then, as if he were recalling a private joke. Strafford, in the back seat, noted the boyish whorl of hair on the crown of his head.

The sun was shining but the air was smoky and dense. It hadn't rained properly in weeks. The trees were parched, their foliage a dingy grayish-green. People were tired of the Indian summer. It wasn't natural, everyone said. The crops would be ruined. Down in the country, priests had begun to offer up prayers for rain after last Mass on Sundays. But still the drought continued. God, it seemed to Strafford, had more pressing things to deal with than the plight of the farmers.

"You can put your foot down, Garda. We're in a hurry."

The young man directed a cool glance at him in the rearview mirror, and said nothing, only smiled his wisp of a smile. He pressed down on the accelerator and the squad car bounded forward like a happy dog.

Strafford was wondering if he should stop at the Garda station in Wicklow and talk to Crowley. But if Crowley had been drunk when the Ruddocks summoned him, he would likely have gone home to sleep it off. The man was a disgrace to the force.

At Newtownmountkennedy, Strafford again tried to remember the joke about the man who wanted that name tattooed on his penis. Perhaps that was all there was to the joke. Who had told it to him? He couldn't remember that, either.

He fell into a half doze, his mind wandering at random. Phoebe with his baby growing inside her, Charlotte Ruddock and her lost child, Wymes and his dog.

At the crossroads he sat up with a start, bleary and feeling slightly nauseous—he should have sat in the front seat.

He looked out at McEntee's pub and thought of Armitage. For a moment, he couldn't recall his first name. Reggie? No: Ronnie. A north of England con masquerading as a lord. He wasn't the first such to walk through the gates of Trinity. Where had his wife run off to? Or had she gone into the water? And if so, had it been by design or accident? From what little he had heard of her, she didn't seem the type to do away with herself. Maybe Armitage had pushed her. Without a body, there was no way of knowing.

The stone house at the top of the slope was quiet. Strafford wasn't sure what he had expected—screams, shouts, doors slamming and windows flung open. It was never like that. Fear always imposed a hush. Even Charlotte Ruddock's shrieks, on the phone, had soon subsided. The ancient dread of provoking the gods, of sending up our cries and drawing down their wrath.

She was in the kitchen, sitting in a low armchair with her elbows on her knees and her face in her hands. Strafford made to touch her, but stopped himself. Whatever there had been between them was severed. That half hour they had spent together in the child's room had been folded up and put away like a toy in a box in an attic.

She let fall her hands and looked up at him. Her face, streaked with dried tears, was as stark as a skull. The large, jutting mouth with its prominent teeth was drawn back at either side in a fierce rictus. He was reminded of those masks worn by the players in Greek tragedy.

"I thought you weren't coming," she said.

"I couldn't get here any sooner. The road—"

"What?"

Her eyes blazed. She seemed incensed, as if he had said something outrageous.

"The road over the mountains, it's very narrow, and—"

"You should have come by the coast!" She had leaped to her feet, and stood before him now, staring into his face with a look at once furious and beseeching. Moments passed, and then, as if something inside her had suddenly shriveled, she went limp and leaned forward, into his arms. "He's gone," she muttered, her mouth pressed against the side of his face, "he's gone."

He made her sit down again, and drew up a chair and sat before her, leaning forward with his hands clasped on his knees.

"Tell me what happened," he said.

She had gone out with the child to walk up the long low slope to the very top of the hill. "You can see Dublin from there, the smoke of the city, and the sun on the roofs, even a pane of glass shining." There was a pine wood at the top, where they often went, the two of them, and a grassy clearing where they always stopped. The child liked to search for pine cones to play with, stacking them up in pyramids and then knocking them down. She had sat on the grass with her back against a rock. The air was hazy, the sun was warm. She was reading a book, and then she must have fallen asleep.

"I looked around and he was gone. The pine cones were there, but he wasn't." She fixed Strafford with a wild-eyed stare. "I didn't know what to do. I ran into the trees, calling out his name. Every few steps, I'd stop and listen. I'll never forget the silence. As if everything was holding its breath and watching me, gloating."

She frowned. She was looking now at the back of her left hand, as if the veins were runes that might be read.

"Go on," Strafford said softly.

"I never wanted to come here. I don't like the country, I'm afraid of it. The trees, the way they just stand there, like the people who stand looking at the scene of an accident. And the birds—the crows, that sound they make, as if they're laughing, jeering." She stood up quickly, wrenching herself from the chair, walked rapidly to the window, stopped, came back, sat down again. "I don't know what to do," she said, in a sort of stricken wonderment, "I don't know what to do."

"Where's your husband?" Strafford asked.

"What?"

"Your husband—where is he?"

"He went off with the Guard, to see about setting up a search party." She looked at her wrist, but she wasn't wearing her watch. "He should be back by now. They should be here, the men who'll do the search."

Strafford nodded in what he hoped was a soothing fashion.

"The child," he said—he couldn't call him Beverly, or Bunny, either, both names equally ridiculous, "did he seem the same as usual?"

She directed her stare at him again.

"What do you mean?"

"He didn't say anything strange, or behave in any unusual way?"

But what way, he thought, with that child, would be usual?

"He's always the same," she said simply. "He's not like other children, he doesn't run about. He only ever plays by himself, never with other children. He doesn't like other children." She paused. "I think he knows how bad his condition is. His blood is very weak. If he were to cut himself—"

She stopped abruptly, and dropped her face into her hands again. She said something, but her voice was muffled. He felt he should attempt to comfort her, if only to lay a hand on her arm, but he didn't dare. She might have been a figure made of the finest crystal, that the slightest touch would shatter.

Now she looked up again.

"I fell asleep," she said, "and now he's gone."

From outside came the sound of voices, one of them Dineen's. Charlotte Ruddock rose again from the armchair with another violent twist of her shoulders, and ran to the door and into the hall. Strafford remembered the little cool dimple at the base of her spine, and his fingertip dipping into it.

21

Crowley, when he came in, had the inveterate drinker's morning aspect, glazed and raw and rumpled, as if he were newly hatched. He appeared first, then Ruddock, then the young Garda with the sticking-out ears. They moved heavily and in silence. To Strafford, they might have been a shooting party returning from the moors and out of sorts, their game bags empty. They gave off a warm, meaty odor. Seeing him, Ruddock halted, scowling. Strafford felt a twinge of unease. Surely Charlotte hadn't told him about that evening in the house in Vesey Place?

She stepped forward and put out a hand to her husband. He scowled at her, too, and the light went out in her eyes. She walked to the sink and filled a kettle from the tap and put it on the stove.

"I'll make tea," she said dully, and wiped her nose on the back of a hand.

"The men are out searching," Crowley said to her. "We got a right lot of volunteers, from all over. They'll find the little fellow, don't you worry."

She said nothing, did not even look at him. He waited a moment, then turned to Strafford and touched a hand to his forehead in what might be a sort of grudging salute.

"Morning," he said shortly.

Ruddock opened a cupboard, took down a full bottle of Bushmills and set about uncorking it. His wife glanced at him.

"You're not going to start on that, are you?" she said. "It's not noon yet."

Ignoring her, he fetched a glass from the dresser by the door, sloshed a double measure of whiskey into it and drank it off in one swallow. He winced, squeezing his eyes shut for a moment and then opening them wide.

"Jesus," he said. He turned to Strafford. "What hole did you creep out of, St. John the Injun?"

Strafford disregarded this.

"What's the situation?" he asked of Crowley.

"I have twenty men searching in the pine wood up there. More volunteers are on the way."

"Who's coordinating the search?"

Crowley glowered.

"I am—who do you think?"

"Shouldn't you be up there with them?"

Ruddock was pouring himself another drink. The kettle came to the boil. Crowley stood with his hands on his hips, looking at the floor. Then he came forward and stood close-up to Strafford. The Guard was the shorter of the two.

"Listen, sonny," he said in a low growl, "don't you come down here telling me how to do my job."

Strafford looked at him as a naturalist would look at a not particularly rare and not at all interesting specimen of wildlife. He stepped back. Although Crowley was not only shorter in stature and lower in rank, he had the advantage of being on his home ground. Nothing was to be gained by continuing this confrontation. Ruddock was enjoying it, leaning against the dresser with his glass of whiskey in his large, tanned fist.

Charlotte Ruddock put the steaming teapot on the table, and stepped past her husband and began to take down cups and saucers from the dresser. Strafford moved away from Crowley. Through the window he could see the squad car outside. Dineen was seated stolidly behind the steering wheel, blank-eyed and unmoving. With his great bulk, he filled the driver's seat to overflowing, making the car seem a size smaller than it was.

I should get out of here, Strafford thought. The air in the room was still rancid with the smell of male sweat; it was as if a noxious gas were seeping up from beneath the floorboards.

Charlotte Ruddock must have read his thought about escaping, for she turned to him and said almost desperately, "Won't you have a cup of tea? Or something?"

"Thank you, no," he answered, not looking at her. "I have some things to do before I go back to Dublin." He tried to think of something kinder, something comforting—he owed her that much at least—but the words wouldn't come. "I'm sure they'll find your son, Mrs. Ruddock. Children wander off all the time, it very rarely comes to anything."

She regarded him with bitter amusement.

"'Very rarely,'" she said. "That's good to know."

Ruddock took another swig from his glass.

"Why don't you come up and join in the search," he said to Strafford. "Bulldog Drummond to the rescue."

The phone in the hall began to ring, and Charlotte raced out to answer it. The three men in the room listened to her speaking.

"Yes yes, what?—" She paused. "Hello, Marjorie. I'm sorry, I can't talk now. What? No, he's not here. I'll explain later." Again, she stopped to listen. "For Christ's sake, Marjorie! I'm hanging up now. Goodbye." She came back, looking more drained and bedraggled than before. "Your sister," she said to her husband. "I told her you weren't here. She asked if you'd left me. The things that woman thinks are funny!"

Crowley was sitting at the table now, with a cup of tea before him. He ran a hand over his close-cropped scalp, and the bristles made a crackling sound.

"You'll keep me informed," Strafford said to him.

It was a command, not a question. Crowley didn't answer, only drank his tea. Strafford moved to the door. Charlotte walked with him out to the car. They stopped. She stood with her hands thrust into the deep pockets of her skirt, looking down along the slope to the gate and the road and the sea far-off. Bundles of purplish clouds were massing on the horizon.

"He's gone, isn't he," she said, flat and matter-of-fact. "I've lost him, I know it."

"You can't know," Strafford said. "It's only been, what, a few hours?"

She was not listening. She nodded slowly, still looking away with narrowed eyes.

"He wasn't meant to be born, that's the fact of it," she said. "He wasn't meant to be here."

She might have been speaking from a long way off. Strafford made to touch her, but let his hand fall back. Dineen watched them through the shadowed windshield. Maybe his smile wasn't a smile but a sort of tic.

"I'll phone later," Strafford said.

Charlotte did not turn to him.

"Will you? You don't know the number."

"Tell me what it is."

But she moved away from him, frowning, preoccupied, and stepped into the dark of the doorway, and was gone.

Denton Wymes was walking with his dog on Kilpatrick beach. Scamp kept running back and forth at a crouch, glancing nervously this way and that. There must be a storm coming, Wymes thought, looking out at the dark clouds boiling up from the horizon.

They were the only ones on the beach. Earlier, when they came down from the dunes, they had met the girl again, the teenager with the sly, provocative smile who had passed them by that other day. Did her parents know she was out here, Wymes wondered, on her own on the beach and smirking at strange men? She could find herself in serious trouble, that one, he thought. He gave her the briefest glance and quickened his pace, anxious to put a good distance between himself and her. He had to be careful. He had no interest whatever in the girl, not that kind of interest, anyway, but it could go badly for him if something happened to her. From the village and the farms around they'd come, hard-faced men, and the women with their sleeves rolled up, a silent, relentless mob, out for his blood.

He smiled wryly to himself. He was letting his imagination run away with him. This wasn't a horror film, and he wasn't M. Who was it that played that part? The German actor with the whispery voice and the lisp. Peter Lorre. M killed the children he molested. Imagine killing a child. Wymes shivered, and looked again out to the horizon. Yes, there would be a storm. The Indian summer was at last at an end.

He thought of the detective who had come to the trailer, asking questions about that fellow's missing wife. She can't have been found yet, or it would have been in the newspapers and on the wireless. Or maybe not—maybe they had found her, or she came back from wherever it was she had run off to, and what's-his-name, the husband, Armitage, had got the whole thing covered up somehow. He was a university professor, he'd be worried about his reputation.

Scamp had run ahead, and was climbing over the rocks that were piled up in the lee of the grassy hill. The tides had eaten away at the base of the hill and the whole side had collapsed, leaving a sandy wall exposed and a sheer drop.

"Come back here!" Wymes called out.

The dog went on, scrambling and tripping on the jagged edges of the rocks. It was strange, he had never ventured along there before. It must be hard on his paws. What was he after, what scent had he caught? A goat, maybe, or a sheep that had lost its footing on the slope and fallen over the edge of the hill and landed on the rocks.

"Scamp! Come back! Here, boy!"

The dog was out of sight now. Wymes was beginning to worry. What if the animal broke a leg, or got trapped in some crevice in the rocks?

"Scamp!"

Don't let him be lost, he prayed, surprised at himself—*please don't*.

How would he live, without Scamp? The creature meant that much to him. He sometimes thought he would have done away with himself by now, if he had not had his friend to keep him company, to keep his spirits up, to save him from despair.

He could hear the dog barking excitedly in the distance. He wouldn't come back until he had done with whatever it was he had found, for he was self-willed, like all his breed. He would have to be caught and brought away on the leash. Wymes eyed the built-up mound of jagged rocks. There was no way to get round them, for at one side they were piled against the sandy cliff, and at the other they ran out into the sea. The hill—he could go back up the lane and climb the hill and at least get a look at the dog and see what he was up to.

It was not an easy climb, for the hill was steep and the grass was slippery. He had to stop twice to rest. A wind had got up, bringing a smell of rain. The damned dog was beside himself by now, barking and barking.

At last, he got to the top of the hill. He stood on the edge where the land had collapsed and looked down. The dog was close in under the cliff, and to see him he had to lean far out and sharply down. He was circling something, his paws slipping and sliding on the rocks. Wymes, who had no head for heights, got to his knees, with his hands on his thighs, and leaned farther out.

What was it? A bit of rag? A cushion with the stuffing spilling out?

No.

Dear Jesus.

22

It was like one of those puzzles in the comics when he was young. There would be a drawing of a tree, and you were supposed to find faces hidden among the foliage. He was never any good at it. He couldn't make himself concentrate for long enough, and anyway the thing was stupid—what was the point of spotting all those idiots grinning at you among the leaves?

At first all he saw was the dog, dancing in a circle around something wedged in a hollow in the rocks. He stared and stared, turning his head this way and that, trying to make out what it was. Not a rag, not a split cushion. Then suddenly the pattern clicked into place. That was a shoulder, and that was human hair, and that, oh Lord, was blood.

He started back, and had to put a hand to the ground to keep from toppling over. He made himself look again. Yes:

a shoulder hunched inside a blue jacket, and a strew of blond hair streaked with red.

Armitage's wife. It had to be.

"Scamp!" he shouted, and the dog stopped circling and looked up at him in surprise. "Be quiet!"

He had to think, he had to decide what to do. Raise the alarm, call the Guards? Or try to get the dog to obey him and come down off the rocks, and then just fade away and say nothing to anyone?

No, no, he couldn't leave her there. He knew she was dead, knew it was a body he was looking at, but all the same it would not be right to abandon her. She might never be found, no one might ever know she was here. No one, except him. And he would be haunted by the thought of her, lost among the rocks on this bleak stretch of coastline where hardly anyone ever came.

What about the girl? What if she climbed up the rocks— she was a bit of a tomboy, he could tell by the look of her— and chanced on that tragic spectacle?

He rose and made his way back down the hill, slipping and sliding and cursing aloud. Damn the dog! Damn him and all his ancestors who over millennia had learned to sniff out lambs fallen into ditches or lost under snowdrifts.

The rocks, when he stepped onto them, were even more treacherous than they looked. Repeatedly, he nearly tripped and fell. Wouldn't that be a thing, if an ankle gave way and he came down and broke an arm or, worse, a leg. The soles of his old rubber boots were worn smooth, and could hardly find a purchase on the smooth-sided lumps of granite, or shale, or whatever it was. In the end, he took off his boots and socks, and went on barefoot—better to sustain a few cuts and grazes on his soles than to fall down and crack his skull.

Seeing him approach, the dog barked more excitedly than ever. Hysterical bloody brute.

"Shut up, for God's sake!"

The animal gave him a look, indignant, offended, accusing. He was right—wasn't he only doing his job, looking out for the strays and the fallen?

Here it was. The body. The remains.

The man knelt unsteadily, and with an effort. Blue velvet jacket, a linen collar, the blood matted in the blond hair. It wasn't a woman, it wasn't that fellow's wife. It was a child.

For a moment he couldn't think. A reddish mist rose up before his eyes and his forehead and his cheeks became flushed. He had dreamed this scene, or variants of it, so many times that for an instant he thought the thing there among the rocks might not be real but a projection of one of his deepest terrors. He couldn't imagine killing a child, but probably no one did, not even the vilest, the most depraved pervert, before it happened. He thought of that film again, the one with Peter Lorre.

He stood up. His feet were numb from the cold. The dog was sitting on its haunches, looking at him with keen expectation. He had calmed down, and was obviously enjoying himself, as if all this were a game his master was playing with him, incomprehensible but great fun.

"Come here," Wymes said to him, and grasped him by the collar and attached the leash to it. "We're going home."

They made their way back over the rocks. When they came onto the beach at last, Wymes sat down and brushed as much sand from his feet as he could—why was sand always so sticky?—and put on his socks and his boots. The dog took the opportunity to lick his ear.

There was no question, he couldn't report what he had

found. They would think he had murdered the child—how would they not, with his record? It wouldn't make any difference that he hadn't hurt, not physically, any of the children he had been charged with molesting.

There's always a first time, they'd say.

No, he would have to keep silent.

It was the little boy from the house on the hill. When he lifted the poor creature's head and saw the face, he recognized him at once. No mistaking that unearthly beauty, despite the blood and the bruising.

He shouldn't have touched the body. That was a stupid thing to do. But how could he not have, in the shock of the moment? Clues. Always in detective stories the killer made some mistake, left some evidence that would convict him later. But he wasn't a killer! That was true, but they would think he was, and all the evidence would be stacked against him.

Would they find his fingerprints? Did fingerprints register on skin? He didn't know. They could do all sorts of things nowadays, with powders and dyes and microscopes.

By now, the wind had driven the clouds in from the horizon and the sky all round was darkly abulge.

Maybe he should go to the Guards. What murderer had ever reported his own crime? He could tell them how the dog found the body, and how he had come straight to the village where there was a phone booth on the corner by Enright's grocery shop, which was where he was calling them from. He was just like any other concerned citizen, wasn't he?

Oh, sure he was, sure. A concerned citizen who just happened to be a former jailbird.

And what was the crime he had been found guilty of? Didn't it involve young children?

Why, yes, that's right, it did—here's his record, have a look.

Right, hold out your wrists. Clink clink, and the cuffs are on, cold, so cold against his skin.

Come this way, my lad, we've a nice warm cell all ready and waiting for you.

He felt the first big splashy drops of rain. Then came a flash out over the sea, followed by a crack and a long untidy rumble of thunder. The dog whined. The dog was afraid of thunder. So was he.

He came to the top of the dunes and looked down into the hollow where the trailer was parked and saw the squad car stopped outside it. He halted, his heart thudding. There were two figures seated behind the windshield, but the rain was coming down hard by now and he couldn't make out who they were.

It would be Crowley, he supposed, and maybe that detective down from Dublin again.

What did they want? Had someone else already ventured out onto the rocks and seen the child's body after all? Surely not—it would be too much of a coincidence, that two people should make the same grim discovery within half an hour of each other on the same day.

And yet, coincidence or no coincidence, maybe someone had spotted the body and raised the alarm. Who would the Guards think of first? The answer to that was easy, and here they were, two of them, sitting down there in the squad car in the rain, waiting for him.

He drew his coat tighter against his ribs. He had no hat, and already the rain had got under his collar at the back and drops of it were slithering down his spine.

Run! a voice inside him urged. *Run.*

Another flash of lightning zipped down the back of the sky, another peal of thunder shook the air. Again the dog whined. The poor animal was beside himself. What angry god did he think it was who was hurling at him these fiery tridents, these awful rumblings?

"Come on, boy," Wymes whispered. "Come on, now, you're all right."

He went back down a little way toward the beach, until he was sure he was out of sight of the squad car and its faceless occupants, then turned left and waded off through the wet and sticky sand, away from the rocks and what they held. Rain dripped from his eyebrows into his eyes, blurring his vision and making everything before him shake and slide, as if he were looking through the joggling lens of a camera. There might be a shed or something he could break into and hide in for a while. The pair in the squad car would soon get fed up sitting in the pouring rain and go away and leave him in peace.

This was another thing he often dreamed of, trying to flee from something over heavy, wet ground into which his feet kept sinking.

Even if they did go, they would come back. Always they came back, slow-moving and implacable.

In a dip in the dunes he came upon a long, humped shape that turned out to be an upturned rowing boat. He hunted about and found a stout piece of bleached driftwood. The dog went into a crouch, forgetting his fear of the storm and thinking they were going to play a game of fetch.

"Don't be an idiot," Wymes said through gritted teeth, and despite everything he almost laughed. Even in a panic he saw the absurd side of things. It was something to do with being a pariah, always looking in from the outer limits.

He lifted up the boat at one side, groaning from the effort, and propped it on the stick, then stepped back. The stick sank some way into the sand under the weight of the boat, but it allowed enough of a gap for him to get through. He lay down full length on his belly and wriggled sideways, his knees and elbows churning in the sand.

Under the low canopy of the upturned hull the air was shadowed, and the ground was dry. Something small scuttled quickly away. A rat? Do rats live in the dunes? There was a briny, tarry smell. He felt like a child playing hide-and-seek. The dog, still outside, looked in at him in puzzlement, its head tilted to one side.

"Come in, Scamp. Come in here—it's all right."

The dog walked around in a circle, whimpering. His coat, wet through, showed the knobbly outlines of backbone and ribs. Wymes spoke to him again, and at last he summoned up his courage and crept in under the perilously suspended gunwale.

They lay together, dog and man, and listened to the rain drumming on the heavy molded planks above them.

He was being ridiculous, Wymes told himself, skulking here in a funk, soaked to the skin and shivering. What had he to be afraid of? He had done nothing wrong. But wait: probably he was in the wrong, technically, by not having gone to the authorities straight off. But no one had seen him out on the rocks, therefore no one knew what he had found there.

Unless there had been someone watching, someone he had not seen but who had seen him, and had gone down to find out what it was he had discovered. And then had called the Guards.

The dog lay cold against him. At brief intervals, a long slow shudder passed along the animal's body, from its shoulders all the way down to the butt of its tail. The whites of its eyes shone starkly in the gloom. He could see the poor thing wondering why they were there, hiding under a boat, while the storm raged outside.

It was a nice question, though, Wymes thought, as to whether he was liable to be charged with failure to report his grim find. Could one break the law by *not* doing something? The answer had to be yes. Didn't the Church say there were sins not only of commission but of omission? No, he couldn't wriggle out of his moral duty by wriggling in under an upturned boat.

More lightning, more thunder. But the intervals between the crack and the crash were lengthening, which meant the storm was moving away, inland. Sure enough, the drumming on the hull began to abate, and after another minute or two the rain abruptly ceased. In its wake, a dripping stillness swelled.

He thought of the broken body over there among the rocks, the blue velvet turned black by the rain, the swatch of golden hair turned dull and brassy.

But really, he must stop this nonsense and return to the trailer, even if the squad car was still there. Imagine if someone were to spy him here, like a little boy hiding away from the big bad men.

It was harder to get out from under the boat than it had been to get in. But he managed it, and set off back along the dunes. The dog went ahead of him, his tail going like the needle in a metronome, glad to be in the open again with the storm ended. Everything looked disheveled and slightly dazed, though the air was fresh and cool and a watery sun was trying to break through.

He poked his head above the crest of the dunes. The car

was gone. Did he really imagine they would have waited for him all this time? He wondered if he was losing his grip on reality.

"A cup of tea for me," he said to the dog, "and a bowl of mincemeat for you."

Once inside the camper, he lighted the little woodstove and sat beside it, his hands wrapped around a mug of strong tea the color and, he suspected, the taste of boot polish. The dog lapped happily at its food. Things could be worse, he told himself. Then he thought of the woman, the child's mother, elegant even in an old smock and bare feet, with her offhand, South Dublin self-assurance, and pictured her big-boned, handsome face collapsing in on itself in grief.

Didn't he have a duty to go to the Guards? he asked himself. And just as he asked it, he heard the sound of a car approaching, and coming to a stop outside. They had come back.

23

She was woken by a cry of pain, her own. Was it her period? It couldn't be, arriving this early and with such force and unheard-of suddenness. For a moment, it was as if she were floating just under the ceiling, looking down at herself where she lay on her back under the bedclothes, clutching her stomach with both hands.

Then she remembered: she was pregnant, so it couldn't be her period.

She sat up, bleary-eyed and confused, and switched on the lamp above the bed and took up her watch from the bedside table and peered at it. Just after four. The darkness all round seemed to be listening, expecting her to cry out again. She pushed back the bedclothes. Her lap was awash with blood.

Again, that searing flash of pain.

Why, she thought, though it was as if it were some other

voice asking the question, *why is pain always a surprise?* Why
don't we get used to it, why don't we come to expect it? No,
always it comes as a sudden blow, a sudden, astonishing assault.

Her mind by now had pulled itself up out of sleep into a
fearful clarity. She knew what had happened. She knew what
all that blood and other, darker fluids signified.

She got out of bed and took off her pajama bottoms and,
with eyes averted, bundled them together with the blood-
ied sheets into a ball and dumped the lot into the handbasin
in the corner behind the door. All that she would deal with
later. Then she wrapped a blanket around herself from waist
to ankle.

At the bedroom door, she paused to listen. Quirke would
be in his room, though she had not heard him coming in.
She hoped he was asleep. Easing the door shut behind her, she
tiptoed swiftly down the stairs to the bathroom on the return
and locked the door behind her. She felt along the windowsill
and was relieved to find three shilling pieces there. She knelt
on one knee, drew open the little door set into wall above
the wainscot, and pressed two coins into the gas meter. Then
she rose to her feet and struck a match and inserted the flame
into the slot in the geyser and turned the knob and the gas
ignited with a *whomp!* She pressed the lever, and hot water
began to pour in steaming gouts from the narrow chrome
spout and fell into the bathtub with what seemed to her the
crash of a cataract.

The bath was old, and there was a brownish stain halfway
up all around the sides. She had tried to scrub it off, but whatever it was—rust, she supposed—had eaten into the enamel
and would not be shifted.

She wiped herself with a facecloth and rinsed the blood out

of it in the sink. Then she sat down on the wooden lid of the toilet and wrapped her arms around herself and rocked back and forth, moaning softly. Intense small pains shot through her like flickers of flame.

The bath was full almost to the brim before she shed her dressing gown and the blanket and stepped in. The water was scalding, but she made herself sit down, exacting a sort of awful, almost pleasurable revenge on the body that had tonight so abjectly failed her.

A moth was circling the light in the ceiling above her, bumping blindly against the cellophane shade. The shade always looked to her as if it were made from dried human skin.

So: it was over. She didn't know what she should feel. Sorrow? Or regret, at least? Relief? There would have been such trouble, such mayhem, if the baby had come to term. Strafford would probably have left her—he would probably leave her anyway, selfish prig that he was—and Quirke would have been so furious it would have sent him straight back on to the drink. She sometimes wondered if her father might be a little mad. She wondered too if it might not be better if he began to drink again—to drink seriously, with grim dedication, as he used to when she was young. On balance, he was less frightening drunk than he was sober.

She reached over the rim of the bath and fished in the pocket of her dressing gown for her cigarettes and lighter. Passing Clouds, for old times' sake. She lighted one, and lay back in the water, which was still hot enough to take her breath away for a second.

What should she do? What was a woman supposed to do, after a miscarriage? Should she call an ambulance, and check herself into a hospital?—*not* the Hospital of the Holy Family. None of the women she knew had lost an unborn baby, or if they had they'd kept quiet about it. Isabel Galloway had gone to England for an abortion at some stage in her colorfully troubled past. "Unpleasant," she had said, when Phoebe asked her about it. "But the alternative would have been unpleasanter still."

She had read somewhere that some women in her situation hold themselves to blame. Did she feel shame, or guilt? No, she didn't. But had she wanted the child, really, in the first place? She had assumed from the start that it would be a girl. Indeed, it hadn't crossed her mind that it might be a boy. If it had been, she wouldn't have known what to do with it. She would have thought of it, him, as a changeling.

She finished her cigarette and doused the butt in the bathwater, taking a tiny, vindictive pleasure in the hiss it gave, like a hiss of pain, as it was extinguished. It was a good thing there wasn't anything alive nearby, a beetle or a spider, for she would have seized it and snuffed out its life, too. She wanted to inflict small damages, small sufferings. Why should she be the only afflicted one?

Don't be ridiculous, she told herself. Think of the thousands, the millions, writhing in agony at this moment, in Soviet jails, or crawling parched through a desert. Think of all the people on their deathbeds, breathing their last.

The moth was still bumping against the shade, softly, with sad, futile relentlessness.

She stood up, the water falling from her in an abrupt cascade. She looked down along herself. She hadn't even begun to show, and wouldn't, now.

In the living room, she switched on a table lamp and poured herself a glass of Quirke's brandy. She carried the glass into the kitchen and sat at the window above the deserted street, partly illuminated by sickly yellow lamplight. She wished she could detach her head from her neck and let the rest of her fall in a heap like a harlequin's discarded costume. The pain now was a general ache shot through with sharp little burning darts.

The brandy seared her throat—she hardly ever drank spirits—but she didn't care.

A couple went by on the other side of the street. The woman was drunk, wobbling along on her high heels, so that the man had to keep a hand firmly under her elbow to stop her from falling over. They must be coming from a party. She wore a tight skirt and a feather boa, and a funny little pillbox hat pinned at a perilous angle to the side of her head. Phoebe used to sell hats like that when she worked for Mrs. Cuffe-Wilkes at the Maison des Chapeaux.

Those days seemed so far-off now. She had been in love then, or in something, with Patrick Ojukwu, before they sent him back to Nigeria. She wondered how he was, and what he was doing. She hoped he had finished his studies and qualified as a doctor out there. Africa needed doctors. He hadn't written to her. He probably felt she could have intervened to stop him being deported. But there was nothing she could have done for him. It was the powers that be, the faceless ones, that had sent him packing.

Imagine if she had got pregnant by him, and had a little Black baby. Quirke would have loved that, oh yes.

She had returned to the living room to pour another drink when she heard a door opening somewhere in the flat. It would be her father—as if her thought had summoned him. He was the last person in the world she wished to see, or be seen by, just now. She drank off the brandy in one swallow, nearly choking on it, and returned to the kitchen and put on the kettle to boil. The water was just starting to boil when he put his head round the door.

"Hello, you," he said. "Can't sleep? You look terrible."

"Thanks."

Her chalk-white face was shrunken somehow, so that her eyes seemed huge, with crescents of deep violet shadow under them. Women's trouble, no doubt. He knew so little about her, even after all these years. He should find a place of his own, an apartment or just a bachelor, and let her get on with her life without him as an encumbrance, him and his unassuageable sadness.

She in her turn was eyeing him. He was wearing his old tartan dressing gown. She rarely saw him like this, his face puffy and hair rumpled. He must have been drinking last night. He gave her arm a squeeze and went and sat at the table and lighted a cigarette. The first intake of smoke caused a coughing fit.

"You know this is the worst possible time of day to be smoking," she said. "Your lungs are defenseless."

He didn't answer. He was looking down into the street. From far-off came the sound of drunken laughter. That would be the woman in the pillbox hat. She hadn't got far. Maybe she had fallen and the man had gone off in disgust and left her sitting on the ground.

She spooned tea into the pot and poured in the water.

"You know this is the worst possible time of day to be drinking tea," Quirke said.

"Very funny," she answered sourly.

"There's more caffeine in tea than there is in coffee. Did you know that?"

"Oh, shut up," she said absently, and carried the pot to the table and set out a cup and saucer.

"There's no milk," he said. "I looked earlier. The bottle in the fridge has gone off."

"I don't take milk."

"Don't you? How did I not know that?" He paused to remove a flake of tobacco from his lower lip. "Funny. You can live with someone and not know all sorts of things."

"You don't take any notice of other people."

"Am I that bad? I suppose I am." *Down among the dead men.* "I'll try harder."

He turned his face again to the window and the street.

"Are you missing Evelyn?" she asked.

"I miss her all the time," he said matter-of-factly. "Some days are worse than others, some nights. Mornings are worst of all."

She saw him looking at her bare legs below the hem of the dressing gown. She thought of Strafford doing the same thing, on the beach that day.

"Can I get you something?" she asked. "A drink?"

"No, thanks," he said. "I notice bold Lochinvar is not about much, these days." This was one of his names for Strafford. "Gone back to the west whence he came, is he? *A laggard in love, and a dastard in war.*"

Tears pricked her eyes. She would not cry—*she would not cry.*

She sipped at the warm bitter brew in the cup. She would swallow her pride and call Strafford. She would wait until nine, then phone him at the office. He hated taking private calls at work. Well, good enough for him. Let him feel wrong-footed, he deserved it.

She surprised herself by her vehemence. But how would she not feel harshly toward him? Not a word from him since the day on the beach. Had he abandoned her for good, or was he just taking time to brood? But he could have sent a note, surely, that much at least. He must know how lonely she was feeling, how isolated, she and her secret.

She would not tell him what had happened an hour ago. Why should she give him that relief? Let him stew for a while longer.

"That fellow stopped me in the street," she said, "the one whose wife disappeared."

"The Trinity fellow? The professor?"

"Armitage. Yes."

"He stopped you?"

"On Grafton Street. I was walking along and he came up behind me and spoke to me. I don't know how he knew me."

"What did he say?"

"I'd spotted him already a couple of times. I wondered if he was following me. He invited me to the Grafton Cinema café and bought me a cup of coffee. He said his wife is still missing. Then he asked me about St. John, how long I'd known him, things like that. It was all very peculiar."

Quirke nodded slowly. She could see he was only half listening. He seemed to be attending to something inside him, some inner register. It was like that with him almost all the time now, since he had lost Evelyn.

"Are you all right?" she asked.

"What?"

"Do you think you'll ever get over it?"

"Over what?" She said nothing. He looked out at the window again. A car went past, going very slowly. On the prowl. Surely there wouldn't still be prostitutes on the street, at this hour of the morning? "Are you sick of my going on about it?" he asked.

"That's not what I meant. As you very well know. I'm sad for you, I wish I could help."

He nodded again.

"There really are only two kinds of people in the world, I've discovered—the bereaved, and the yet-to-be bereaved." He was lighting another cigarette from the butt of the previous one. "I wouldn't have anything to do with that fellow, if I were you."

"Who? Armitage?"

"An unsavory type, from what I've heard of him."

Now it was she who was half listening. She was debating with herself whether she might tell him about the baby, about losing it. Here they were, sleepless together in the hour before dawn, brooding on their losses. Such a moment might never come again. If she did tell him, he'd make her go to the hospital. But maybe she should? She had lost a lot of blood— when she was getting out of the bath, she had thought she might faint. And her insides were paining her again, since the mildly anesthetizing effects of the brandy had worn off.

Was it a boy or a girl? she wondered again. Strange not to know. Girl or boy, it had been a life, another life, growing inside her. And something of it would be there always, through all her days, a pinprick of sorrow aglow in her inner firmament, like the enduring light of a long-dead star.

"I'm going back to bed," she said. "I'm tired."

Yet she hesitated. Would she have the strength to stand up? What if she got lightheaded again? What if she left a puddle of blood after her on the chair?

Quirke put a hand over hers, where it rested on the table. She was startled. They almost never touched. In the flat they maneuvered carefully around each other, like two passengers meeting in the corridor of a train.

"You're very good to me," Quirke said. "I don't show my appreciation enough, and I should."

"Yes. Well."

And so they sat there, his hand on hers, above the lamplit street, where it had begun to rain, in silence, absent-mindedly.

24

Strafford knocked on the trailer door, but by the time Wymes opened it he had moved back to stand by the squad car, the left-hand back door of which stood open. He was wearing his gray gabardine raincoat and his brown hat with the squashed crown. Over his shoes were black rubber galoshes stuck with sand. A lock of hair hung in a limp diagonal across his fore-head. He was holding an outsize black umbrella, furled. The galoshes: had he brought them with him because he had guessed the weather was going to break, or was a pair kept in the boot of all squad cars, a standard part of Garda equip-ment? Wymes would like to know. There was something faintly comical about this finical, unsmiling young-old man, with his drab hair and drab clothes and drably careful manner.

"Have a word?" he said, blank-eyed.

"A word about what?" Wymes responded, surprised at his

own daring, though his voice, he noted, was not entirely steady.

The dog, remembering the detective, had jumped down from the trailer and approached him, wagging his tail.

Wymes wasn't sure what to do, how to behave. He knew he must keep up the pretense of being surprised, perhaps even indignant, at being called on by the police for a second time. Whatever there was in his past, he was a law-abiding citizen nowadays, and didn't care to be harassed like this by the police—he should say something like that, and strike an attitude, one hand on his hip. But what would be the use? His eyes would give him away, his eyes, and the tremor in his hands.

Strafford came forward, and Wymes moved out of the doorway and back into the trailer. The driver got out of the car, in his uniform, with his cap in his hand. His head was remarkably large, the size of a shoebox. Wymes gestured for them both to come in, which they did, Strafford first and then the driver.

"This is Garda Dineen," Strafford said.

Wymes nodded to the young man.

Strafford was looking for somewhere to put down his dripping umbrella. Wymes took it from him and stood it by the door on a rush mat.

Without preamble, Strafford said, "The Ruddocks' child has gone missing. The little boy."

"Missing?" Wymes said, putting on a large frown. "How do you mean?"

"His mother took him up on the hill above the house. They were having a picnic or something. At some point, the mother noticed he was gone. There's a search party out looking for him."

"This is incredible—twice in, what, a matter of days, in the same place, first the woman and now the child?"

"Yes."

The wind was high again, and now and then the camper gave a sort of shiver as the gale buffeted it. Rain was beating against the back window. The Garda with the big head had produced a notebook and a pencil. *What would they do without their props?* Wymes thought with sour amusement.

"Where were you this morning, Mr. Wymes," Strafford asked, "between, say, ten o'clock and noon?"

"I was here. In the caravan."

"You didn't go out at all? Even to walk the dog?" He glanced at the towel that Wymes had used to dry himself when he came in earlier, thrown across the back of a chair. "You look as if you got a wetting."

"That was later. After lunch. There was a thunderstorm, it went on for ages. I had to take shelter in a hut over on the dunes."

Scamp was sitting on the floor in front of the stove, looking from one of the men to the other and squirming on his haunches in anxious excitement. It must be strange for dogs, Wymes thought, trying all the time to understand the unaccountable behavior of their human overlords.

"You went out in the storm?"

"No, the storm came on while I was out. The dog had been restless, the way he always is when there's a turn in the weather. I suppose they can hear the thunder while it's still miles away. Maybe too they smell the rain."

Garda Dineen was writing all this down in his notebook.

Strafford glanced about, frowning. He seemed to have lost his train of thought.

"She's very upset, the mother," he said.

"That's hardly surprising."

"I didn't say it was surprising." This was spoken without emphasis. "She blames herself for letting her attention stray. She thinks she may have fallen asleep."

"Yes, no doubt," Wymes said vaguely. He knew he should feel sympathy for the woman, but he didn't. She was a spoiled bitch, from what he had seen of her. "Very hard, to lose a child."

Strafford stood in silence, gazing at him. Wymes turned aside and looked at the dog, at its shinily inquiring eyes, its twitching ears. What would happen to the poor thing, he thought, if he were to be arrested and taken away? Who would look after him? He couldn't bear to think of the poor brute caged up in some awful pound with scores of other stray or abandoned animals.

"You say that as if you think the child is lost for good," Strafford said. "There's no reason to think that's the case. Children wander off all the time, and then turn up again."

"No, I just meant—" He was stammering, and told himself to shut up.

The detective was still watching him with his pale dead eyes.

"Did anyone come by here this morning, between ten and twelve?" he asked. "Did you talk to anyone?"

"No, I don't see people."

"No one at all?"

"You mean someone who could vouch for me, and give me an alibi? Why don't you ask the dog? He can vouch for me."

But the show of bravado fell flat. Strafford looked at the floor for a moment in silence, then stepped forward and put a hand on Wymes's shoulder and turned him about and walked with him to the far end of the caravan.

"Mr. Wymes," he said quietly, out of the hearing of the Garda with the notebook, "I'm trying to help you, you understand that?"

"Why would I need help?" Wymes said, surprised at his own continuing boldness. Maybe he would get out of this after all. Stupid to hide under a boat.

"Because," Strafford said, in what was hardly more than a murmur, "a child has gone missing, and you have a criminal record."

"I've done nothing," Wymes insisted. "I never harmed a child. I wouldn't."

Garda Dineen, whose hearing must have been sharp, gave a soft snigger. So he too knows who I am, Wymes thought, and what I am.

"You think the child has been harmed?"

"I don't know. How would I know?"

Strafford considered the floor again, lips pursed, then abruptly turned and walked to the door and opened it, picking up his umbrella. The dog looked up at him and beat his tail expectantly on the linoleum.

The young Garda put away his notebook. Strafford, in the doorway, looked back at Wymes.

"You have no plans to leave the area, yes?"

"What do you mean, to leave the area? Where would I go?"

"We might need to talk to you again," Strafford said. He paused briefly. "If the child isn't found."

"I'm going nowhere," Wymes said sullenly, and took up from the chair the still-damp towel.

The two men stepped down onto the sand and walked toward the squad car, shoulder to shoulder under the umbrella. Wymes stood at the door and watched them go. The

rain had begun to stop, the last random drops scattering before the wind. Low down in the sky inland there was a rent
in the clouds, showing a strip of glaring magnesium light.

"Wait," Wymes said, and Strafford stopped, and turned.

It was hard going, over the soggy sand, and it took them
fifteen minutes to get to the rocks. The rain had fully stopped,
but the sky was in turmoil, the windswept clouds tumbling
over each other like smoke from a burning building. Wymes
leaned down and took off his shoes, and urged the other two
to do the same. Both men looked doubtful.

"Shoe leather is too slippery," he said. "You could trip and
break something."

So they went forward barefoot, the three of them. Strafford thought what a comical sight they must be, grown men
picking their way daintily over the big, sharp-edged rocks,
their trouser legs rolled, carrying their shoes and socks in
their hands.

They came to where the child's body was wedged in the
sandy hollow between two leaning outcrops of shale.

"It was the dog that found him," Wymes said. "Otherwise
I wouldn't have known he was here."

Strafford was looking at the sandy cliff face.

"He must have fallen from up there. That's why the search
party missed him—he's too close in to the bank to be seen."
He turned to Wymes. "Did you move the body?"

"No. Only to lift up the head, to make sure it was him.
First I thought it was that man's wife."

"You didn't touch anything else? Move anything, take
anything away?"

Wymes shook his head.

The young Guard was leaning forward with his hands braced on his knees.

"The neck is broke, looks like," he said. It was the first time Wymes had heard him speak. He had a strong west of Ireland accent. Slowly he shook that outsize head of his. "Poor lad."

To the embarrassment of the other two, he lowered himself to one knee on the rocks, made the sign of the cross and mouthed a silent prayer.

Wymes turned to Strafford and said, "I'm sorry. I should have told you right away. I panicked when I heard the squad car outside the trailer."

Strafford nodded. "Was there anyone else around?"

"No. Or yes—I met a girl, fifteen or so."

"What was she doing?"

"Just walking along."

"Shouldn't she have been in school?"

"Playing truant, maybe. Or maybe she's left school. I've seen her here before, but I don't know her. Someone local."

"How do you know?"

"What?"

"How do you know she's local?"

"She just looks like someone from around here."

Strafford now turned to Dineen.

"Get on to Radio Éireann, tell them to put it on the six o'clock news that we're anxious to talk to anyone who was on Kilpatrick strand this morning, especially a girl of fifteen or so." He addressed Wymes again. "You're sure there was no one else? Think back."

"I don't need to. There's never anyone out at that time of the morning, in November. Except—"

"Yes?"

"There's a couple of young fellows who exercise horses along the beach."

"Do you know them?"

"They're from Keenan's stables, up toward Arklow. One of them I think is Keenan's son. But they come out early, and don't stay long. I think it's the law that they have to be gone by nine."

Dineen was balancing his notebook with difficulty against the front of his right thigh and trying to write in it.

"Keenan's," he murmured.

They made their way back along the rocks. When they had come to the sand and were putting on their shoes, Wymes asked of Strafford, "Are you going to arrest me?" He was surprised how calm he was. He supposed he must be resigned to his fate.

"Should I arrest you?" Strafford asked, with what seemed an amused flicker of the eyes.

Wymes did not reply.

They set off along the beach the way they had come. Wymes's feet were damp and cold in his shoes, and there was sand between his toes. He thought of the lupins, and the man waiting. So many years had passed, and yet it was all as clear as if it had happened an hour ago. He had left the florins and the half crowns buried in the sand under the wooden steps outside the chalet. He had been afraid to spend the money, for surely his parents would have demanded to know where he had got it. It could be there still, his treasure trove, for all he knew.

The man, the lupin man, did not tell him his name.

Strafford had Garda Dineen drive him to the village, and on the phone in McEntee's he called Crowley at the Garda station in Wicklow and told him what had happened.

"An accident, by the look of it," he said.

"Did you question Wymes?" Crowley asked in his gravelly voice.

"The parents will have to be informed," Strafford said. "Don't use the phone, go over and tell them." He was remembering Charlotte in the house in Dublin, her cold calm gaze, her broad strong shapely hands. "Maybe tell the husband first, on his own, and he can tell the wife." He could hear Crowley breathing on the line. "Go easy on them."

Mr. McEntee, who had been listening from behind the bar, gravely bowed his head.

25

Quirke went with her in the ambulance. She was cold, despite the blanket they had wrapped around her and tucked in at the sides and under her feet. *Why is the blanket always red?* she wondered. *To camouflage the blood, when there was blood?*

It was daylight by now, and though it was still early, the morning rush hour had started, and the driver had to keep the siren going continuously. So many times in her life she had heard that sound and not given a thought to who it was inside the ambulance, swaddled in a blood-red blanket.

She had been back in bed only a few minutes when the pain intensified with such suddenness that again she thought she might faint. Her teeth were clenched and she was panting like a hunted animal run to ground. A hot stickiness again flooded her lap. She thought it must be a hemorrhage. She gave in, and called out to Quirke, but so weakly that she was surprised he heard her—had he been listening outside the bedroom door? He came in at a rush, and she was glad of the warmth of his bulk leaning over her.

"I'm bleeding," she told him.

"What kind of bleeding?" he asked, and laid a hand on her forehead, which was bathed in sweat.

"You'd better call someone," she said in a tiny voice, a voice out of childhood.

Ten minutes later the ambulance pulled up at the pastry shop downstairs, siren blaring. Everything was happening with dreamlike promptness, as if it had all been arranged in advance.

Where were they taking her? There was a hospital just down the street, a maternity hospital, at that: why wasn't she brought there? The ambulance wove through the traffic at frightening speed. When it came to a halt at last and she was lifted out on the stretcher, she saw that she was at the Hospital of the Holy Family after all. Quirke wanted her near him. She wasn't at all sure she wanted to be near him. He would want to know everything, and how would she resist telling him?

But of course he knew already. He was a doctor, he could recognize a miscarriage and its consequences. Yet to her surprise he said nothing, except to tell her not to worry, he would speak to the head nun, and call a consultant he knew. He would not look at her. She would have to find a way to keep him from going after Strafford. She knew how violent her father could be.

Yet he didn't seem angry. He was attentive, even tender. He held her hand as she was wheeled along. The seemingly endless, glistening corridors were painted the color of yellow phlegm.

The bleeding had stopped. She was put to bed—Quirke had arranged a private room for her—and given a sedative. The doctor was grave but kindly, the nurses brisk and efficient. The matron came, a gaunt nun with a sharp face and skin as pale and parched as bone. She noted Phoebe's bare ring finger and pursed her bloodless lips.

It was all so banal, so predictable—Phoebe felt like the errant daughter in a third-rate movie.

Quirke sat with her until she fell asleep.

Next day she was transferred—again the ambulance, again the blanket, but no siren this time—to a private nursing home in Clontarf. It was run by a tall and strikingly handsome woman, whom Quirke seemed to have known at some time in the past. His manner with her was tentative, even shy. Phoebe guessed she was one of his old flames, of which there were many. Her name was Mrs. White. Her eyes were hard, the irises black. She had the air of one harboring an old hurt. Was it Quirke, was it he who had hurt her?

Phoebe was put into a spacious upstairs room. There was a narrow bed with a blue spread, a chintz-covered armchair, and a highboy on which stood a pitcher and an enamel basin. The lace curtains at the window were frilled at top and bottom. The still air smelled of lavender. It all seemed familiar, somehow, familiar and yet remote, Phoebe thought. It was as if she had come all this way to find herself in her parents' bedroom. Her imaginary parents.

And indeed Mrs. White, however remote her manner, might have been a relative, close and yet not close—might be her stepmother, say.

There were two nurses, one tall and raw-boned and timid, the other freckled and bouncy and bright. Both recently up from the country, Phoebe guessed, with work-worn hands and plain, unmade-up faces. They were, it seemed, a little in awe of Phoebe, of her fragile beauty and calm assurance. They knew why she was here and couldn't understand how she could be as coolly unapologetic as obviously she was.

Mrs. White brought her up a cup of beef tea herself.

"We'll have to get your strength up," she said.

She did not mention the miscarriage.

In the afternoon, Strafford came to visit her. She was surprised. He had not called to say he was coming. Siobhan, the tall nurse, knocked on her door and told her she had a visitor, and Strafford walked in almost on her heels, with his hat in his hand. He had on that awful gabardine raincoat that made him look even more thin and gaunt than he was.

Phoebe was sitting up, propped against pillows, wearing a cardigan over a calico nightdress. Strafford approached the bed hesitantly, unsure of his welcome, she could see. She was not going to make things easy for him.

"Hello," she said, her tone deliberately flat, her look neither hostile nor welcoming.

"Your father told me you were here."

"Did he."

Strafford turned the brim of the hat in his hands.

"How are you?"

"I'm all right."

A silence.

"I phoned the flat this morning. I called half a dozen times. I wanted to see you."

"Did you."

He looked down at the hat.

"Please," he murmured.

"Please what?"

"Don't be like this."

"Like what?"

She knew she was overdoing it, but she couldn't stop. She hadn't realized until this moment how angry she was at him. So what if he had phoned half a dozen times? He had let days go past without a word, without a sign. Did he expect her now to be grateful to him?

He brought forward a straight-backed chair and set it beside the bed and sat down. In that raincoat, the good but shabby suit, the waistcoat and watch chain, he might be a solicitor's clerk, Phoebe thought, come to take instructions from a bed-bound client in some delicate legal matter.

It was stormy outside, and now a squall of rain clattered against the windowpanes like handfuls of flung gravel, and the casement rattled.

"I've come to ask you to marry me," Strafford said.

It sounded so affectless, he might have been remarking on the weather. Phoebe gave a brief cold laugh.

"Did your divorce come through already? That was quick."

To this he made no response, only sat erect on the straight chair, regarding her with that lugubrious, clerkly gaze.

Again the wind shook the window frame, again the rain flung quick hard drops against the glass.

"I lost the baby," Phoebe said.

"So I gathered."

"How did you gather it?"

"From your father. He didn't say it in so many words, but I guessed."

"What did he say, in so many words?"

Strafford thought about this, his head to one side.

"He was shocked. And worried. You know he loves you very much."

"Oh, yes, I know that," she said with heavy sarcasm. "So much, he pretended for the first two decades of my life that I wasn't his daughter at all."

"People make mistakes."

She was about to make a riposte, but closed her lips tight and stared straight before her, like a thwarted child. Then she said, "So when you heard what happened, you thought it was safe to make contact with me again, is that it?"

"I had called you before I spoke to your father."

"Was he drunk, by the way?"

"It was the middle of the morning."

"He can get drunk at any time of day. He has had a lot of practice, over the years."

And then, abrupt as a sneeze, the tears came on. Within seconds she was choking on big blurted openmouthed sobs. He put out a hand to her, but she batted it aside with a furious sweep of her arm.

"Don't touch me!" she gasped. "Don't you dare touch me!"

He sat back on the chair, aghast and helpless.

"I'm sorry, darling, I'm so sorry to have hurt you."

Even in her distress, she was inwardly calm enough to note that this was the first time he had called her darling. That was progress.

"Do you really think I'd marry"—sob—"a dry stick like you"—sob—"do you?"

He said nothing, just sat there looking at her with that stupid owlish gaze. She wanted to hit him. Meanwhile, he was thinking that if this helpless anguish churning inside him was an aspect of love, then it must be that he did love her.

"Do you want me to go, or shall I stay?" he asked at last.

"Go or stay—I don't care."

He looked to the rain-streaked window, then back to her again.

"Are you in pain?"

"Yes, I'm in pain!" she snapped. "I had a miscarriage. It's painful."

"I'm sorry."

"Please stop saying that," she muttered through gritted teeth. "You're sorry, I'm sorry, we're all sorry." She had stopped weeping. Suddenly, she laughed. "I'm surprised he didn't knock your block off."

"Who?"

"Who do you think?" Pain darted through her like a streak of boiling liquid, and she winced. "He may yet. You ruined his daughter, after all—didn't you, Lothario? That's what he calls you, you know. It's one of his more polite names for you."

The door opened and the freckled nurse put in her head and asked Phoebe if she should bring tea for her and Strafford. Phoebe thanked her and said no.

"Are you sure?" she said, eyeing Strafford with interest. "There'll be nothing else now until six o'clock."

"Thank you, Sadie," Phoebe said again. "I'm fine."

Rain dashed against the window. Winter has arrived at last, Strafford thought. He rather welcomed it, this year.

"You owe it to me to give me a proper answer to my proposal," he said mildly. "I'm serious, you know."

"Oh, you're serious, yes—you're always serious."

He waited a moment, looking at his hands.

"I'm not good at this kind of thing. Perhaps no one is. I was brought up to keep my emotions in check."

She snorted.

"Your emotions!"

Never before in his life had he known such acute, helpless misery. He supposed he deserved it. He had let himself drift into the affair with Phoebe. He had not expected her to love him, or that he would love her. Then, what had he expected?

He rose from the chair and stood beside the bed with his hat in his hands.

"I'll have to go," he said. "There's a bit of a crisis going on."

"What sort of a crisis?" she asked sullenly, not caring.

"A child's body was found yesterday morning."

"Where?"

"Place in Wicklow, by the sea. Kilpatrick."

"Whose child was it?"

"Little boy. People called Ruddock."

"Why do I know that name?"

"When that Trinity professor's wife disappeared, it was to them he went for help."

"And now their own child is dead? Christ, that's an unlucky corner of the Emerald Isle, for sure. Is there a connection?"

"I don't know. That's one of the things I have to find out."

Human beings are so strange, he thought. A minute ago we were fighting each other like animals, now we're talking calmly about other people's troubles.

He was still standing beside the bed. Phoebe leaned back against the cushions and closed her eyes.

"Pain again?" Strafford asked.

"He stopped me in the street, that fellow," she said, without opening her eyes.

"What fellow? Armitage?"

"He put a hand on my shoulder and invited me to come for a coffee."

"Did you go?"

"Yes. God knows why. I was curious, I suppose." She opened one eye and looked up at him. "I'm not in the habit of going to cafés with strange men, in case you're wondering."

"What did he want?"

"Don't know. Not the obvious, anyway." Now she opened the other eye and made an exaggerated pout. "I was rather miffed. The least he could have done was make a pass at a girl." He said nothing, and she looked up at him again. "He asked about you."

"What did he ask?"

"How long I'd known you, how we met. Things like that. It was all very peculiar."

Yes, Strafford thought, very peculiar indeed. Perhaps it was time to have another talk with Professor Armitage. He checked his watch.

"I really must go."

"Bye for now," Phoebe said. "And by the way, I will." He cocked a questioning eye at her. "Marry you. '"I will,'" she said.'" She smiled, wrinkling her nose. "You did ask. Haven't forgotten already, I hope."

The thought occurred to him, absurd yet oddly compelling, that her way of teasing him could be a stone in the foundation of a life together. Marguerite was incapable of teasing, and didn't recognize it when she was being teased herself.

"I haven't forgotten," he said. "Thank you."

He leaned down and kissed her lightly on the forehead. When she smiled up at him, he was surprised to realize that he had not noticed before how fine and white and even were her squarish little teeth.

Well then, it was done.

Phoebe was not the only one to suffer a hemorrhage that day. At 4:37 in the afternoon, in the big white bed in the room in St. James's Hospital, Chief Inspector Hackett felt a sudden fullness in his chest, before passing into a profound and soundless sleep. His left lung had filled up with blood. He was wheeled to the operating room, where he regained consciousness briefly and asked, firmly but politely, that his wife, May, be summoned. At just before five o'clock, the surgeon made the first incision. The operation had been proceeding for just under seventeen minutes, and a tumor almost two inches in diameter was being excised from the superior lobe of the left lung, when the patient died.

26

Strafford came out of the nursing home and walked down Castle Avenue to the front. It had stopped raining, but boilings of lead-blue cloud were sweeping in across the bay. He turned up the collar of his raincoat and crossed the road, buffeted by a cold and brackish wind. He stood in the inadequate shelter of a palm tree—they weren't really palms, but he couldn't remember the correct name for them—and looked along the road in hope of flagging a taxi.

He felt like a character in a cinema cartoon who had just run smack into a brick wall. There must be a halo of stars spinning around his head.

The truth was, he hadn't expected Phoebe to accept his proposal. He hadn't meant it to be accepted. He had made it out of a mixture of guilt, confusion and embarrassment. That didn't mean he had changed his mind about Phoebe. His love for her, or whatever to call it, was the same as it had been. Only, the thought of being married to her, actually married and living with her, seemed unreal. He simply couldn't imagine getting up in the morning and sitting opposite her at the breakfast table, of putting on his hat and coat and kissing her goodbye, of walking to the bus stop and turning to wave to her, where she stood in the doorway, waving too, smiling a smile of connubial bliss.

At the same time, he couldn't imagine his life going on without her. He had got used in no time to Marguerite's not being there, but Phoebe had somehow become the fixed point for him that his wife had never been. How was that?

The fact was, he did not understand himself, or Phoebe, or anyone. The vagaries of the human heart baffled him.

Here was a taxi, at last. He flung up an arm, and a wet gust from the sea smacked him full in the face.

The driver, old and wizened, was wearing a fur hat like a Russian soldier's.

"That wind would skin you," he said, and peered rheumy-eyed at Strafford in the rearview mirror.

"Pearse Street Garda station," Strafford said, and the old man looked at him with a sharper eye. The police were still regarded warily, after eight centuries of colonization.

And then there was Quirke to be reckoned with. Strafford almost laughed as he tried to picture himself asking that irascible and violent man for his daughter's hand in marriage.

No, he would leave it to Phoebe to convey to him the happy tidings of her engagement to Detective Inspector St. John Strafford, of Roslea House in the barony of Talgarth in the northwest corner of County Wexford.

On O'Connell Bridge, a double-decker bus had collided with a coalman's dray. A crowd had gathered, despite the rain, and a Guard in an oilskin cape and white gloves was diverting the traffic.

The taxi driver chuckled.

"Them bus drivers," he said, "are fucking eejits."

Strafford left the taxi at Pearse Street and went into the station, and was lifting the counter flap to go through to the stairs when the desk sergeant signaled to him. Crowley had been on the telephone three times in the past hour. A body had been discovered in a cove just down the coast from Courtown in County Wexford. It was the body of a woman, estimated to have been in the sea for at least a week, and badly decomposed.

What was the name of Armitage's wife? Doris? Dearbhla? No: Deirdre. Yes.

The news came at once that the chief was dead, and the station went into a strange hushed state that was part paralysis and part excitement. Nothing comparably momentous had occurred here since a young rookie—Devlin, something Devlin, his first name was long forgotten—had hanged himself from a crossbeam in the lean-to off Townsend Street where the squad cars were parked.

But Devlin's suicide couldn't be compared with the death of the chief. The chief had seemed immortal.

Over recent months, though, he had largely withdrawn into his stuffy little office high up at the back of the building. Strafford had become the de facto officer in charge. Now and then the chief would ask for a file to be brought up, or he would phone up one of the younger detectives to ask about the progress of a case, though from the tone of his voice it was clear his heart wasn't in it, and that he was only going through the motions.

No one knew how he had passed his time up there in his aerie. Occasionally, the internal phone on the duty sergeant's desk would jangle and it would be the old man, coughing and spluttering and gasping for breath, asking for someone to fetch him a ham and cheese sandwich and a bottle of stout from Mooney's over on College Green, or a pack of Player's and a box of matches, or a copy of the *Evening Mail*.

It was suspected these errands were an excuse to have someone come up to the office and visit him in his isolation, if only for a minute or two. At first he would seem eager to talk, then he would grow vague and scrabble about in the mound of papers on his desk, mumbling under his breath. On occasion he would even turn about in his swivel chair and gaze out of the window behind the desk, leaving whoever it was he had summoned to back out of the room and shut the door soundlessly.

Yet his going left a vast and unfillable absence. It was as if a sacred idol, present for so long that even the attendant priests had ceased to take much notice of it, had been stolen by some sacrilegious vandal, and suddenly the great, glittering temple was reduced to bricks and mortar, and nothing remained of its former sanctity, save a wisp of incense and a gleam of light through one corner of a stained glass window.

Strafford, when he heard the news, sat motionless at his desk for a full five minutes, gazing at nothing. Then he roused himself and put through a call to the Hospital of the Holy Family, and asked for the pathology lab. Quirke himself picked up the phone; this meant he was in his office, which was as cramped and musty as Hackett's, and the air as thick with the stench of immemorial cigarette smoke.

"Dead?" Quirke said. "No."

"There was some kind of emergency. Had a hemorrhage, I think. He died on the operating table."

"Jesus."

There was a long silence. Strafford heard the scrape and flare of a match, then the soft hiss of cigarette smoke being expelled.

"His wife was on the way to the hospital when it happened," Strafford said.

"I suppose we'll have to pay her a visit."

"Yes."

Another pause. Then Quirke said, "The end of an era."

It was not, as both men knew. It was just something one said, on such occasions.

"There's another thing," Strafford said. "Two things, in fact. A woman's body has been found in the sea down in Wicklow."

"The Armitage woman?"

"It looks like it."

"And the second thing?"

"The Ruddock child was killed."

"Killed?"

"Fell onto the rocks at Kilpatrick strand. An accident, so it seems."

27

In a gruesome conjunction, the remains of Armitage's wife and the Ruddocks' child were brought in the same ambulance to Dublin, and deposited together at the City Morgue. Quirke could not face carrying out a postmortem on the little boy. He called in David Hillmore, a young pathologist lately qualified and moved over from London, who was ambitious and would take any work that was going. Why he was in Ireland was nobody's business but his own.

"A hemophiliac," Hillmore said, with one of his sardonic half smiles, "and the little guy goes and breaks his neck. What are the odds?"

Deirdre Armitage's body had been in the sea for more than a week and was unrecognizable even to her husband. Every stitch of clothing was gone, of course, and some underwater creature, or a seabird perhaps, had got at her eyes. However, the string of pearls she had been wearing somehow survived, and that was how she was identified.

Strafford came down to the morgue, but Quirke advised him against viewing the corpse—"if you want to hold on to your lunch."

The two men went across to Molloy's on Talbot Street. Strafford could never be at ease in Quirke's company, but today he had more cause than ever to be wary of him, especially when he was drinking.

Phoebe was still in the nursing home in Clontarf. Despite her having accepted Strafford's proposal of marriage, the circumstances in which he had made it, and her almost offhand acceptance, had left him wondering if she had been serious or if she was just toying with him. He did not understand Phoebe's sense of humor, and never would, he suspected.

"The chief is to be buried in Leitrim," Strafford said.

They both looked aside. Given the distance, time and inconvenience, they would not have to attend Hackett's funeral, and to their shame they were glad of it. There had been talk in the station of a memorial drink-up at Mooney's across the road. But everyone knew they would be commemorating a man who in the final months of his life had become his own ghost.

Quirke ordered a gin and tonic, to Strafford's surprise and faint unease. He had never known him to drink anything other than whiskey, or brandy. Any deviation in Quirke's fixed ways made him especially wary.

"Good for the innards," he said, tapping a fingernail against the miniature Schweppes bottle. "Preventive of the Bombay tummy."

To this, Strafford could think of no response. Was it a joke? Was he supposed to smile, or laugh, even? He had not known what to expect of Quirke, after Phoebe's miscarriage. Rage, recrimination, violence perhaps. Instead, the man seemed to be in what for him was a quiet, even meditative, mood. At first, Strafford took it to be the calm before the storm. However, as they sat face-to-face on two high stools in front of a tall gilt-framed mirror, Quirke sipping his gin and Strafford toying with a cup of undrinkable, dark brown treacly stuff made from coffee essence, all was calm between them— almost, indeed, companionable.

"It was your child, I take it," Quirke said, frowning at his glass.

Again, Strafford made no reply, since any reply would be wholly inadequate.

Quirke brought out a cigarette and lighted it with slow, pensive movements. A horse and cart went by in the street. They listened to the unhurried clip-clopping of the horse's hooves and the grinding sound of the metal wheel-bands harshing on the tarmacadam. It sometimes seemed to Strafford that his life was a series of tableaux as elaborate, studied and unreal as a staged performance at Versailles at the height of the reign of the Sun King. This was one of those times.

The silence became intolerable, and he was compelled to break it, for fear of other, more consequential breakages.

"Yes, it was," he heard himself say. "And I've asked her to marry me."

Oh, a veritable Tartuffe.

"But you're married already," Quirke said. "Aren't you?"

"My wife is divorcing me. We were married in England, so it will be relatively easy."

"You'll still be regarded as a married man here."

"Only by the Church—the Catholic Church. Or so

Marguerite—that's my wife—assures me. She has looked into it."

Quirke set his glass on the bar and turned it slowly round and round on its base.

"What did Phoebe say? When you proposed to her."

"She said yes."

"Did she, now. That calls for another drink."

He signaled to the barman, pointing to his emptied glass.

Again there was silence, and again it was Strafford who spoke.

"I wish things could have been otherwise."

"You mean, you wish Phoebe hadn't got pregnant and you wouldn't have to offer to marry her?"

"No."

But what had he meant? Didn't he wish Phoebe hadn't got pregnant, didn't he wish he hadn't felt he had to propose to her?

Quirke said nothing for a long minute, then "You're not serious about this, are you? You're not going to marry Phoebe. You're nearly twice her age."

"I don't see what age has to do with it."

"Do you not?" Quirke was fiddling with his cigarettes. His hands had a faint tremor, Strafford noted. "If you won't think about her, think about yourself. When you're starting to get old, she'll be in her prime. Few things more laughable than an old man stuck with a young wife."

"If you look far enough ahead, everything becomes laughable. Even death, viewed from a certain perspective."

Quirke splashed the last gulp of tonic water from the little bottle into his glass, where it fizzed and frothed. The drink, suggestive to Strafford of nightclubs and feather boas, was as incongruous as everything else that was happening here. Cer-

tain moments, Strafford thought, detach themselves from the
flow of time and become legend on the spot. All his life he
would remember being here this afternoon, in this bar, with
the rain pattering against the window and the soft daylight
gleaming on mirrors, on brass, on polished oak, and Quirke
sitting hunched around himself, with his cigarette in his fingers and his flapper's bubbly drink before him.

"Phoebe has had troubles before," Quirke said. "Enough
for a lifetime."

"I don't intend to be a trouble to her."

Quirke nodded, but his look was bleak.

"She's all I have," he said.

Strafford thought about this. Quirke's daughter, whom he
had denied for twenty years, was not all he had. And anyway, she wasn't his, not any longer, if she ever had been. She
was a grown woman, with her own life, her own concerns,
her own joys and sorrows. He had no right to make so gross
a claim. He had forfeited her.

"I think," he said, slowing down his voice, "I think you
should move out of her flat."

It surprised him more than it seemed to surprise Quirke,
who only said, with a sort of laugh, "Why, so you can move
in?"

"Of course not."

What, then? Would Phoebe come to live with him, in the
flat on Mespil Road? Impossible. He thought of the Claridges,
Mr. and Mrs. and their surreptitious daughters. He thought of
Mr. Singh. He even thought of the unseen but ever-prompt
postman. As well introduce a woman—and a wife, at that—
into the meager midst of his domestic arrangement as lob a
small bomb onto the swirling purples and oranges of Mrs.
Claridge's hall carpet.

Then Quirke said, "She's all I have left in the world, you see."

He spoke without a trace of pathos or self-pity, but in an oddly brisk fashion, as if merely to illustrate some point made earlier.

Strafford looked at his shoes. Oxblood brogues, made by hand and to measure a quarter of a century ago by John Lobb of St. James's Street, London. They were in fact his father's shoes, or had been, before gout and ingrown toenails made them unwearable, and he had with bad grace passed them on to his son. They were a size too large for Strafford, but they fitted well enough if he wore two pairs of socks.

Something had happened, Strafford realized. Something in Quirke's matter-of-fact statement had flipped everything over, like a book being closed, or a mirror being turned to the wall. Quirke was right, not about Phoebe being the last thing left to him—that was just a clumsy attempt at emotional blackmail—but about the improbability, about the impossibility, of the entire thing. He would not marry Phoebe. Had he ever meant to, really? The notion was absurd—more, it was mad.

He would have to fix it somehow, would have to patch something together.

Maybe pretend Marguerite had changed her mind about the divorce. Or say his father had threatened to disinherit him if he married a Catholic, even though she had never practiced the faith. Not that there was much to disinherit him of, but Phoebe wasn't to know that.

Claim Quirke had threatened to have him kicked off the force?

Or maybe he should just run away, quit the flat on Mespil Road, put his few possessions in storage, and stay on in London after the divorce. He could look for a job at Scotland

Yard, or if not there then in one of the big northern cities, Liverpool, or Manchester. Or even in Scotland. What was the northernmost Scottish city, Dundee? Inverness? Or why not the islands, the Orkneys, or Shetlands—surely there would be an opening in Kirkwall, say, or Lerwick, for a no longer young but far from burned-out middle-ranking detective inspector.

Oh, come off it, he told himself.

"Have another coffee," Quirke said.

Strafford had returned to Pearse Street and was idling at his desk when the call came through. It was from the commissioner himself.

"That fellow, what's his name, the child molester—have you brought him in?"

"No, sir."

"Why not?"

Strafford turned in his chair and looked out of the window. The view, if it could be called a view, was much the same as in the office next door, which used to be Hackett's. Slanted rooftops, jostling chimney pots, distant spires, the very tip of the gable end of St. Mark's Church, then roiling clouds, and rain, and seabirds.

"I spoke to him. It was he who found the body. He took me to the spot." He could hear Phelan on the line, breathing, waiting. "I don't think he had anything to do with the child's death."

"You don't *think*?" Phelan said heavily.

Strafford could picture him at his desk, his big head and buffalo's shoulders thrust forward as if into a rugby scrum, bushy eyebrows bristling, the receiver dwarfed in his meaty, freckled fist. Same type as Charles Ruddock. He disliked

Strafford, the lapsed Protestant, and Strafford despised him, one of the leading lights of the Knights of St. Patrick.

"I don't believe he would be capable of killing a child, sir."

"Have you looked at his record?" There was the sound of pages flipping. "Couldn't keep his hands off them."

"Yes, but—"

"Bring him in," Phelan said. "Bring him in and grill him. That's an order."

Grill him. Phelan had seen too many Hollywood gangster films.

"Right, sir. I'll send someone down to fetch him."

"Down where?"

"County Wicklow. He lives in a trailer, Kilpatrick beach."

"Where's that? Where's it near?"

"Wicklow town."

"Toss Crowley is there, isn't he?"

"Yes, sir."

"Get on to him." More heavy breathing. "Kilpatrick. Isn't that where that woman disappeared, the one that was found yesterday?"

"The same area, yes."

"What the bloody hell is going on? Is there a maniac on the loose?"

Strafford watched lines of rain wriggling across the windowpanes. Must be windy out there. The second summer was already a fading memory.

"The thing is, sir, there's no evidence of any wrongdoing."

"Wrongdoing?" Phelan said, and snorted.

"It appears the woman drowned, and the child fell and was killed. I'm waiting for the postmortem results."

Phelan snorted again.

"Quirke on the job?"

"Yes, the woman. Dr. Hillmore is doing the child."

"Who's he?"

"He's new."

He heard Phelan putting his hand over the phone and turning away to speak to someone in the room. Then he came back.

"What?"

"I said, he's new here. Dr. Hillmore."

"Yes. Right." A humid pause. "Listen, Strafford, I want you to bring in that fellow Wymes or whatever he's called, bring him in today and go through him like a dose of salts. Understood?"

"Yes, sir."

The receiver at the other end dropped onto its cradle with what sounded to Strafford like a rancorous click.

He waited a minute, still turned to the window, still watching the raindrops slanted on the glass. Phelan hadn't actually ordered him to direct Crowley to bring in Wymes. Crowley would probably stop off somewhere to get himself tanked up, then haul Wymes into the station and throw him in a cell and beat the daylights out of him.

No.

He dialed the sergeant on duty downstairs.

"Send Garda Dineen down to Kilpatrick beach, pick up Denton Wymes—what?" He spelled the name. "It's pronounced Weems. Dineen will know where to find him. He's to bring him back here. What? Yes, now. This afternoon. Commissioner's orders."

At five o'clock, the commissioner was put through again. Strafford assumed he would be asked for a progress report on Wymes's arrest, but he was wrong.

"Paddy Carson will be taking over from Hackett, temporarily. Arrange for Hackett's office to be cleaned, will you? Still a rubbish heap, I suppose?"

"It's a bit untidy, sir, yes. I'll get on to the cleaners."

"Good. Oh, and sorry about the old man."

"Thank you, sir."

"At least he went quick."

"Yes."

Chief Inspector Patrick Carson hailed from the Falls Road in Belfast. Despite his second name, and as indicated by his first, he was a Catholic. He had been stationed along the border since leaving Templemore Garda Training College some fifteen years ago. He had risen rapidly through the ranks, and had been the youngest chief inspector on record. He was a bully, and a bigot.

"He's coming down from Dundalk next week," Phelan said. "He'll be taking up his duties immediately. And listen. He's a rough diamond, but he's a fine officer nevertheless. Mind you show him respect."

This time, the clatter of the receiver on its cradle sounded like a bark of derisive laughter.

Poor Strafford.

He was putting on his coat and about to leave for the evening when the phone rang again. He thought of leaving it unanswered, but picked it up instead. It was Quirke.

"The Armitage woman," he said. "I've just finished the PM."

"And?"

"She didn't die in the sea. She drowned in fresh water."

28

He was halfway there before he realized where he was going. When he did, he laughed out loud and smacked the steering wheel with the palm of his right hand. The murderer returning to the scene of the crime! Ha!

But why the surprise? It wasn't the first time, after all. Hadn't he gone back to have a sniff around the lock-up in Herbert Lane where he'd left Rosa Jacobs choking on the exhaust fumes from her own car? And years and years before that, didn't he used to loiter in the great hall of the railway station in Manchester where one bleak winter midnight he pushed Doreen Huckstable off a deserted platform No. 1, his poor, simple, kindhearted but inconveniently pregnant Doreen, and watched her tumble under the wheels of the Edinburgh express? And now here he was, on the way to that bleak shore in Wicklow and the spot where just over a week ago he had dumped his wife's limp, damp and unexpectedly cumbersome corpse. He was incorrigible, he really was.

It was madness, of course, but he felt like doing something mad. He had become increasingly concerned, as the days went on and Dee's body still hadn't been found. He wasn't sure why it should matter, but it did. It worried him. It was a loose end, and he didn't like loose ends. When the call came—he was in his office, wading through a pile of half-witted undergraduate essays—he almost cheered, which wouldn't have done at all. You couldn't sneeze in that building without someone coming to your door to complain about the noise.

"Poulshone Bay, near Courtown," the voice on the phone had said. "Do you know the area, sir?"

"What?" Honestly, the names they give to these places. "No, no, I haven't been there." Nor had he.

"A woman was out early, walking her dog, and spotted the body washed up in a cove."

"You're sure it's her?"

"We're not sure, sir, no. But the height and age match, and no one else has been reported missing in those parts." A pause, then a considerate little cough. "There was a necklace."

"What sort of necklace?"

"Pearls."

He left the essays sitting on the desk and took a taxi to the City Morgue. What a ghastly hole that was, worse even than he would have expected.

That plainclothes cop was there, what was his name? Stafford?

Dee was lying on her back on a trolley under a white nylon sheet. He managed not to look at her face for more than a second or two, before the sheet was replaced. He would hardly have recognized her, except for the hair. She had always

been proud of her hair. Auburn, she said it was, "my auburn
tresses." More the color of melted toffee, to his eye. When
they were in bed, she liked him to take hold of a swatch of it
and wrap it around his fist and tug it hard a few times as the
crucial moment approached. Those little squeals she gave,
half of pleasure and half of pain. Ah well.

They showed him the pearls.

"Yes, yes, they're hers," he said, and produced a sob so
heartfelt he was almost convinced himself.

"Sit down here for a minute, sir, and the porter will bring
you a cup of tea."

Thanks, he felt like saying, *but could you make it a glass of
champagne instead?*

He drank the tea, he nibbled at the digestive cookie that
came with it.

Everybody was so polite and kind, he almost shed a real
tear. He tried out a sniffle, but it was harder to do than a sob,
and he didn't repeat it.

They offered to call a taxi for him, and asked if there was
anyone at home. He didn't understand—what did they mean?

"You've had a shock, sir, you shouldn't be on your own."

"I'll be fine." He gazed soulfully into the middle distance.
"I'm just glad she's been found at last. My poor Dee."

He enjoyed his performance—he should have been an
actor—but told himself not to overdo it. On the way out he
stumbled, and had to lean against the wall for a moment to
recover himself. They were right, he was in shock, only not
the kind of shock they meant. It was only now that he realized
how tense he had been this past week, longing for news and
at the same time dreading it. Now he was giddy with relief.
He had got away with it. He was free. And he had Deirdre's
money all to himself. When he walked out through the gate

into a gray drizzle, he felt like skipping a few steps for simple joy. He felt as if he were eighteen again.

The police, or the Gardai, or whatever to call them, had brought up the car from Wicklow. Thank you very much, I'm sure. The Garda driver, a taciturn fellow with an enormous head, advised him in an oddly confidential tone that the right front tire was bald, and should be replaced. He had thanked him, and looked away again, tragically, as he had done in the morgue, and Garda Humpty-Dumpty had cleared his throat, made a sort of salute, handed over the car key, and taken himself off.

What to do then? It would look odd if he went back to the office. He felt like strolling up to the Hibernian Hotel and ordering a steak and chips and a nice bottle of claret. But what if somebody he knew were to see him, tucking into the funeral baked meats and swilling down expensive plonk?

What ho, Ronnie, you're looking cheery and bright.

Yes, just been to view the trouble and strife, sodden and swollen and laid out on a slab like a sack of blubber.

So he went home instead, and cooked himself a lamb chop and ate it with cold potatoes from the fridge and half a tomato. No wine in the house, but plenty of whiskey. He sat in the living room listening to *Workers' Playtime* on the radio. Anne Shelton sang a song, then Charlie Chester did his routine. The audience roared. The Stargazers did "Broken Wings," as usual—their one big hit. Dee used to sneer at him for listening to "that stuff," but he didn't care. He had no ear for music, and the jokes were awful, but the show made him feel gently nostalgic for his young days. Silly, of course—he had long ago shaken the dust of Salford from his heels and intended never to set eyes on the place again.

He went into the lounge to pour another whiskey and discovered he was still wearing the apron he had put on when he was preparing his lunch. It was made of blue cotton, or was it linen, heart-shaped, with a scalloped edge. He had tried once to get Dee to wear it in bed—"you know, like a French maid"—but she made a disgusted face and said if he wanted that kind of thing, he should go down to that place in Temple Bar and hire a tart.

The whiskey made him feel drowsy, so he turned off the radio—the news was on next, then *Mrs. Dale's Diary*—and had a lie-down in the front bedroom upstairs. He couldn't sleep, though, and after ten minutes he got up again and wandered restlessly through the empty rooms. Something had happened to the house after Deirdre's departure; a great silence had settled on it, or better say a *soundlessness*, as if something were being withheld, a word, a cry, a plea.

Back in the living room, he tried to make himself sit down with a book, but then he glanced out of the window and saw the Merc parked outside. Why not take her for a spin? The rain had stopped, or paused, at least.

What was it called, where her body was found? Poulsomething. He hunted around for the RAC touring map of Ireland, and found it at last in a drawer in the kitchen. He spread it out on the table and ran his finger down the line of the east coast. Poulshone. How had the fellow on the phone pronounced it? Something like *Powellshown*. Ridiculous country, with its ridiculous place names.

He tootled happily along the sea road, whistling the tune of "Broken Wings." Big bundles of lead-blue cloud out over the bay threatened rain—for a change. The tide was a mile out. Why so shallow, along here? Booterstown, Blackrock, Monkstown. There was a restaurant along here where he and

Deirdre used to go, before everything went stale between them. What was it called? The Guinea Fowl, something like that. Good mussels, oysters if they were flush, bit of cod or a nice grilled sole. Happy times.

At Dún Laoghaire, or Kingstown, as it used to be, the rain came on in a cloudburst, sliding down the sky like curtains of soiled lace. In Bray he stopped at a pub and drank another whiskey. At the other end of the bar, a blowsy blonde with crooked lipstick sat alone with a gin and tonic in front of her. She gave him the eye, and he smiled back at her. Rare to see, a woman drinking on her own in the middle of the afternoon. Maybe he should go and sit beside her and tell her all about his great loss, boo-hoo. Poor old Dee, with her flat chest, her little cold hands, her toffee-colored hair. Pity she had to go.

It was a spur-of-the-moment thing. He had barged into the bathroom by mistake—she never would lock that blasted door—and there she was, lying full length in the bath with only her head above the surface of the lightly steaming water. She looked up at him, wide-eyed, and said not a word. She seemed less startled than guilty. Maybe she'd been having a go at herself, thinking dirty thoughts about her hunk of a lover.

It was simple. He just put a hand gently on the top of her head and pushed her under not so gently and kept her there until she stopped thrashing about. The strength of her! He had to sit on the side of the bath for a minute to get his breath back.

Then his troubles started. She was, literally, a dead weight, and slippery besides, until he got the towel around her. He had to clean her up, something he hadn't expected, and which almost made him vomit. How he got her into a dress he didn't know, but somehow he managed it.

The grisliest moment of all was when he had laid her on the bed and was fastening the necklace round her neck and he glanced up and caught his reflection in the mirror above her dressing table. Didn't seem himself at all, with that look in his eyes and his side teeth bared. Dr. Crippen, or who was that other fellow, in the house on Rillington Place. Was he like them? No, not at all. Not at all.

He made sure the coast was clear—Sandymount was a quiet spot on a weekday afternoon—and carried her out and sat her in the passenger seat and shut the door. Her head fell over and bumped against the glass. He thought of throwing a blanket or a coat over her, but decided against it, and left her that way, slumped to the side with her mouth open. Anyone seeing her would think she was asleep. In real life, people weren't as alert and nosy as they are in detective stories.

What was going through his head? He couldn't remember now. When he thought back, it seemed to him his mind had been a blank. He drove along like a robot, sitting up very stiff and straight in the seat with both hands set firmly on the steering wheel, his eyes fixed on the road unwinding ahead of him like a roll of linoleum.

Was I mad that day? he wondered. *Am I mad now? Have I always been mad?* He found the question interesting. He had not entertained it before. Wasn't it said that lunatics didn't know they were lunatics, and that it was a mark of their lunacy? But you couldn't be mad and be this calm, could you?

Poulshone was a bleak spot. There was a bit of strand, and a few holiday homes behind, and that was it. He couldn't see much of it, since the rain was still coming down in sheets. All the same, he parked the car above the dunes and stayed there for half an hour or more, sitting behind the wheel and gazing through the streaming windshield, thinking, remembering.

He had known for weeks, for months, that something was going on. At the end of the summer, Dee had suddenly started being extra nice to him. He would come home from work and she'd meet him at the door and kiss him and smile, wrinkling her nose in the way she had seen some film star do. She prepared special dinners for him, with things she knew he particularly liked, veal chops with spinach and fried potatoes, rolled pork stuffed with breadcrumbs and sage, thick sirloin steaks fried until they were crunchy on both sides.

She would sit with him while he was eating—she was on a diet herself, though she never put on weight—and listen with smiling attentiveness while he told her about his day and the shits in the department whom he was in the process of shafting before they got a chance to shaft him. She was different in bed, too, unrestrained, rough at times, biting his lips and raking her nails along his back and asking him to hit her. But all the time her mind, he could see, was elsewhere.

Then he found the letter.

He often took a little peek in her handbag, out of curiosity more than any desire to spy on her. A woman's handbag is a world apart. That day, though, he was only looking for change for the gas meter. The strangest thing was that the letter, folded into a zipped-up side pocket of the bag, was not from her lover to her, but from her to her lover. And it was not as if she had forgotten to send it, or had thought better of it at the last minute, for it was postmarked and had been delivered, opened and, surely, read. Why had she got it back from him? Maybe there had been a row and she had demanded that he return all her correspondence. Were there others like this one, hidden somewhere in the house? He did

a thorough search, but found nothing. The little mystery remained, and he was sorry now he hadn't confronted her and
forced her to tell him the truth. But then there wouldn't have
been the element of surprise, and she would have been ready
for him in the bathroom that day, and would have fought
back even harder.

When he finished reading the letter, his mouth went so
dry he had to drink three full glasses of water, straight off,
one after the other, standing at the kitchen sink and staring at a window box full of geraniums on the sill outside.
The flowers were lavishly in bloom, but he didn't even see
them. He was upset. He was very upset. He was more upset
than he had ever been in his life, which was saying a lot, for
in his life he had been required to deal with some serious
annoyances—one of them being a certain Jewish bitch who
one day out of the blue had announced that she was pregnant and that the child was his. Turned out it was a fib, but
by then he had already dealt with her.

And how was he to deal with this latest blow? His wife,
having it off with a rugby player. That could not be allowed
to stand, no, it could not.

It was handy, the letter, since it gave him not only the bastard's name but his address, too.

He immediately put an investigation in train. There was
a former student of his who had gone bad, whom he had
helped, and who still owed him a few favors. It was he who
had supplied the stuff needed to neutralize Jezebel Jacobs the
Unpregnant, and now he called on his services again. Less
risky, this time: just some background info on this Ruddock character, the rugby player who was shagging his wife
in secret.

It came to him that between them they had made him a

cuckold. This was a position he had never expected to find himself in, and he didn't like it, not one bit.

Cuckold. Ugly word, silly too. Was there a term, he wondered, for the one who does the cuckolding?

Now, at Poulshone beach, he sat listening to the rain clattering on the roof of the car and faced, for the first time really, a shaming fact. It was Ruddock he should have bumped off, not poor old Dee. But Dee had been an easier target. The evening he came back from dumping her body on that rocky beach and went up to the house and got his first look at the usurper, he realized he had been right to take his revenge on Dee and leave this fellow alone. Bloody great brute, he was, thighs as thick as tree trunks and a chin like Desperate Dan's.

It was absurd, as he knew now, but at the time he had not doubted for a moment that it would be Ruddock who would discover Dee's body, first thing next morning. How could he have been so deluded? The morning came, then the evening, then the next day and the next, and nothing happened. Dee had simply vanished, taken by the sea, as they say. Had something attacked her and eaten her? He had heard there were basking sharks in these waters. Or maybe she had got lodged under a rock, or been washed far out and swept away by the currents.

Nobody suspected him of having got rid of her. Maybe the possibility had crossed Ruddock's mind—he had given him some funny looks that evening at the house—but if so, he had said nothing. But then, why would he? He would have been determined to stay as far away from the thing as possible. A bit of clandestine hanky-panky now and then did no one any harm, but if she was dead, that could be serious for him and his reputation.

His missus, the tall chick with the fancy accent, looked as if she was having some suspicions of her own.

Only afterward did he come to realize what a risk he had taken that night. It was one thing doing in poor Dee—no wife of his was going to have it off with a rugby player and get away with it—but dumping her body on the shore just down from the house where her paramour was staying over Halloween, that had been, to say the least, unwise. What if Ruddock, or the wife, Mrs. Hoity-Toity, *had* found the body? He would have had to confess he'd been screwing her, it would have been too risky not to, since it would have been bound to come out sooner or later. And surely the cops, even though they were stupid Micks, would have put two and two together.

So all in all it was best the way it had turned out, the body found way up here and nothing to connect Dee with Ruddock, except that he had gone up to the house that night, along with the fisherman. But why then was he on his way back to the said scene of the said crime? He knew it was madness, yet something was drawing him on, irresistibly.

Madness. There was that word again.

Yet he felt he could indulge himself a little. He was feeling remarkably confident. Three times he had done it now, and three times he had come through scot-free. He supposed that in murder, as in everything else, one's skills only improved with practice. Certainly, the first time, he hadn't been anything like as cocky as he was now. There was hardly a moment went past when he wasn't thinking about Doreen, reliving that moment when she disappeared under the train. What if the driver had spotted him on the platform the second before he pushed her? But no, no—at that speed, everything would be a blur. He knew that, and yet he worried.

He thought up all kinds of crazy schemes. He would forge a suicide note in Doreen's handwriting. He would get his friend Eddie in Hull to say he had been up there visiting him that night. He would put the word around that it was someone else's baby Doreen was carrying. In the end he did nothing, only waited, biting his nails, sweating, listening for the heavy hand of the law to come knocking. But no knock came, and eventually he was able to sleep at night again.

So strange, though, one minute she was there, babbling away, telling him how much she loved him and what a wonderful baby they were going to have, the next she was gone.

The only worry he had this time was that lanky detective with the lock of hair hanging over his forehead. He looked like a dope, but there was something about him, an edge, a sharpness, that said he wasn't dopey at all.

His girlfriend—why had he stopped her in the street like that?

When he was a kid, someone brought a shock machine into school one day. A copper coil, a winder, a battery, two wires tipped with solder. He was the one who had held on longest. It was like having a wet dream, the electricity going through him gave him the same kind of jolts. It had been like that with the girl. It was a big risk, accosting her like that.

Her name was Phoebe. He hadn't expected her to come with him to the café, but she had. He must have made an impression on her. Some women were able to feel the darkness in you, and the pent-up, smoldering rage. It excited them. He'd look out for her again. Yes, that could be interesting. She was skinny, with not much in the way of hips or tits, but she wasn't bad-looking. That pale neck. Just look out for Limp Lock, he told himself.

He drove away from Poulshone in the rain that at last had

begun to slacken. What did he intend to do? No question of his returning to that house on the hill, certainly not, but what was to stop him calling in to that pub where he had stayed? He could say that Dee's body had been found and that he was retracing her last steps on this side of eternity.

My heart is broken, I can't believe she's gone, lend me a hankie.
Aw, you poor chap—have another, on the house.
Thanks, I don't mind if I do.

McEntee's was full. There had been a soccer match, which the local team had won, and the hicks had come in from all over for a celebration. When he had finally managed to push his way to the bar, McEntee looked as if he would swallow his false teeth.

"Is it yourself, sir?" he said, putting on a big smile, though his eyes flicked this way and that and he licked his lips with a fat gray tongue-tip. Word had got round already about Dee having been found. "Aw, God, sorry for your trouble," the publican mumbled, and he turned away to pour a glass of Bushmills. Which he charged for. *Wasn't all that sorry for my troubles, then.*

He stayed too long, and drank too much—four, or was it five, whiskeys? And the measures here were about a third larger than on the mainland. He stood all that time in the same spot, an elbow on the bar and the heel of his shoe hooked on the footrail. The more of the spirits he downed, the lower his own spirits sank. What was he doing here, among these noisy, red-faced local yokels, knocking back Bushmills as if there were no tomorrow and grinning like a loon at his reflection in the mirror behind the bar?

Then he spotted the sandy-haired sergeant, what was his name? Cowley—no, Crowley. He was in the thick of it, red-

faced and shouting louder than the rest. Their eyes met, and
the fellow shut his mouth and stood there swaying and staring.

He pushed through the crowd and stopped in front of him.

"Have a drink," he growled, phlegm rattling in his throat.

*No thanks, honestly, I've had more than my measure as it is,
must be on my way, nighty-night.*

This was ignored.

"I hear they found your missus." *Yes, they found her.*
"Drowning your sorrows, are you?" *Something like that, yes.*

Then he leaned in, close enough to be smelled.

"I know you did it, you fucker."

Did what?

"She didn't drown in the sea."

"No?"

"No. She drowned, she *was* drowned, in fresh water."

That was enough, that was that. He paid for the whiskeys
and turned and fled, barging his way through the crowd.
Crowley was saying something behind him but he didn't
listen, didn't hear.

Outside, the night glistened. The rain had stopped but
the air felt like liquid. He started up the car, and as he drove
away he saw Crowley coming out of the pub with a raincoat
pulled over his head.

Drive, you fool!—drive!

And drive he did, too fast, far too fast. After he had gone
a mile or so, he realized he had gone the wrong way at the
cross. He found a gap in which to turn the car, and drove
back all the way to the pub, and this time turned left onto
the back road toward Dublin.

It was a black night. Trees at either side of the road sprang
up in the headlights and loomed inward like waving arms. He
met no other cars. The sea was somewhere out to his right,

he could smell it, and once or twice he spotted a lightship flashing in the distance.

A bird swooped down and quickly up. An owl? Bad omen.

What an idiot he had been, coming down here to flaunt himself in front of a crowd of drunken hicks. *Hubris*, he told himself: that was the word.

He didn't recognize the road. Surely he hadn't gone wrong again?

There was something ahead, a bridge, or a narrow causeway. A car was slewed at an angle in front of it, the lights off. He braked, but the wheels skidded sideways—he heard again the Guard with the sticking-out ears murmuring about the tire being bald—and sank into the ditch and the world at the left tilted up at a steep angle. The engine had died, and in the sudden silence he heard himself give a little moan.

It was a Garda car, there in front of him, blocking his way. A figure stood beside it. Short, squat, with a bulldog's blunt head.

Yes, *hubris*.

The man standing at the car came forward with a hand lifted, palm forward.

Crowley.

29

It turned out that Crowley had arrested Wymes, or detained him at least, and he was being held at the Garda station in Wicklow town. So Strafford took the Rosslare Harbour train and got off at Wicklow. He had telephoned ahead, and Billie the stand-in cab driver was waiting for him outside the station. The dose of flu that had put her father off the road was a bad one, and he hadn't yet recovered from it.

"Just to the barracks, is it?" she said.

"The Garda barracks, yes. Will you wait?"

"There won't be a train back to Dublin until tonight."

"I'll take the bus."

She started the engine, and they pulled out of the bleak forecourt and headed toward the town.

"I hear that man is under arrest," Billie said, glancing up

into the rearview mirror. "The one you came down to see last time."

"How do you know?"

She glanced up again, her mouth lifted at one corner.

"It's a small place, word gets around." She paused. "Is it about the child, the one that was found out at Kilpatrick strand?" He said nothing. She shrugged.

"I hope to God he didn't do it."

"There was no evidence of foul play."

"Is that so? They're saying in the town he was pushed off the bank and broke his neck, the poor little fellow."

"As I say, there's no evidence of such a thing."

"Right."

She seemed slightly offended, as if he had accused her of spreading false rumors.

A middle-aged Guard was on duty. His manner was surly. A visitor from Pearse Street wasn't welcome here.

Sergeant Crowley was off sick, he said.

"What's wrong with him?"

The Guard shrugged.

"He's sick," he said. "His missus phoned in. She didn't say what was wrong."

Strafford gazed at him, nodding slowly.

"Mr. Wymes," he said then, "I'd like to talk to him. You are holding him here, yes?"

"He's here. But I'd have to check with the sergeant as to whether I can let you see him."

"Will you phone, then, and check?"

"His wife said he wouldn't be available."

"I've no wish to avail of him," Strafford said. He was determined not to let himself get angry, or angrier than he already was. "I'm asking you to ask him—to tell him—that I'm here to speak to Mr. Wymes."

The Guard stood a moment, stony-faced, a muscle in his jaw working. Then he shrugged, opened a drawer in his desk and brought out a set of large, old-fashioned keys strung on a metal hoop.

"Come on," he said shortly, and turned away, rattling the keys.

Strafford followed him along a corridor painted a bilious shade of green. At the end, on either side of a frosted-glass window, there were two cells, facing each other. Wymes was lying on the narrow, bare bunk, with his arms lifted and the backs of his hands resting on his forehead. He wore a pair of thin cotton trousers and an old padded jacket with a tear in one sleeve. His belt and shoelaces had been taken from him. He rose slowly from the bunk, clutching the front of his trousers with one hand to hold them up. He was ashen-faced, and his eyes kept flickering here and there, as if there were small creatures scurrying about that only he could see. Strafford had noticed how he winced when he stood up.

"Are you all right?" he asked.

Wymes's glance darted toward the Guard, who was standing behind Strafford. Strafford could hear him breathing.

"I'm all right," Wymes said.

It was plain he was afraid of the Guard. Strafford turned.

"Could you leave us alone, please?"

The Guard stared at him, hesitated a moment, then stepped forward and unlocked the cell.

"I'll be in the day room," he said, making it sound like a threat. Then he went off.

Strafford opened the heavy, barred door and stepped into the cell.

"Did they beat you?" he asked.

The man before him looked aside.

"A few punches," he said. "I've had worse."

"Did Sergeant Crowley charge you?"

Wymes stared at him.

"What would he charge me with? I didn't lay a finger on that child. The first I saw of him was when I found him in among the rocks."

"Yes," Strafford said. "The postmortem was carried out last evening. There's no sign of violence, other than the fall. The pathologist's opinion is that the death was accidental."

This news had no visible effect on Wymes. He sighed, and pressed a hand to his ribs on the right.

"Crowley told me he has witnesses who say they saw me with the child, up on the grassy bank."

"What witnesses?" Strafford asked sharply. "This is news to me. Who are they?"

"McEntee, the publican, and the fellow who has the shop in the village. Mulrooney." He looked at the floor. "They're lying," he said, without emphasis, as if he were repeating a statement he had made already and did not expect anyone to take notice of it.

"Sit down for a moment," Strafford said. They sat side by side on the bunk. A sudden gust outside smacked against the window in the corridor, making it rattle. "I'm going to have them release you. They have no reason to hold you here."

"What about McEntee, and the other fellow? They'll tes-tify against me." He paused, then said wearily and without a trace of bitterness, "I'm not wanted around here." He gave a sort of laugh. "Not that I'm wanted anywhere else, either."

Strafford sat with his elbows on his knees and his hands clasped before him. He was wearing his raincoat, and had placed his hat beside him on the bunk. Wymes picked up the hat and transferred it to a three-legged stool.

"Bad luck," he said, "a hat on a bed."

Now Strafford stood up and paced the length of the cell twice. He stopped.

"None of this is right," he said. "Did Crowley caution you?"

Wymes shook his head, and again gave a brief laugh.

"No. Not unless you count a punch in the ribs. That felt like caution enough."

A thought occurred to Strafford. He stopped pacing.

"What about your dog?" he asked. "Where is he?"

"In the trailer. He'll be in an awful state." Wymes touched a hand to his forehead. "Would you do something for me? Would you arrange for him to be put down? Bill Cullen, the vet, is a decent man. I'll give you his number."

"Is the dog sick?"

Wymes looked up with an awful smile.

"No. But there'll be no one to look after him." Strafford was about to protest, but Wymes lifted a hand to silence him. "I'm finished," he said. "They'll put me away, you'll see. You're not from round here, you don't understand. I'm a thorn in their side, a standing offense to respectable people."

Strafford was shaking his head.

"I'm going to get you out of here," he said. "I've no intention of leaving you to the mercy of a lynch mob."

But they both heard how unconvincing he sounded.

He was thinking of a moment at the house, with the Ruddocks, and with Charlotte in particular, the day the child disappeared. He was in the kitchen with her, and she was sitting on a chair, with her face in her hands. Ruddock had come in from outside, with Crowley behind him, and she

had looked up at her husband with an expression that Strafford could not interpret. He had thought about it afterward,
and was still thinking about it. There was expectation in her
eyes, and a mixture of hope and fear, but something else as
well. Of course, she was afraid of what Ruddock might have
to say to her, afraid that he would tell her she must brace herself, that the child had been found, and that she would not
see him again alive. But it had seemed somehow that this
was not her first concern. Her eyes were asking something
of Ruddock, a silent something that nevertheless he heard,
and which he declined to answer.

What had she asked? What disclosure was she begging
him not to make? And what had happened on that grassy
slope above the rocks onto which the child had plummeted,
and died?

He felt as if he were staring into an abyss, where a dark
thing stirred. He did not know what to do. He could not
speak out on the basis of a look, a look from a woman gripped
by terror and awful foreboding. If Crowley brought forward
his witnesses—what debts did those two owe to him, what
favors were they returning?—Wymes could well be con-
victed of killing the child, given his record. They would put
him away for life this time. He would die in prison, that almost went without saying. *Could I save him?* Strafford asked
himself. Would the court take account of testimony based
on nothing more than a look from Charlotte Ruddock, and
his suspicion based on that look?

He had slept with her, in her and her husband's house, in
their child's bed. What if that fact were somehow to be revealed?

The Guard was coming back, they heard the door of the

day room opening and his footsteps approaching along the corridor.

Wymes stood with the front of his trousers bunched in his fist, watching Strafford.

I must do something, Strafford told himself.

But he did not know what.

Armitage's body wasn't found until early that afternoon, and so the evening papers got the story. "THIRD DEATH IN COUNTY WICKLOW," the *Mail* bellowed on its front page. The subheading was more specific: "Widowed Trinity Professor Recovered from Sea." There was a tacit agreement among journalists not to report suicides, so as to spare the feelings of the families. More to the point, no one wanted to give the insurance companies an excuse to renege on standing policies on the lives of the deceased.

All the same, the circumlocutions the reporters employed were easily deciphered, intentionally so.

An Englishman, Professor Ronald Armitage (46), whose body was found this afternoon washed up on the beach at Poulshone, Co. Wicklow, had recently suffered the loss of his wife, Deirdre. She too died by drowning, just over a week ago, and her body was discovered yesterday, also at Poulshone.

Professor Armitage, a native of Salford, was the Lecky Professor of History at Trinity College, Dublin, for the past eight years. It is thought he had been suffering from depression since the disappearance of his wife, and those close to him said the discovery of her body yesterday would have been a crushing blow to the bereaved man.

Gardai say their investigations are continuing, and

foul play is not suspected, and no one else was involved in Professor Armitage's demise. The alarm was raised after his car, a Mercedes sports, was noticed seemingly abandoned at Bansha Bridge close to Poulshone with its right wheels sunk in a culvert.

Fr. Eamon Murphy, parish priest of Wicklow town, said this double drowning, along with the tragic death of little Beverly Ruddock, had left people in the area reeling from shock. "We pray for the souls of Professor and Mrs. Armitage," Fr. Murphy said, "and offer sincere condolences to the families of the deceased."

30

Late on a wet Friday afternoon, Quirke went out by taxi to collect Phoebe from the nursing home on Castle Avenue. The moisture drifting slantways across the bay was more mist than rain, and sat on the shoulders and lapels of Quirke's overcoat like beads of clouded glass. Kate White herself opened the front door. She gave him a smile, sardonic yet intimate, as she used to, in the old days. Over the past week, she had warmed to Phoebe.

"She's her father's daughter, but I like her."

Quirke raised his eyebrows.

"Does that mean you don't like me?"

At the end of the hall she handed him over to Sadie with the freckles, who led him up to Phoebe's room. She was sitting on an upright chair, dressed and with her bag at her feet, waiting for him. Pale and drawn still, he saw. She had lost weight, too. But she was smiling, and when he came in she rose from the chair and kissed him, which she did not often do.

"How are you?"

"All the better for getting out of here."

"Oh, now!" said Sadie the nurse, putting on a face.

"I don't mean you," Phoebe told her. She opened her purse and took out a rust-colored ten-shilling note. "Here, this is for you."

Sadie lifted her hands and took a step back, saying she couldn't take the money, Mrs. White was very strict on that. Phoebe said that in that case she would send her a box of chocolates instead. But as they were driving away down the avenue, it occurred to her that she didn't know the nurse's surname.

"Send it to Kate—to Mrs. White. She'll pass it on."

Phoebe was watching him.

"You and 'Kate,' do I take it you were—?" She left the question hanging, and he smiled, and wouldn't look at her. "I do believe you're blushing," she said.

When they arrived in Mount Street and she got out of the car, he noticed how carefully she carried herself, watching the sidewalk and taking short, delicate steps. It was as if she were carrying about her person some small, precious vessel made of the most fragile crystal. Phoebe picked up a small pile of post from the hall table. In the flat, she stood in the middle of the living-room floor and looked around, nodding.

"Funny," she said, "no matter how short a time you're away, when you come back everything looks slightly changed. Even the smell is different, somehow."

She was cold, she said. He made her sit in front of the gas fire, and fetched a blanket from the bedroom and put it over her shoulders. She looked suddenly young, huddled there, warming her hands on a mug of coffee and gazing at the gas jets dancing. He stood over her, feeling helpless yet strangely pleased, with her, with himself, with the damp light of evening in the window.

"How are you?" he asked. "I mean, in general, overall."

"You make me sound like the weather. Which I suppose I should be under, but I'm not, or not badly."

He was lighting a cigarette.

"I'm going to move out," he said.

Phoebe stared at him, then looked away.

"Where will you go?"

"I'll sell Evelyn's house, and rent something."

And then there was nothing more to say on that subject.

Quirke went into the kitchen to fetch a glass, and came back and poured himself a whiskey from the bottle on the sideboard. Without turning, he asked, "Will you marry him?"

She looked up. "Don't be shy, go ahead and ask," she said.

"I have asked."

He tried to smile and couldn't, but only because his face would not make the required adjustments. She asked for more coffee. He carried the mug into the kitchen. Once there, he felt lightheaded suddenly, and had to put a hand on the back of a chair and close his eyes for a moment. Then he poured the tea and went back to the living room.

"I can't see it, myself," Phoebe said. "Can you?"

He switched on a standing lamp, and the room took on a melancholy aspect. How the past crowds in, he thought, in lamplight, on autumn evenings.

"No, I suppose I can't."

She put her mug on the floor beside her chair.

"Give me one of those cigarettes, will you?" she asked.

"You know I don't approve of you smoking."

"You didn't approve of me being pregnant either," she shot back.

"True. But you put a stop to that."

"I didn't really—Mother Nature stepped in and did it for me." And she laughed. Yes, he thought, she was her father's daughter, all right. "Tell you what," she said, blowing a cone of cigarette smoke at the hissing fire. "You stop being awful to him, and I won't marry him. What do you say?"

She was looking up at him again. He touched the tips of his fingers lightly to her cheek.

"I think," he said, "we should go and have a fancy dinner at the Russell Hotel, the way we used to. We'll eat steak and drink a disgracefully expensive bottle of wine."

This she considered for some moments, then said, "I've a better idea."

So they went on the bus into the city center and then took a taxi up to Leo Burdock's fish-and-chips shop on Werburgh Street. The shop was busy, and the customers eyed Quirke's Crombie overcoat and fancy shoes with envious disdain. He felt both ridiculous and ridiculously happy. They bought a one-and-one each, and walked down past Christchurch, eating with their fingers out of the steaming greaseproof bags. The chips burned their tongues, and the fish left slimy deposits on their hands. They spoke little, and were content with silence.

"By the way," Phoebe said, "there was a letter for you."

"A letter?"

"Yes. It was with those ones I picked up in the hall. I forgot to give it to you. London postmark." She paused. "I think it might be from Molly Jacobs."

The cathedral bell was tolling the hour, the reverberations rippling out upon the air like broad silk ribbons.

Flat 5
12 Grantley Terrace
Maida Vale
London W9

Dear Quirke

Yes, it's me. I hope you won't be too startled when you get this, if you get it. I was going to phone you, or try to, but I couldn't work up the courage. So a letter will have to do. I'll send it to your daughter's flat, in hopes that you're still there. My news is that I'm coming home, back to Ireland. My father is not well. He hasn't got over Rosa's death, and is in a depression that shows no sign of lifting. I'm not sure what I can do for him. Rosa was the apple of his eye, as you know. But I feel I have to be near him and give him whatever support I can. Therefore I

Damn! I was going to stop and tear this up, but I've started so I may as well go on. If I'm to be honest, my father is not the real reason for my decision to return to Ireland. I'm finished here. London has lost whatever glamour it used to have for me. I've given my notice at the paper. Also, I've broken up with Adrian. Or to be more precise, he broke up with me. I don't mind, or not much, anyway. We had got from each other as much as there was to get, I mean as much as we had to offer, so it's for the best, I think. I've applied for a job on the Cork Examiner. Yes, I know. And of course the money is pitiful. But I can live at home, on the cheap, and Cork is ten times less expensive than London. I suppose I must be fond of the old place, the city on "my own lovely Lee," as that awful song has it. I remember us at the Imperial Hotel, and I smile to myself and think

Damn again! What I really want to say is that I'm coming back because of you. I haven't been able to get you out of my mind, or out of my heart—I know you'll laugh at that, but I don't care. Maybe I'm making a fool of myself, and you won't want to see me. Maybe you've moved on to a new life, a new love, or even new loves. But the other day something came back to me, something you told me once, about Freud. A patient of his, a woman whose mind was very sick, asked him if he could cure her. "I can't cure you," he told her, "but I can get you back to where you'll be ordinarily unhappy." Or words to that effect. You thought this was very wise of the old boy, very realistic and not unkind. I was appalled, though I hadn't the nerve to say so. But now, since I'm writing to you and so I won't have to see you looking at me the way you used to, as if I was a complete, pathetic and utter idiot, I'm going to steel myself and ask you a question. Do you think we could be ordinarily happy together, you and I? I mean, if we really tried? Will you think about it? And please don't be angry with me.

Oh God, this is awful. I don't know whether I'll post this or not. I know I shouldn't. But I won't get many chances in life to offer what I've offered here. And this chance I want to take.

With love
Molly

★ ★ ★ ★ ★